CHRIS RYAN

ENDGAME

D0766600

RED FOX

Also available by Chris Ryan

The One That Got Away

AGENT 21 series
Agent 21
Agent 21: Reloaded
Agent 21: Codebreaker
Deadfall
Under Cover

CODE RED series
Flash Flood
Wildfire
Outbreak
Vortex
Twister
Battleground

ALPHA FORCE series
Survival
Rat-Catcher
Desert Pursuit
Hostage
Red Centre
Hunted
Blood Money
Fault Line
Black Gold
Untouchable

ENDGAME

RED FOX

UK | USA | Canada | Ireland | Australia
India | New Zealand | South Africa

Red Fox is part of the Penguin Random House group of companies
whose addresses can be found at global.penguinrandomhouse.com.

www.penguin.co.uk
www.puffin.co.uk
www.ladybird.co.uk

Penguin
Random House
UK

First published 2016

001

Text copyright © Chris Ryan, 2016
Cover artwork copyright © Collaborations JS, 2016

The moral right of the author and illustrator has been asserted

Set in Adobe Garamond 13/16.5pt by Falcon Oast Graphic Art Ltd.
Printed and bound in Great Britain by Clays Ltd, St Ives plc

A CIP catalogue record for this book is available from the British Library

ISBN: 978-1-849-41012-0

All correspondence to:
Red Fox
Penguin Random House Children's
80 Strand, London WC2R 0RL

CONTENTS

AGENT 21

Real name: Zak Darke

Known pseudonyms: Harry Gold, Jason Cole

Age: 15

Date of birth: March 27

Parents: Al and Janet Darke [DECEASED]

Operational skills: Weapons handling, navigation, excellent facility with languages, excellent computer and technical skills.

AGENT 22

Real name: Ricky Mahoney

Age: 14

Date of birth: August 8

Parents: Fred and Elaine Mahoney [DECEASED]

Operational skills: Pickpocketing, covert entry, weapons handling, self-defence.

AGENT 17

Real name: classified

Known pseudonyms: 'Gabriella', 'Gabs'

Age: 27

Operational skills: Advanced combat and self-defence, surveillance, tracking.

Currently charged with ongoing training of Agent 21 on remote Scottish island of St Peter's Crag.

AGENT 16

Real name: classified

Known pseudonyms: 'Raphael', 'Raf'

Age: 30

Operational skills: Advanced combat and self-defence, sub-aqua, land-vehicle control.

Currently charged with ongoing training of Agent 21 on remote Scottish island of St Peter's Crag.

'MICHAEL'

Real name: classified

Known pseudonyms: 'Mr Bartholomew'

Age: classified

Recruited Agent 21 after death of
his parents. Currently his handler.
Has links with MI5, but represents a
classified government agency.

'FELIX'

Real name: classified

Age: classified

Recruited Agent 22 after identifying
his potential during a chance encounter.
Currently his handler. Represents the
same classified government agency as
'Michael'.

CRUZ MARTINEZ

Age: 17

Significant information: Succeeded Cesar Martinez as head of largest Mexican drug cartel. Ruthless, possibly psychopathic. Thought to blame Agent 21 for death of father. Highly intelligent.

MALCOLM MANN

Age: 14

Significant information: Borderline autistic computer hacker. Known to have cracked the security of a number of intelligence agencies. Has provided help to Agent 21 in the past.

1

STUPID OLD MAN

It's always dark at night. But some places are darker than others. St Peter's Crag was one of those places.

It was 2 a.m. on 3 January. Christmas was long forgotten, as were any New Year celebrations. Not that many celebrations ever occurred here. A strong wind howled as it circled this bleak rocky outcrop in the North Sea. Waves crashed against the sharp rocks that surrounded the island. Even in fine weather, it was very difficult to approach by sea. Tonight it would be impossible.

A solitary figure in a black oilskin coat struggled across the barren terrain towards the building that sat alone in the middle of St Peter's Crag. His name was Stan. Stan had learned long ago that, on nights like this, it was better to stay in the warm protection of his small stone house on the north of the island.

But on this particular night, he had work to do, so he was braving the storm.

Stan thought of himself as a caretaker. As a young man he had been a soldier, and this job suited someone who was used to taking orders and not asking questions. He looked after the strange inhabitants of this island. There were three of them, most of the time. A man and a woman in their late-twenties, who called themselves Raf and Gabs, though Stan strongly suspected these were not their real names. And a teenager called Zak. Occasionally a fourth man, who called himself Michael, would arrive. The others looked up to him – he was obviously their boss. From time to time, a helicopter would arrive to ferry everyone except Stan from the island. Sometimes they were gone for weeks. Whenever they returned they were tired and grimy, and in need of the food and other supplies with which Stan kept the house well stocked.

Stan wasn't stupid. He knew that Raf, Gabs and Zak had jobs that could only be described as 'secret' – although what a kid like Zak could offer this secret world, Stan had no idea. He also understood that he would never know the whole story.

At first he hadn't minded being kept in the dark. His job was simply to look after the place. But as time passed he had grown resentful. He didn't like the way conversations suddenly stopped when he entered the room. He didn't like the way he was expected to stay, by himself, in his lonely quarters while the others had the thing that was in shortest supply on this desolate island: company. He didn't like how, whenever his fellow islanders saw him, they said to each other: 'It's only Stan.'

So when, during one of his infrequent trips to the mainland, someone had approached Stan and offered him a life-changing amount of money to perform them a certain service, they'd got lucky. Stan wanted to retire, and his paltry pension wouldn't cover much. Even worse, in his solitude he'd developed a habit for online poker. An expensive habit. He now owed more than he could ever repay.

I heard you had some money troubles, Stan, the man had said. *You think your employers will help you with that? You think they care about your problems? But we can, Stan. We can make those troubles go away just like that* . . . The man had clicked his fingers. *You just need to do us a little favour* . . .

'This blimmin' wind,' Stan muttered to himself as he struggled against the elements. It felt like the gale was pushing him back from the house. He slipped and fell, jarring his knee badly and making him drop the briefcase he was holding. He cursed, then pushed himself to his feet again and continued towards the house.

The big main door was firmly locked. To its side there was an electronic keypad. Stan faced it and typed in a number. A beam of red light shot from the keypad and scanned his retina. Stan's eyeball allowed him to gain access to this secret place.

It has to be you, you see, Stan? You're the only person who can get around that island without raising suspicion.

The main door clicked open. Stan stepped inside.

Water dripped from his oilskin onto the chequerboard floor of the dark hallway as he closed the door behind him. The howling of the wind immediately stopped. This was a solid old house. He removed his wet coat, let it fall to the floor, then put the briefcase down and opened it up. It contained two hypodermic syringes in plastic casings, and a torch. Stan took the syringes and headed through the pitch black towards the big old staircase leading up from the hallway.

Thirty seconds later he was walking along a first-floor corridor. At the very end of the corridor was the room young Zak used. But Zak wasn't here tonight. He was off doing something 'secret', whisked off just after noon that very day by helicopter.

It will be when the kid isn't there, the man had said. *That's very important, Stan. Do you understand?*

Soon as we see him leave, it needs to happen.

Of the three of them, he liked Zak best. Stan was glad he wasn't on the island tonight.

He continued along the corridor and stopped outside the third door on the left. He touched his thumb to the white doorknob. It recognized his fingerprint and clicked quietly open.

Stan knew better than to step inside immediately. This was Raf's bedroom, and Raf would be aware of an intruder immediately. Sure enough, as the door swung open, he made out the silhouette of a broad-shouldered figure approaching him.

''S only me,' said Stan.

The figure stopped two metres from the doorway. Stan could see that he was wearing pyjama bottoms, but was bare-chested.

'Blimey, mate,' said Raf. 'What are you doing here in the middle of the night?'

'Intruders on the island, sir. Thought you ought to know.'

Stan could just make out Raf's blond hair and chiselled face. Raf frowned. 'I didn't hear any air-craft,' he said as he strode through the doorway. Stan stepped aside to let him past. Then, as soon as Raf had his back to him, he lifted one of the syringes and stabbed it firmly into the muscular flesh of Raf's shoulder blades just as he'd been instructed.

Time slowed down. Stan's stomach sank as he saw Raf spin round, his face suddenly creased with anger.

The injection hadn't worked.

But a fraction of a second later, the broad-shouldered man's eyes rolled into the top of his head and he collapsed.

Stan was breathing deeply, and sweating. He knew he didn't have time to regain his breath. He walked to the next door on the right. Once again, he pressed his thumbprint onto the white doorknob. Once again, it clicked open.

''S only Stan,' he said.

There was even less time now. Clearly alerted by the noise in the corridor, Gabs was already in the doorway. She wore a tight vest top and pyjama bottoms, and her blonde, shoulder-length hair was messy. But she moved like lightning, straight past Stan, whom she barely acknowledged.

Stan raised his second syringe and stabbed it into her shoulder. The muscles here were not as big as Raf's, but they were at least as tough. For a horrific moment, Stan thought the needle hadn't entered her body. She spun round and raised one hand, palm out, fingers together. She struck him hard in the neck. Stan's knees went immediately. Gasping for breath, and losing his grip on the syringe, he sank to the floor.

But so did Gabs. With the syringe still sticking out of her shoulder, she collapsed unconscious, just as Raf had done.

Silence.

Stan rubbed his neck as he got to his feet. He shuffled on the spot for a moment, then suddenly kicked Gabs as hard as he could. Her prone body didn't move.

Muttering to himself, Stan stumbled back along the corridor, down the stairs and into the hallway, where his oilskin and briefcase were still lying on the floor by the door. He pulled the wet coat on again, then retrieved the torch from the case and opened the door.

Make sure they're both unconscious before you make the sign. That's very important, Stan. Can you remember that?

The howling of the wind hit his ears again as he stepped outside. It had grown stronger, and the clouds up above were scudding quickly across the sky. Standing on the threshold of the house, he raised the torch. Using the pulse button, he shot three short beams towards the heavens. There was no visible light – this was an infra-red torch – and although Stan wasn't expecting any, he still found himself examining it carefully before repeating the sign. He hoped the torch was working, because if

Raf and Gabs woke up before reinforcements came, he'd *really* be in trouble . . . Stan had seen them training, and he knew how fit and strong they were.

A silent sheet of lightning filled the sky. A few seconds later there was a boom of thunder from many miles off. Then a helicopter emerged suddenly from the boiling clouds.

It was clearly having difficulty in the high winds. Stan had seen many helicopters land on St Peter's Crag. In general, they avoided weather like this, and with good reason. Stan had never seen a helicopter shake and spin so violently as it struggled to land on the open ground in front of the house. He felt his mouth go dry.

You'll come with us in the helicopter when we leave, the man had said. *We'll give you your money then, and help you disappear . . .*

Stan didn't want to get into the chopper in these high winds, but he knew that staying on the island was no longer an option. He wrapped his oilskin more tightly around him as he watched the chopper touch down and two men emerge. He squinted to see what they looked like. They were wearing black clothes and balaclavas. Ugly-looking guns hung across their chests from slings. With their heads bowed against the downdraught of the helicopter, they sprinted towards the house.

It only took them a few seconds to reach Stan. They said nothing, but one of the masked men put his head to one side, as though asking a question.

'F-first floor,' Stan said nervously. ''S all done, just like he said.' He pointed toward the helicopter. 'Should I . . . ?'

'Stay there, old man,' said one of the figures. He seemed a lot less friendly than the guy Stan had made the deal with. He had a foreign accent. Spanish, maybe. Or Mexican.

Stan nodded. 'Right,' he said. 'Right you are.'

But the men had already slipped into the house, leaving Stan out in the wind, still clutching the infra-red torch. He shuffled on the spot again for a couple of minutes. The men returned. Each of them had a body over his shoulder – Raf and Gabs. They looked very limp. If Stan hadn't known they were unconscious, he might have thought they were . . .

'Wait there,' said one of the masked men.

'Right,' Stan muttered. 'Righto . . .'

The figures hurried with their cargo towards the helicopter. Through the darkness, Stan could just make out some more figures dragging Raf and Gabs into the chopper. He found he was holding his breath. He looked over his shoulder, then back to the chopper. A horrible thought crossed his mind – maybe they weren't intending to come back for him.

Maybe they were just going to fly off and leave him here . . .

But no. With relief, he saw the two figures running back up towards him from the chopper. When they were about ten metres away, they slowed down.

'Shall I come, then?' Stan asked. 'Shall I come along to the heli— W-what – what are you doing?'

Stan's stomach had turned to ice. One of the two men had lifted his gun and was pointing it directly at him. The other pulled off his balaclava. He was a thin young man – too young, Stan thought, to be carrying a gun – with cold, cruel eyes. He was standing five metres from Stan's position.

'Who . . . who are you?' Stan stammered.

The young man inclined his head. 'My name is Cruz Martinez.' His tone of voice indicated that he thought Stan should recognize the name. But Stan didn't, and it obviously showed in his face. 'I'm a little disappointed that your precious Agent 21 hasn't mentioned me.'

Stan blinked heavily. 'Put them guns down,' he said.

They didn't.

Stan staggered backwards. His limbs were heavy with fear.

''S only me,' he said. ''S only Stan.' He was

terrified by the fierce, keen look in the young man's eyes.

'You,' Cruz Martinez said, lowering his gun so that it was pointing at Stan's knees, and speaking as insultingly as possible, 'are a *stupid* . . .'

He fired as he said the word. A single shot that echoed through the air and slammed straight into Stan's right knee. A shriek of pain shot through him as he collapsed. Blood oozed down his shin.

'*Old* . . .' Cruz said, and he fired a second round into Stan's left knee.

The pain was beyond imagining. Stan tried to shout out, but the sudden violence had robbed him of his voice.

Cruz Martinez stood above him. Now he was pointing the gun at Stan's head, the wind blowing his hair wildly, and his cold eyes were brighter than ever.

'*Man*,' he said.

If anyone had been watching from a distance of more than fifty metres, they wouldn't have heard the bark of Cruz Martinez's firearm above the howling of the wind. They would simply have seen a muzzle flash as the third round slammed into Stan's head. And Cruz heartlessly kicking the old man's body.

They would not have heard him turn to his

companion and say, in Spanish: 'Phase one complete.' Nor would they have heard the response: 'Phase two is underway, Señor Martinez.'

They would have seen the two figures turning their back on Stan's lifeless corpse and running back to the helicopter. And the aircraft lifting shakily into the sky before disappearing quickly behind the thick bank of clouds.

And if they had waited for a few hours, until the wind dropped and the sun rose, they would have seen a single black bird landing on the corpse, and pecking at its wounded flesh, since there was nobody around to shoo it away.

2

INCARCERATION UNIT 3B

Wormwood Scrubs. Strangeways. Parkhurst. They give weird names to ordinary prisons. But special prisons – the prisons nobody really knows about – have very ordinary names.

It was 2 a.m. on the morning of 3 January. Zak Darke stood outside a prison that was a secret to almost everyone. Including Zak, up until the moment fourteen hours previously when he had been summoned, alone, to Incarceration Unit 3B.

From the outside, this building on the Caledonian Road in North London looked like a warehouse. Only a trained eye would pick out the security cameras fitted to its walls. They covered every square inch of the building and its grounds. And only a suspicious mind would wonder why the high wire fence was topped with bundles of razor wire that would be more in keeping at a military base.

Zak had a trained eye *and* a suspicious mind. He'd picked out the camera and the razor wire immediately.

It felt odd being in this part of town. He had once lived just half a mile from here, after he had been orphaned and sent to stay with his aunt and uncle. That part of his life seemed like a distant memory. He'd been plucked from it by a strange old man who sometimes called himself Mr Bartholomew and sometimes plain old 'Michael'. Michael had offered him the chance to join a top-secret government department – Zak thought of it simply as The Agency – and since then, his life had become . . . unusual.

Which was why, while most teenagers were tucked up in bed, making the most of their last chance of a lie-in before school or college began again any day now, Zak was here, outside this top-secret, high-security prison. And although he was used to peculiar circumstances, he couldn't help a twinge of anxiety in his gut. It's always nerve-racking, visiting a prisoner you've helped put behind bars, and Zak had more reason than most to be wary of one of the inmates of this institution.

But Michael had thought it would be a good idea. *He's made a request to see you*, Zak's handler had said. *Alone. Maybe he's decided he wants to talk, to give us information. It could be useful. And it could be good for you too. Sometimes the best way to deal with your demons is to confront them . . .*

Zak had a whole load of demons. He guessed it wouldn't hurt to cross one off the list.

There was a brick reception building set into the perimeter fence. Zak pressed a buzzer. A moment later the door clicked open. He stepped inside to see a uniformed guard standing behind a desk. On the far side of the room there was an iron door. Zak knew it would be heavily locked. On its right-hand side was an iPad-sized screen, but it was blank. Behind him, he heard a click as the first door locked.

As Zak approached the desk, the guard walked round from the other side. He looked suspicious. Zak scanned him up and down. He immediately noticed the slight bulge on the left-hand side of his torso that told him the guy was carrying a firearm. Probably a pistol, though Zak assumed the guard could call on heavier reinforcements if he needed them.

Zak stopped two metres from where the guard was standing. He knew better than to invade the personal space of a man with a gun.

'Harry Gold,' he said, using one of the many false names for which he had full paperwork, and about whose life he knew every tiny detail. 'I'm expected.'

The guard looked even more suspicious. 'Shouldn't you still be playing with your Christmas presents?' he said. And then, when Zak raised an eyebrow: 'I wasn't expecting a kid.'

'I can't help what you were expecting,' said Zak. But realizing his nerves had made him sound surly, which wasn't the way to get what he wanted, he smiled. 'I've got a baby face,' he said. 'Always have done. Didn't start shaving till my eighteenth birthday.'

Zak's eighteenth birthday was a long way off.

'ID?' the guard said.

Zak handed over a passport in the name of Harry Gold. The guard flicked through it, then walked back round to the other side of the desk and scanned the passport while watching a screen. He nodded a few seconds later and handed the passport back. Zak stuck it in his back pocket. 'You're good to go,' the man said. 'I'll call someone to take you in.' He picked up a radio handset. 'All right, Ern,' he said. 'That fella's here for the Cyclops.' He gave Zak another meaningful look. 'Well, I say *fella* . . . more like a pipsqueak . . .'

The guard put the radio back on the desk. 'You'll have to empty out your pockets. No phones, coins, nothing sharp or metal.'

Zak had come prepared. Aside from an iPhone, which he laid on the desk, he only had notes in his pocket. Six fifties – because in Zak's line of work, you never knew when you'd need some ready cash. The guard's eyes widened at the sight of all that money, but he didn't insist that Zak hand it in. Zak returned the notes to his back pocket.

'Dunno why the Cyclops finds you so damn interesting,' said the guard. 'Hasn't spoken a bleedin' word to any of us all the time he's been here. Hasn't had a visitor. Hasn't even received or sent a letter. Just stays in that cell of his, working out sometimes or just staring at the wall. Gives me the creeps.' He peered at Zak a bit more closely. 'What are you?' he asked. 'Family or something like that?'

'Something like that,' Zak agreed with a smile.

The guard didn't get a chance to ask another question. There was a hissing sound, and the door on the far side swung open. A black guy in uniform walked in. Zak supposed this was Ern. He was about the same height as Zak, but twice as broad. Zak had the impression it would be as hard to get past him as to get past the metal door itself – which was already swinging shut.

Ern looked Zak up and down, much like the guard had done. 'This our midnight visitor, is it? This the one keeping us from our beauty sleep?' He smiled, to reveal several missing teeth. Zak reckoned they hadn't been removed by the dentist. 'Arms above your head, please, son.'

Zak did as he was told, and let Ern frisk him down. It only took a few seconds. Zak wasn't hiding anything.

'Come on then, son, let's get this over with.' Ern turned and placed his right palm against the screen to the right of the door. The hissing sound came again as the door swung open. Ern walked back through it.

Zak followed. The door automatically locked behind him.

They were in a tarmac'd open space. 'Exercise yard,' said Ern. 'Not that any of our lot are allowed to use it.' They crossed the yard towards the large, warehouse-type building. 'Want to know what makes this place different to other prisons, son?'

'More secure building?'

Ern smiled. 'Ain't no such thing as a totally secure building. Not if you know what you're doing. And what's to stop a prisoner trying to escape, if they know they ain't got no chance of seeing the light of day again any other way?' As they walked he opened up his jacket. Zak immediately recognized the MP5 sub-machine gun holstered to his body. 'Much better deterrent,' Ern said. 'Ain't a single prison guard not armed to the teeth. And the prisoners know we won't hesitate to shoot if we see anything resembling an escape attempt.' He paused for a moment, before adding: 'I always mention that to the visitors, just in case they get any funny ideas, you know.'

He gave Zak a sidelong look full of meaning.

Zak almost replied. He almost told Ern that he was barking up the wrong tree if he thought Zak was here to help anyone escape. He was here to see the prisoner that the jailers called the Cyclops. Zak knew him as Calaca. He had been the right-hand man of Zak's arch-enemy, Cruz Martinez. Calaca had tried to kill Zak, and he'd tried to kill someone very dear to him. But then he'd made the mistake of trying to cross Zak's Guardian Angels, Raf and Gabs. As mistakes went, that was a pretty big one. It had ended up with Calaca detained at Her Majesty's pleasure – although Zak wasn't entirely sure that Her Majesty knew of the existence of such places as Incarceration Unit 3B.

But Zak's training had taught him never to release more information than was strictly necessary. 'I'm glad he's not going anywhere,' was all he said.

Ern led Zak into the building, through another door that required his palm print to open. Zak noted that he used his left palm this time. Clearly the system was programmed to recognize both of Ern's hands. The inside of the building was as warehouse-like as the outside – just a huge open space. In the middle, however, was a small metal structure, about the size of a Transit van, with yet another palm-print door. Ern opened it up. It contained nothing but a flight of steps leading into the ground.

Zak followed his guide down the steps. They entered a sterile, brightly lit, hexagonal room. On each of the six sides was a door, and at each door were two armed men – these guys didn't bother to conceal their MP5s. They all looked suspiciously at Zak, who had the impression that visitors were rare. 'These doors guard the six most dangerous men in the country,' Ern said. 'One way into their cells, one way out. Two armed men per prisoner, guarding every entrance and exit. Everything that goes in and out of these corridors is *rigorously* searched. It's impossible to deliver an illicit item to any of the six.'

As Ern spoke, Zak happened to be watching one of the guards. He had a brown beard and bushy eyebrows. He glanced down at the floor and then looked quickly up again.

Zak had been trained to recognize the facial expressions of a dishonest man. Had he just seen one? His muscles tensed up as Ern led him to one of the doors – it had a burnished steel number one just above it – and raised his hand to open it. But before he pressed his palm to the pad, he spoke.

'I don't know who you are, son. I don't know why a guy like the Cyclops should ask to see a kid like you, or why the authorities would allow it. But you've got five minutes with him, and not a second longer. I don't trust this guy. Nobody trusts him. I'll be with you at all times. Don't get too close to the glass, and for God's sake don't accept anything from him. Understood?'

Zak nodded. 'Understood,' he said.

Ern put his palm to the pad. The door slid open. Together they walked over the threshold. The door slid closed behind them.

They were in a bunker-like corridor, about twenty metres long and three metres wide. The walls were solid concrete, and there was strip lighting along the ceiling. On the left-hand side, halfway along the corridor, was a floor-to-ceiling clear panel. As Zak stepped forward he saw that this panel was the front wall of a large cell. Here and there were little ventilation holes in the glass, and in the middle, at about head height, was a grille for speaking through.

The cell behind the glass was sparse. A single bed. A desk, piled high with books. A toilet with no seat in the corner. A TV fixed to the wall. And a chair, which was positioned a couple of metres back from the speaker grille.

And on the chair sat Calaca. The Cyclops.

They called him the Cyclops because he only had one eye. The other eye socket was covered with pale skin.

He looked half the man he had been when Zak had last seen him. He had a blanket wrapped around his body and over his head, like a little old man trying to keep warm. His skin, once tanned, was pasty. His good eye was bloodshot and his lips were pale. The name 'Calaca' meant 'skeleton' in Spanish. Today, he more than lived up to it.

He watched Zak walk towards him with his single eye, and made no attempt to hide the dislike on his face. Zak did his best to look cool, but the truth was that the sight of Calaca made him feel slightly sick, and slightly weak. He knew that the one-eyed man would happily kill him if he got his hands on him. Although the glass looked tough, Zak couldn't help wondering if it was tough enough.

Ern had remained by the door, leaving Zak to approach the grille by himself. His footsteps echoed against the concrete as he walked, then fell silent.

'You wanted to see me?'

Calaca remained seated, and said nothing.

'Here's the deal,' Zak said. 'I don't know why I'm

here, and frankly I don't care. I've got five minutes, and if I think you're wasting my time, I'll just walk away now. It'll be the last you ever see of me.'

A pause. Zak noticed that Calaca seemed to be clenching something in his right fist. He remembered what Ern had said about it being impossible to smuggle anything illicit into one of these cells. His eyes flickered to the left, where the prison warder was standing by the palm-print door.

But then his focus shifted. Calaca was standing up.

Zak felt his pulse thumping.

The one-eyed man moved to the grille. He put his lips very close to it and whispered something. His voice was quiet. Zak couldn't make it out.

He drew closer to the glass. Calaca spoke again. Zak still couldn't hear.

He looked at Calaca, whose lip curled into a nasty grin. He held up the forefinger of his left hand and used it to beckon Zak even closer to the glass.

Zak swallowed hard. He was doing his best to hide how on edge he was. But he moved closer, so that his ear was just an inch from the glass.

Calaca spoke for a third time. His voice was louder now, and Zak fully understood every word he said.

'If you want to live, hit the floor!'

Zak's instincts kicked in. He fell immediately to

the floor, winding himself as his body slammed against the concrete. He was aware of Calaca doing the same.

And it wasn't a second too soon.

The explosion was deafening: a sudden, ear-splitting, destructive blast that came, Zak sensed, from inside the cell. The moments that followed passed in sickening slow motion. There was an enormous shattering of glass, and the ominous sound of cracking concrete. The shock waves from the blast battered Zak's whole body, as though he was being pummelled by someone's fist. Hot, acrid smoke filled his lungs as splintered glass rained down over his body.

Then he passed out.

3

PALM PRINT

The next sixty seconds were like a dream. Zak
teetered on the edge of consciousness. The noise of
falling debris sounded deep and low, like a slowed-
down recording. He forced his eyes open. All the
lights in this underground bunker had shattered.
Grit scraped his eyeballs. He closed his eyes again to
clear them. When he opened them for a second time,
he was aware of someone leaning over him. It was
too dark to see clearly, but he knew it had to be
Calaca.

Zak felt a burning mass of fear in his chest. How
would Calaca kill him? Did he have a gun or a knife?
Or would he grab a shard of the broken glass and slit
his throat?

Zak knew he should fight. Jolt his body into
action. But he found he couldn't move.

Calaca leaned in closer. His face was only inches from Zak's. He spoke, but Zak couldn't understand him; his words sounded slow and distorted. He felt sick. The room started to spin. Calaca grabbed his right hand and put something into it. Then Zak passed out again.

He didn't know how long he was out. Perhaps another minute. In the depths of his mind he felt as though he was screaming. Agonized, panicked screams. His eyes suddenly pinged open and he realized that the screams were real. They were coming from back along the corridor.

It took a titanic effort for Zak to get to his feet. His knees buckled as he straightened up, and he nearly collapsed again. Almost unconsciously, he stuffed into his pocket the object Calaca had put in his hand. He saw that there was more light in the corridor again now. It came from the direction of the central hexagonal room – and it was from this direction that the screaming was coming. A blood-curdling sound. Zak turned to look towards it. Smoke and dust obscured his view. He could see that the sliding metal door was half open. It cast a long shadow along the corridor.

Zak groped his way through the dust. The floor was littered with shadowy debris. He picked his way carefully along it, towards the screaming sound.

After he had moved five metres, he saw where it was coming from. There was a figure lying across the threshold of the corridor, stopping the sliding metal door from closing. Now that Zak was closer to the light, he could see that it was Ern.

And as he moved another five metres, he could see why Ern was screaming.

The prison warder was clutching his right arm. But the arm was not complete. His right hand had been severed. A catastrophic amount of blood was seeping from the wound and soaking into the sleeve of his uniform.

Zak's eyes flickered to the palm-print panel by the side of the door. It was smeared with blood. In an instant, he knew what had happened.

Calaca had needed a palm print to escape. So he had helped himself to a palm.

Zak shot forward. All his sluggishness had fallen away. As he moved, he pulled his belt from around his trousers. He knelt down over Ern, whose screaming had now changed to a desperate panting. 'Can you hear me?' he asked the prison warder urgently.

'Y-y-yes . . .'

'You need to raise your bad arm. I'm going to try to stop the bleeding.'

'You . . . you helped him escape . . .' Despite the

27

pain he was obviously in, Ern still managed to sound furious.

Zak didn't have time to argue with the guy. He needed to stem the bleeding, otherwise Ern had served his last shift. He wrapped his belt just above Ern's elbow, then pulled it tight. Ern gasped, but was clearly too weak to struggle. As Zak went about his work, he noticed that Ern's MP5 was missing. Not a good sign. He tightened the belt as hard as he could. With all his strength, he punctured an extra hole through the leather using the buckle. It was a very rudimentary tourniquet, but it was the best he could do until proper medical attention arrived.

Only then did he stand up again and take in the devastation of the hexagonal room.

The remaining doors were all shut, but that didn't mean anything. Calaca could have freed the other prisoners. In fact, Zak bet that was what had happened – it would cause more chaos, and chaos would make it easier to escape. There were bodies strewn everywhere. Surely Calaca couldn't have overpowered them all. He couldn't tell if the guards were dead or alive. But there was no blood, so he figured he couldn't do anything for them either way. They'd either wake up, or they wouldn't. His eyes tried to pick out the guard with the brown beard and bushy eyebrows, and he wasn't surprised to find him missing.

Several of the guards had obviously tried to grab their weapons before they were put down. Their jackets were open and their hands were resting on their MP5s. Zak strode over to the nearest guard and grabbed his firearm.

He heard Ern calling out weakly: 'That's not a toy, son!'

Zak turned. With a single, skilled movement he released then re-engaged the weapon's magazine. 'No,' he said firmly. 'It's not.'

His mind turned back to Calaca. He *had* to stop him escaping.

The door that led to the staircase was shut. Zak needed a palm print to get out of there. Ern, despite his terrible state, was the only conscious guard. Zak turned to him. 'Do you think you can walk?' he asked.

Ern was white and trembling. Zak wasn't even sure he'd heard him. There was no time to waste. He bent down and grabbed the huge prison warder under both arms, then hauled him with great difficulty to his feet. He slung Ern's good arm around his neck and dragged him, shivering and shaking, towards the door. When they were in sight of the palm-print panel, Zak manoeuvred Ern's good hand against it. The door slid open.

'You didn't help him?' Ern asked.

'No way,' Zak said. His voice was fervent, and Ern nodded in acceptance.

'I think I can walk,' the jailer said.

Zak let go of his patient. It was a relief to lose the weight. Ern was unsteady on his feet, but managed to climb the stairs after him. Zak flicked off the safety switch of his stolen weapon, then burst out into the warehouse with sweat pouring down his grimy forehead.

The warehouse was empty. No sign of Calaca. But Zak's sharp eyes quickly picked out a few spots of blood leading to the exit. Perhaps Calaca had been injured in the blast. If so, it would slow him down. He looked over his shoulder. Ern was still coming behind him, but he looked like a ghoul. His eyes were rolling.

'We have to run!' Zak barked.

But it was clear that Ern wasn't running anywhere. His knees crumpled beneath him, and he fell heavily to the floor, unconscious.

At the same time, Zak heard sirens in the distance. He swore under his breath. The emergency services were arriving. The last thing Zak wanted was to become involved with them. They would ask him questions he couldn't answer. And they would slow him down in his hunt for Calaca . . .

He felt in his pocket for his phone, then cursed

again when he remembered he had left it at reception. Instead, he ran over to where Ern was lying and felt inside his jacket. The prison warder had his own iPhone tucked in a pocket. Zak swiped it open. When it requested a fingerprint to access, he touched the thumb of Ern's good hand to the start button. Seconds later he was dialling a number.

In the time since Zak had become Agent 21, it had been necessary for him to learn many things by heart. One of these was an emergency number that would put him in direct contact with his handler, Michael. It was understood that he should only ever dial this number in emergency situations. Zak reckoned this qualified. The phone only rang once before it was answered.

Zak didn't wait for a voice. 'Calaca's escaped,' he stated briskly. 'The police are on their way. I'm stuck inside Incarceration Unit Three B. You need to upload my palm print to the unit's security system.'

There was barely a pause. 'Done,' said a voice at the end. 'Proceed to Meeting Point Three.'

'I need to find Calaca!'

'Negative. Proceed to Meeting Point Three. Do *not* allow the emergency services to question you. Repeat, do *not*—'

'You need to get medics on site immediately,'

Zak interrupted. There was no time for repetition. 'Multiple severe casualties.'

There was no more to say. Zak hung up, then threw the phone back down where Ern was lying. He felt himself burning with anger that the Agency didn't want him to go after Calaca. But he had learned that it was best to follow instructions, because sometimes you don't know the whole story. He had a feeling that this was one of those times . . .

He sprinted towards the exit and slammed his hand against the palm-print panel. The door slid open. Zak looked out onto the exercise yard and winced. It was brightly lit by floodlights on the roof of the warehouse building. The scream of sirens was even louder here, and Zak could see the flashing blue neon of several emergency vehicles pulling up outside the perimeter of the prison.

He glanced down at the MP5 in his hand. If anybody saw him carrying a weapon, they could get the wrong idea. He decided he had to lose it. He made the weapon safe, removed the magazine again and laid the gun on the floor. Then he took a deep breath and sprinted across the exercise yard.

The floodlights cast multiple shadows all around him. His footsteps were silent. Dazzled by the bright lights, he reached the reception building in less than ten seconds. Once more he slammed his palm onto the panel. The door slid open. He stepped inside, then stopped dead in his tracks.

The guard who had let him in was sitting behind his desk. He was sprawled out in his seat and his head was lolling to one side. His throat had been cut. Rivulets of fresh blood were dripping down his neck. Zak reckoned he had only been killed in the last couple of minutes.

He tried to ignore the sickening chill that was creeping down his spine. Taking a deep breath, he drew back his shoulders and strode for the main entrance. For a third time he slammed his hand against the palm panel, and the main entrance to the prison clicked open.

He stepped outside.

Three police cars had pulled up onto the kerb. Their doors were open, their sirens flashing. Zak found himself face to face with five uniformed officers. Twenty metres along the road was an unmarked black van. Its rear doors were open, and a unit of armed response officers were spilling out. They wore flak jackets and carried MP5s, just like the prison officers.

Zak raised his chin. 'You need to get in there,' he shouted, before anyone could start asking him awkward questions. 'There's a load of badly wounded men inside.'

One of the five uniformed officers started talking into the radio clipped to his chest. The armed response officers ran at Zak. Two of them got down in the firing position covering the entrance, while the others stormed past him and made their way into the prison. A second uniformed officer grabbed Zak by the arm and pulled him away. 'What's your name, kid?' he demanded. 'What the hell were you doing in there?'

Zak looked him straight in the eye, because he knew that was the most convincing way of lying to someone. And the bigger the lie, the more confident you have to sound when delivering it. 'My dad works here,' he said. 'His name's Ern. Sometimes I have to sleep over.'

The policeman narrowed his eyes, but seemed to accept Zak's story. 'Stand over there, kid,' he said, indicating the section of pavement alongside the armed response unit van. 'And try not to get in the way, OK?'

'Right,' Zak said quietly. He sidled over to the van, his heart thumping inside his chest. When he got there, he saw that one of the other policemen was watching him carefully.

Proceed to Meeting Point Three. Do not allow the emergency services to question you.

Zak bowed his head, but kept his gaze on the third

policeman. He could tell, just by the expression on his face, that he had overheard Zak's story and didn't believe it. The policeman started walking in his direction. Zak's body tensed up.

Gunshots in the distance. A single burst of fire coming from the opposite end of the street. All five policemen turned, as did the two armed response unit guys covering the entrance.

Zak knew he wouldn't get another chance. While everyone else was looking the other way, he turned and ran.

Ten seconds later he heard a shout from behind. *'That kid's running away! Stop him!'*

4

MEETING POINT 3

In the early days back on St Peter's Crag, there had been times when Zak Darke had truly hated his Guardian Angels. Those times lasted for approximately ninety minutes a day – the time set aside for his fitness regime.

On many occasions, with his lungs burning and his muscles on fire, and with Raf barking at him to push his body through feats of endurance that felt impossible at the time, he'd felt like throwing in the towel. And on those occasions, his Guardian Angels had been strict with him. 'Look, sweetie,' Gabs had told him more than once. 'All the other stuff doesn't matter. So what if you know your way around an assault rifle? So what if you can fly a plane? So what if you can speak four languages? If your fitness isn't up to scratch, you're out of the game.'

It was only when Zak was out in the field that he fully understood what she meant. And right now he was grateful for every gut-busting training session they'd put him through.

He pounded the street, running fast, breathing slow, just like he'd been taught. His trainers barely made a sound as they hit the pavement. After fifteen seconds, he looked over his shoulder to see if the police officers were following. Two were sprinting after him on foot, but he could tell at a glance that they would never catch him. The police car pulling out with its siren flashing might be more of a problem. Zak could outrun most people, but he couldn't outrun a car.

He looked ahead. Twenty metres from his position, a main street cut across at right angles. During the day it would be very busy. Zak could have easily got lost in the commotion. But at this time of night there was just the occasional flash of headlamps passing. Not easy. He'd have to think of something better.

The police siren grew louder. Zak felt like it was right on his shoulder, and he had to suppress his panic. When he hit the main road, he turned left. Past Boots – closed. Past KFC – closed. He caught glimpses of tired Christmas trees and tinsel in shop windows. And as he continued to run, he scanned the pavement ahead. It was deserted. He'd be very obvious, sprinting down it. He needed to blend in – and quickly.

Then he saw him – an old homeless guy with a long, messy beard, sitting on the pavement ten metres ahead, just outside Costa Coffee, whose window showed a jolly Santa holding a steaming mug. The homeless guy wore a heavy but shabby coat, a threadbare woollen hat and gloves with the fingertips cut off. A thin, hungry-looking bull terrier was lying at his feet.

Zak sprinted towards him, pulling the sheaf of fifty-pound notes from his back pocket as he ran. The homeless guy looked up. For a moment, he seemed terrified. But his face changed when he saw the money.

'Here's a hundred quid,' Zak said urgently, pressing two notes into his hand. 'I need to borrow your coat for two minutes.'

The homeless guy couldn't move fast enough. He wriggled out of his overcoat and handed it to Zak, who quickly pulled it over his shoulders, then sat next to him, his shoulders hunched and his head down. The bull terrier sniffed curiously at his feet, but didn't move.

Zak had hit the pavement just in time. A police car screamed up to the corner, closely followed by a second one. They'd obviously seen Zak turn left, because they swung round in that direction, their tyres screeching as they did so.

'Robbed somewhere?' the homeless guy asked.

Zak kept his head down. The two police cars had slowed down. They were thirty metres away and suddenly moving at a crawl as their occupants scanned the street, left and right.

'Don't worry, lad,' the homeless guy muttered. 'We sometimes do bad things when we're hungry. Lie down. The cops don't normally move us on when we're asleep.'

Zak gave him a grateful look, then quickly lay down, covering his body and half his head with the coat, facing the shop window with his back to the road. He felt the dog nuzzling up to him.

The seconds ticked by, agonizingly slowly. The sirens were silent now, but he could see the flashing neon reflected in the shop window.

Suddenly, a voice from the road. 'You seen a kid running this way, pal? About five eight, blue jeans, brown jacket?'

'That way, officer,' the homeless guy said. To Zak's surprise, his voice was slurring – he was doing a very good impression of being drunk. He belched loudly. Zak saw the neon reflection of the policeman moving on. 'Don't get up yet, lad,' the man said quietly. 'They're still watching.'

Zak waited.

Thirty seconds passed.

A minute.

'All right, lad. They've gone.'

Zak sat up quickly. He uncovered himself and handed the coat back to the homeless guy. The grizzled old man was looking at him with sharp, clear eyes. 'I've seen a lot of bad 'uns in my time,' he said. 'You're not one of them. I can tell.'

Zak didn't reply. He shoved his hand into his back pocket and pulled out the remaining four fifty-pound notes. He knew it was bad tradecraft – that he might *need* that money at some point. But the old homeless guy looked like he needed it more. He thrust the money into the man's dirty hand. The man looked shocked, but also thankful. Zak nodded gratefully at him.

Then he turned, and ran in the opposite direction.

Meeting Point 1 was a kiosk in Waterloo Station that sold pasties and sausage rolls. If the contact was holding a bottle of water, it was safe to meet. If they were holding a cup of coffee, it was a sign to abort the RV.

Meeting Point 2 was the steps of St Paul's Cathedral. If the contact was holding a newspaper, all clear. If they were reading something on their phone, abort.

Meeting Point 3 was a bench by the Serpentine in Hyde Park. If the contact was wearing a hat, it was safe to go ahead with the RV. If not, get the hell out of there.

Distance to Meeting Point 3: approximately three kilometres. Once Zak was sure he was no longer being followed, he dropped down to a steady jog – as much to keep warm as to get there quickly – and covered the distance in about twenty minutes.

The park was empty. Hardly surprising, in the middle of this cold night. As he approached the Serpentine, he checked the time. Quarter past three. The air was piercingly chill, and the visibility was poor. He stood, hidden, in the shelter of a copse of trees, observing the bench from a distance of 100 metres. There was nobody there.

Zak didn't miss a beat. The first rule of an RV was this: if your contact hasn't shown, don't hang around. Nothing looks more obvious than someone milling about, keeping surveillance on an otherwise unsuspicious location, even when you think you are hidden and unobserved. Zak immediately turned and walked in the opposite direction from the bench. There was a standard operating procedure for moments like this. He would return at 4 a.m. If his handler was still not there he would return at 5 a.m. – and then every hour, on the hour, until he made contact.

Head down, shoulders hunched, his senses acutely sharpened, Zak strode through the park. The cold was really getting to him now. It seemed to creep into his bones. Or maybe it was the memory of the horrific events at Incarceration Unit 3B. He couldn't help thinking about the awful bleeding stump of Ern's arm, or the look of pained horror on his face. He thought of Calaca, and the way he had warned him.

Then he remembered: Calaca had put something in his hand.

He dug around in his pocket until he found the object. It was a tiny USB flash drive. Zak stopped and stared at it. Then, aware that he'd look strange if anyone was watching, he continued to walk.

And he continued to think.

Why had Calaca wanted Zak there on the night he intended to escape prison? And why hadn't he killed him? The answer had to be on this flash drive.

Zak thought about heading into the centre of town, finding a PC at an internet café and plugging in the flash drive to see what information it held.

But he quickly discarded that idea. It would be too insecure. He needed to wait until he'd made contact with Michael. He'd know what to do with it.

Four o'clock came and went with no sign of anyone at Meeting Point 3. By 5 a.m. Zak was shivering with cold. He wished he hadn't given the homeless guy all his money, because now he couldn't even find a coffee shop in which to kill time. So he kept walking, trying to put the cold from his mind by analysing the events of the night, and by keeping his mind on high alert.

And hoping that the RV would occur at 6 a.m.

At five minutes to six, he found himself hiding in the copse of trees again. The sky was beginning to lighten, although it was, if anything, even colder now. In the murky half-light, from the distance of 100 metres, Zak could just make out the shape of not one, but two figures sitting on the bench. He squinted. He thought both of them were wearing woolly hats, though it was hard to tell from this distance. But he hesitated anyway. If the first rule of an RV was not to hang around if your contact hadn't shown, the second rule was this: if things don't look like you expect them to, assume that your secrecy has been compromised and abort the mission.

Zak was expecting only one person: his handler, Michael. Why, then, were there two people waiting?

Maybe they were just random people sitting by the water. It was, after all, a public bench. But as Zak watched, one of the figures stood up. Zak thought he'd recognize the stoop of Michael's shoulders. He decided to move a little closer.

Distance, fifty metres. The guy standing up was definitely Michael, and he was definitely wearing a woolly hat. He was looking at his watch, and his breath was condensing in the cold morning air. Zak decided to make contact.

He strode towards the bench, his eyes flickering left and right to check he wasn't being observed. Two joggers – one male, one female – cut across him at a distance of about fifteen metres, but there were no other people in sight. Zak realized that the dawn chorus had just started. Pretty enough, but extremely loud and a distraction once he'd noticed it.

By the time Zak reached the bench, Michael had sat down again. Approaching from behind, Zak saw that he and his companion had moved to opposite ends of the bench. They'd clearly spotted Zak, and had cleared a space for him to sit down.

Zak walked round to the front of the bench. He could smell the aroma of cherry tobacco that always lingered around Michael. He nodded at his handler. The older man looked very tired. Older than usual. Something was obviously wrong. He looked at the second man and immediately recognized him. His name was Felix and he ran another agent – code name Agent 22, real name Ricky – whom Zak had met once. Felix was balding on top, with wild hair above his ears. He wore a blue cagoule, and was clutching a walking stick. His face was as grim as Michael's.

'Sit down,' Michael said.

Zak did as he was told. A solitary duck swooped onto the water a few metres in front of them. Zak looked at the two men in turn. 'What's wrong?' he asked. No reply. 'Don't give me the silent treatment,' Zak said, his voice trembling slightly. 'This is turning into a really rotten day.'

Michael gave him a severe look. 'I'm sorry, Zak,' he said. 'But it's about to get worse.'

5

SNIPER

'How can it get any worse?' Zak demanded. He started to tell them about everything that had happened that night, but Michael held up one hand to interrupt him.

'I know all about Calaca,' he said.

'No you don't,' Zak said, a bit impatiently. 'I mean, he could have killed me, but he decided to—'

'Rafael and Gabriella have been abducted.'

Zak stared hard at him. '*What?* How? They were on the island just a few hours ago. Nobody can take them from there.'

'They had help.'

'Who from?'

'Stan,' Michael said shortly.

Zak blinked. '*Stan?*'

'He betrayed us.'

Zak sat in stunned silence for a moment. The duck that had just landed waddled out of the water and started pecking at his feet. 'When did this happen?' he asked.

'About the time your friend Calaca was blowing up Incarceration Unit Three B,' Michael said. 'Our people noticed an unexpected radar splash above St Peter's Crag. We sent a unit to investigate. They found the house empty, and Stan's body lying at the front door.'

'Stan's *body*?' Zak said. 'You mean he's—'

'Our working theory is that they used Stan to disable Raf and Gabs, then killed him when he was of no more use to them.'

'We've got to find them,' Zak said. All thoughts of Calaca had left his mind. 'Which way did the aircraft fly? We've got to start looking, now . . .' Michael surveyed him carefully, saying nothing more, and Zak suddenly felt irrationally angry that his handler seemed to be taking all this so calmly. He got to his feet. '*Now*, Michael.'

Michael turned to Felix. 'That's the trouble with these young agents,' he observed. 'They're so hot-headed.'

'You've noticed?' Felix said.

'Sit down, Zak. I haven't finished.'

'So what? Raf and Gabs are missing. Don't you even care?'

Michael stood too. His face was suddenly angry, with deep frown lines on his forehead. 'I care more than you can possibly imagine, Zak. Now sit down.'

Zak took a deep breath, then sat down again. Michael joined him. 'He doesn't understand how this looks,' he said to Felix.

'That's hardly surprising, old friend,' said Felix. 'Like you said, they're very young. They haven't had time to become as untrusting as we have.'

'To trust nobody is the first thing we teach them,' Michael pointed out.

'It's a long lesson to learn,' Felix said. 'A very long lesson to learn.'

'Will you two stop talking as if I'm not here?' Zak said. 'What do you mean, I don't understand how this looks?'

Michael took a deep breath. 'At midday yesterday, January second, Agent 21 left St Peter's Crag. Fourteen hours later, his Guardian Angels are abducted thanks to a traitor within the agency. How very convenient that Agent 21 himself happened not to be there that night.'

Zak stared at him. Was Michael saying what he thought he was?

'At the same time as the abduction was taking

place, Agent 21 walks into a high-security incarceration unit. Ten minutes later, an extremely dangerous convict has escaped, several men are wounded or dead and Agent 21 is on the run from the police.'

'You *told* me to run from the police!' Zak half shouted.

'I know,' Michael said calmly.

'Then why the hell are you suggesting *I'm* the traitor?'

'I'm suggesting nothing of the sort, Zak. I'm just telling you how it looks.' He glanced at Felix again. 'I'm just telling you how *other* people in our agency are seeing the situation.'

'How could *I* be a traitor?' Zak demanded. 'Look at all the things I've done for the Agency. All the missions . . .'

'To someone with a suspicious turn of mind,' Felix interrupted, 'that doesn't mean you're not a traitor. That means you've got good cover.'

Silence. Zak considered what Michael and Felix had just said. He had to admit that they were right. 'Are you handing me in?' he asked quietly.

Michael shook his head. 'That's what the Agency thinks we're here to do. We won't, of course. But we're running a risk. You don't know anybody else in the Agency apart from us, for very good reasons of secrecy. But they know who you are, and every one of them has agreed in the last four hours that you need to be deactivated.'

'Deactivated?' Zak repeated.

'Permanently.'

'But that's insane.'

'Not if you look at it from their point of view, Zak. They don't know you personally. They just look at the facts. Now maybe – *maybe* – I'll be able to talk them round. But in the meantime, you need to disappear. And I mean, *disappear*. You need to be totally off the grid. You know how good the Agency is at finding people. That's why I've brought Felix along. He's in the middle of training up Agent 22, but that will have to wait. He'll help you.'

'I don't *need* any help,' Zak said. 'I'm *not* disappearing. Surely they'll see sense . . .' His voice trailed off for a moment. 'I've been set up,' he said finally. 'Someone's set this up to make it look like I've gone bad.'

Michael nodded seriously.

'But who would . . .' Zak's voice trailed off again as the answer dawned on him. 'Cruz,' he breathed.

'It can't be a coincidence,' Michael said, 'that Cruz's right-hand man escapes from prison the very same night that two of our agents are abducted and a third, whom Cruz loathes, is – forgive the phrase – stitched up like a kipper.'

'But when they see Cruz is involved, surely the Agency will realize that I'm not a traitor.'

'The Agency,' Michael said, 'has it on file that several times in the past you've been in a position to deal with Cruz permanently, and on each occasion you failed to do so. It hardly helps your cause, Zak. Now listen carefully. Felix is going to take you away right now and install you in a safe house a long way from London. I can't promise that it will be very comfortable, but it was the best we could come up with at short notice. Don't worry about Calaca: we'll find him. And don't worry about Rafael or Gabriella. We'll find them too. All we need to do is—'

Zak didn't hear what they needed to do. At that precise moment two shots rang out in quick succession from the other side of the Serpentine. An entire flock of ducks rose noisily up from the water, squawking and screaming as they took to the air. A dog barked somewhere nearby.

Zak reacted instinctively. The gunshot had come from behind them. He slid off the bench and onto the ground, bunching himself up in order to present a smaller target, protected by the bench itself. He was momentarily surprised that Michael and Felix hadn't done the same. 'Get down!' he hissed. '*Get down . . .*'

He sensed movement on either side of the bench.

But neither Michael nor Felix joined him on the ground.

Zak looked to his right. Michael was slumped where he sat. His chin was resting on his chest. The bench itself was spattered with blood.

He looked left. Felix was in the same position. More blood. And from this angle he could see a wound in the back of Felix's head.

Zak wanted to shout out – '*No!*' – but the word stuck in his throat. For the second time that morning, the world seemed to spin. He quickly grabbed Michael's wrist and checked his pulse.

Nothing.

He did the same for Felix.

Nothing.

A hot wave of anger washed over him. He spun round and raised his head over the back of the bench. High risk, but he *had* to know what was going on. At a distance of 100 metres, he spotted movement in the same copse of trees from which he had observed Michael and Felix.

It went against all his training, where rule number one was: stay alive. But someone had just killed his handler, and he was fuelled with anger. He jumped over the back of the bench and sprinted as fast and as hard as he could towards the trees. Everything around him was a blur. His eyes were filling with hot tears. Through them, he could only just make out the copse ahead. And though there was, he thought, still movement there, it was obscured by the tears. When he wiped them away, more came. They made it impossible to spot the gunman.

Zak burst through the tree line, gasping as he inhaled great lungfuls of air, and ferociously wiping his eyes as he looked around desperately for any sign of the shooter.

None.

He spun round again and looked down. Instantly, his well-trained eyes picked up two cartridge cases. He touched them, and found that they were still warm. The evidence of the gunman was here, but the gunman himself was gone.

Panic surged through him. What should he do? He had nobody to go to. Nobody to call. He found himself, almost by instinct, running back towards the bench. When he was thirty metres out, he saw Michael's body move, and for a wild moment of hope he thought he was still alive. But as he drew nearer, he realized that the corpse had simply slipped further down on the bench. And now he could see the terrible entry wounds in the back of each man's skull. Nobody could have survived that. He averted his eyes from the horror.

Someone was shouting. Zak looked over his shoulder and saw three people huddled together, about fifty metres away, pointing at him. One of them was on the phone. And as he looked, Zak heard sirens for the second time that morning.

He froze.

From what Michael had said, the police already suspected him of helping Calaca escape. The Agency suspected him of being a traitor. Now he was at the scene of the brutal murder of two of their top men.

His world was collapsing. He needed to think fast and clearly.

His eyes fell on Felix.

With Raf and Gabs out of the game, Felix's agent, Ricky, was one of the few people he could think of who understood who and what Zak was. And with Felix dead, Ricky was now in the same boat as him.

But he had no way to contact him.

The sirens were getting louder. The police would be here any second. He needed to get away.

First, though, he hurried round to Felix's slumped body. He started patting down his clothes, trying to ignore the sticky blood spatter and the gruesome smell of a freshly dead body. He heard more shouts from the group of people watching him. With a single glance, he saw that one of them was filming him with his phone, though they did all keep their distance. That video footage wouldn't look good for Zak. He'd appear to be looting Felix's body.

Which, in a way, he was.

He found Felix's phone after about ten seconds. It was locked, of course, so Zak grabbed the dead man's left hand and pressed his thumb against the start button. Within seconds, Zak was scrolling through his recently dialled calls. He didn't think for a moment that Felix would have Ricky's name programmed into his address book. Instead, over the course of the next ten seconds, he identified the five numbers Felix had called most often in the past few days. Back on St Peter's Crag, Raf and Gabs had trained him to recall lists of numbers after reading them only once. It had seemed a useless skill back then. Now, yet again, he was grateful to his Guardian Angels for their instruction.

There was no point taking Felix's phone with him. Without the fingerprint it was inaccessible, and in any case it could be used to track him. Looking across the park, he could see neon lights flashing in the distance. The sirens were louder than ever.

He had to go.

He stepped over to where Michael's body lay

slumped, and put a trembling palm on his handler's shoulder. He felt he should say something. But then he heard Michael's voice ringing in his head. It was urgent and waspish. *Run, Agent 21*, it said. *Run!*

Zak ran.

6

GREASY SPOON

'Listen up, Coco. I'm going under the radar for a while. It means I won't be around. Don't bother trying to call.'

Felix always called Ricky 'Coco'. Ricky didn't like it at all. But when Felix had called at 5 a.m. that morning, his voice was taut and he'd sounded stressed, so Ricky hadn't made a thing of it.

'How long for?' Ricky had asked – rather groggily, as the phone call had woken him up.

'Could be a few days, could be a few weeks. Could even be a few months. Just try not to get into trouble, OK? Remember, you're not a petty thief any more, but you're not a fully-fledged agent yet either. I know you think you're quite the big shot, but your training is only half complete and you've got a lot to learn. Got it?'

'Got it,' Ricky had replied in a mock-tired voice. 'Holiday . . . no trouble . . . not a petty thief . . . lots to learn.' He considered concluding with 'blah blah blah', but Felix had already hung up.

After a call like that, further sleep was impossible. Ricky had hauled himself out of bed, pulled on his jeans and the hooded top Felix had given him as a present ('reversible, in case you need to change appearance quickly') and padded out into the main room of his flat, where he dumped his mobile phone on the glass-topped coffee table. He looked around. He'd come to the conclusion that his flat was flash, but bland. He'd wanted to put up a few photos of his dead sister on the wall, but Felix had put his foot down about that – he said it made him too easy to identify. And there simply hadn't been time to go shopping for pictures to hang. The only thing approaching decoration was a line of ten different coloured baseball caps hanging on the wall. Ricky liked baseball caps. Stick a new one on, or turn it backwards, and you could change your appearance in an instant. A useful trick, in his line of work.

He still sometimes couldn't quite believe he lived here, in the penthouse suite of this flash tower block overlooking London. The apartment came with the job. A lot of people would think that Ricky was too young to be in a job that came with its own flat – or indeed in any job at all. But this wasn't an ordinary job, and Ricky wasn't an ordinary kid. Felix had plucked him from the streets and persuaded him to stop pickpocketing and do something more worthwhile. He'd certainly done that. His first mission had been completed over Christmas. Thanks to Ricky, a young girl had escaped an abusive father; a traitor had been brought to justice; and everyone in the UK was just a little bit safer.

The bottom line was that Ricky owed Felix. Big time.

He watched dawn creep over the London skyline as cold air blew in from the open window, giving him goose bumps. He always kept this window open, even when it was very cold out. It made him feel like he had a way out. He felt strangely uneasy as he stood there. His days were normally so filled with training exercises that he barely ever had time to himself. Now that the day stretched emptily ahead of him, he didn't quite know what to do. At 7 a.m. he glanced over at the free weights sitting on the floor in the corner of the room.

– You could do a workout.

There existed in Ricky's mind a little voice, which was always questioning and – more often than not – arguing with him. Ricky had even given the voice a name: Ziggy. And Ziggy was about to be overruled, because Ricky's stomach was rumbling.

– *Yeah, I could* do a workout. *Or I could eat a big breakfast and go back to bed. I'm on holiday, remember?*

He walked to the fridge. It was crammed full of food, as always. But after a few seconds he swung the door shut.

– *I thought you were hungry.*

– *I am hungry. But maybe I'll go out for breakfast. That's what people do on vacation, right?*

Ricky was just grabbing his coat when his mobile – still sitting on the coffee table – started to buzz. It shifted along the glass table top with each ring. Ricky's eyes narrowed. Nobody ever called that number apart from Felix, and he'd gone 'under the radar', as he put it.

Ricky stepped over to the phone. The screen said 'Number withheld'.

– *Probably just a junk caller.*

– *What if it's Felix?*

– *Felix just told me he has to go under the radar. I hardly think he'd be calling so soon after that. Anyway, I'm starving, let's go.*

The phone was still ringing as Ricky locked the apartment door behind him.

At the front of the building in which Ricky lived there was a large plaza. It was busy. Ricky pulled his hood over his head, hunched his shoulders and started to cross it. He was halfway across when something made him stop. He'd seen something from the corner of his eye that didn't make sense. He looked back at the apartment block.

A building like that had a lot of windows that needed cleaning. From time to time, a large cradle lifted the window cleaners up the entire height of the building. The cradle was there this morning. It was about halfway up, but there was nobody in it.

— *That's weird. If there's nobody in the cradle, who's operating it?*

— *Maybe it's just malfunctioning.*

— *Yeah. Maybe.*

He turned again, and continued on his way. At the far side of the plaza, he noticed a man sitting on a bench, reading a copy of *The Times*. For the briefest moment, their eyes met. The man immediately pulled his gaze back to the newspaper. Ricky felt a little uneasy. This was turning into an odd morning.

Ricky had a bit of a problem with cafés. Last time he'd been in one, exactly a week ago, a man had died and Ricky had been lucky to escape with his life — thanks to a kid his own age who went by 'Agent 21'. Agent 21 had got him out of there by smashing the whole glass frontage of the café to smithereens.

But surely something bad couldn't happen *every* time he went into a café. There was a greasy spoon just five minutes' walk away. He reckoned today was as good a day as any to try it. What could possibly go wrong?

It was steaming and busy inside. Rihanna was playing on the radio in the background. There was only one table left, next to the window. Ricky took a seat and, two minutes later, had ordered himself tea and breakfast.

Ricky had always been observant. But since he'd met Felix, his observation skills had improved tenfold. So much so that he found himself recording minute details of everything around him without even knowing it. He noticed how the old man by the window had his knife and fork in the wrong hand, but his watch still on his left wrist. He noticed how the girl at the table opposite, with a sleeping child in a pushchair, had two ear studs in her left ear and only one in her right. She looked exhausted, and her purse was lying on the table, teetering on the very edge. He noticed how three guys in their early twenties, sitting together with mugs of tea, had newspapers open on the table, but weren't reading them. They were all looking in different directions: one towards the kitchen, one towards the door and one directly at the young mum's teetering purse . . .

— They're casing her. They're going to try to steal her purse.

— Very observant. It's her own fault for leaving it on display like that.

— She looks knackered. I bet the last thing she needs is for her purse to go missing.

— Not your problem, Ricky. Isn't Felix always saying you shouldn't use your skills to get involved with things that aren't your concern?

This was true. Felix was like a stuck record about stuff like that. The Rihanna song finished on the radio, and a news bulletin started. Ricky felt his ears tuning in.

'*Reports are coming in of a shooting in Hyde Park. Two men are suspected dead, and police are actively searching a teenage boy to help them with their enquiries . . .*'

Ricky frowned. Right then, his food and tea arrived. As the guy serving him walked away, he saw the three young men nod imperceptibly at each other. They stood up. And as Ricky cut into his sausage, they walked over to where the mum and her child were sitting. One of them started making a real fuss of the kid. The little boy cooed delightedly at him. Another loitered a metre or so away, while the third engaged the mum in conversation.

'He's very cute,' the guy said in a pronounced London accent. 'What's his name?'

Ricky ate, but his eyes were firmly on the woman's purse.

'Andrew,' said the woman.

'Hey, that's *my* name!' said the young man. He turned to the baby. 'All the best people are called Andrew,' he said.

Ricky had to admit grudgingly that it was a good take. Just as the woman looked proudly at her cooing baby, the guy deftly took the purse. He immediately passed it on to the guy loitering by the door, who slipped it into the right-hand pocket of his coat. Then he straightened, making ready to leave.

Ricky stood up.

– *Mate, stay out of it. It's nothing to do with you.*

– *Trust me. I can deal with these jokers.*

– *Ricky, what is it with you and cafés? You're on holiday, remember?*

But Ricky was already stepping towards the door. 'Excuse me, mate,' he said to the guy who had the purse.

The pickpocket's expression changed. His eyes looked wary, and as Ricky stood right in front of him, he could feel the guy's muscles tensing up. Flight or fight.

'What?' The guy raised his arms, palms outwards, as if to say: *I didn't do anything.*

'You left your newspaper at your table. Mind if I

take it?' As Ricky spoke, he looked over the pick-pocket's left shoulder, knowing full well that the guy would follow his gaze. It gave him the fraction of a second he needed. Ricky slipped one hand into the guy's pocket and retrieved the woman's purse.

'Whatever.' The guy shrugged.

Ricky smiled at him. 'Thanks very much, mate,' he said brightly. He pushed past the others and retrieved one of the newspapers. By the time he was walking back past the woman's table, the three guys were outside, striding hurriedly away. Ricky bent down and pretended to pick up the purse. 'I think this fell off your table,' he said, and he handed it to the woman. She looked a bit flustered, but grateful.

— *Very flash.*

— *Thanks. I thought so.*

— *Any chance you could stop looking quite so smug? It'll put the other diners off their food.*

Ricky took his seat again and started wolfing down his breakfast. As he ate, he saw the three guys on the other side of the street. Two of them had turned on the third — the one they expected to have the purse — and were shoving him in the chest. Looked like he was in for a bad morning.

Couldn't happen to a nicer guy, Ricky thought.

When he'd finished, he folded up his newspaper, shoved it under his arm and wandered up to the counter to pay. Then he made to leave the café. Just as he was stepping outside, however, he froze. The three guys were no longer on the other side of the street. They had crossed over, were standing just a few metres from the entrance to the café, and they seemed to have made up their differences.

They also seemed to have worked out what had just happened.

Not good news for Ricky. He'd just broken the first law of the street: don't mess with someone else's job.

Ricky gave them his most winning smile. 'All right, lads?' he said, holding their gaze so that they didn't notice how he was tightly rolling up his newspaper.

'What's your game?' the guy on the left said.

All three of them stepped a little closer to Ricky.

Ricky thought about Felix. His handler was always telling him to be careful how he used his recently acquired skills. That if he found himself getting into street fights, he was turning back into the boy he once was.

But Felix wasn't here now, surrounded by three pickpocketing thugs who wanted to teach him a lesson.

'Think you can stick your nose in where it's not wanted?' said the guy in the middle. And as he spoke, he pulled a flick knife from his pocket. A click, and the blade shot out.

Ricky eyed the weapon carefully. The guy was holding it low, like he knew how to use it.

Ricky raised his rolled-up newspaper. The guys sniggered. He didn't blame them. A flick knife against a copy of the *Daily Mirror*? That was no contest, was it?

But these three lads hadn't been trained by Felix. They hadn't learned that sometimes the best weapon is the one that doesn't look like a weapon at all.

Ricky didn't wait for the others to attack. With a sudden sharp swipe, he whacked the stiff end of the rolled-up newspaper against his assailant's wrist. The force was stronger than the guy expected, and it caused him to drop the flick knife, which clattered onto the pavement. Now Ricky raised his arm and slammed the stiff end of the newspaper directly into the knife guy's face. Blood spurted from his nose as he cried out and staggered back. Ricky took his chance. Shoving one of the other surprised lads out of the way, he sprinted off down the street.

– *That was a great start to the New Year.*

– *If you could spare me the wise-guy comments, I'm trying to run away here.*

But Ricky knew that the chances of anyone catching him up were non-existent. He was fast, he was lean, he was clever. And he'd been taught well by his Guardian Angel . . .

He was damp with sweat when he arrived back at the plaza outside his apartment block, but scarcely out of breath. There were fewer people here now that the morning rush hour had passed. Instinctively, however, his eyes picked out the guy he'd noticed sitting on the bench reading *The Times*.

– *He hasn't moved.*

– *Maybe he's reading an interesting article.*

– *Sure. Or maybe he's not reading at all.*

Ricky strode past the guy. As he walked, he looked up at the apartment block. His eyes narrowed. The window-cleaning cradle had moved to the very top.

Halfway across the plaza, he suddenly looked back over his shoulder. The guy reading *The Times* was watching him, but immediately looked down again.

– *Ever get the feeling you're being watched?*

– *I have now.*

He took the elevator to the penthouse and let himself back into his flat. For some reason, it felt very good to lock the door behind him. As he stepped over the threshold he heard his phone buzzing again. Striding over to the coffee table, he saw that the phone had shifted to the very edge of the glass. That was weird. It must have been buzzing a lot.

The phone fell silent just as he picked it up.

A banner on the home screen read: '17 missed calls'.

Ricky frowned. He'd barely been gone an hour. Who needed to get hold of him so badly?

– Something's going on. A weird call from Felix. The cradle. The guy with The Times. *Seventeen missed calls . . .*

And as Ricky was holding the phone, it buzzed again.

This time he answered it.

7

DECOY

'Who's this?' Ricky demanded.

'Your friend from the café.'

A puzzled look crossed Ricky's face. How could the guys from the café possibly know his number? He opened his mouth to ask exactly that question.

Then he stopped. He realized that he recognized this voice, and not from just now. The caller was referring to a *previous* incident in a café. An incident exactly a week ago.

It was Agent 21 – Zak Darke.

'You need to meet me,' said the caller.

'I don't take my orders from you,' Ricky said uncertainly. He felt out of control, and it wasn't a feeling he liked.

'Where Regent Street meets Oxford Street, zero nine hundred hours.'

Ricky looked at his watch. It was 8:15 exactly. 'That doesn't give me much time,' he said.

But the caller had already hung up.

Ricky had been warm from running. Now, for some reason, he was ice cold. There had been a strange, strained tone to the caller's voice. It did nothing for Ricky's nerves.

– Do we meet him?

– I don't see that we have a choice. Not if we want to know what's going on.

He decided to grab a coat before he left. 'This is insane,' he muttered as he turned towards his bedroom.

'Tell me about it,' said a cracked voice from behind him.

Ricky's muscles tensed up. Someone was in his flat. Who? How? The answers to both questions came quickly. 'You got in using the window-cleaning cradle, right?' he breathed.

'The other entrances are being watched.'

Ricky turned slowly. There, standing in the middle of the room, which had been empty just seconds before, was a figure he recognized.

Zak Darke looked terrible. His hair was scruffy. There were black rings under his eyes. Ricky wasn't sure, but he thought he could see tear tracks down the dirty skin of his face. He was very sure that Zak was as tense as a tightly coiled spring. He was ready to defend himself if Ricky went for him – which, for a brief, irrational moment, he felt like doing.

– If he'd wanted to hurt you, he'd have done it when your back was turned.

'What do you want?' Ricky said. Zak didn't answer. 'Look, mate, I've had a pretty trying morning.'

'You know what?' Zak said. His voice was hoarse. 'So have I.'

'What was all that business with the phone call?' Ricky asked warily.

Zak nodded at the window. 'Check out our friend reading *The Times* on the other side of the plaza.' Ricky hesitated, and Zak said, with a grim kind of smile: 'Don't tell me you didn't see him.'

Ricky edged over towards the window. He looked out over the plaza. His sharp eyes picked out the guy on the bench. He had folded up his newspaper and was now standing, holding his phone to his ear. Ten seconds later, he turned and hurried out of sight.

Zak joined him at the window. 'He's just received a call telling him to get to the corner of Regent Street and Oxford Street. And right now I reckon there's an armed response unit on its way. Maybe two.'

Ricky blinked at him. 'What for? Why are they sending an armed response unit to apprehend me, when they know I'm in my flat?' Then he silently cursed his own stupidity. 'It's not me they're after, is it? It's you.'

Zak nodded. 'They're monitoring your phone,' he said. 'They figured I might make contact and I needed a way to throw them off the scent. It was a decoy, not a message. Which reminds me . . .' Zak took his phone from his pocket, opened up the back and removed the battery. Ricky understood why – without the battery, the phone couldn't be tracked.

'Is this something to do with Felix? He called this morning, before it got light. Said he was going off the grid for a while . . .' Ricky's voice petered out. He didn't like the way Zak was looking at him. He had the stony expression of someone about to deliver bad news. 'What is it?' Ricky demanded. 'What's happened?'

'There's no good way to say this,' Zak replied. 'Felix is dead. He was shot this morning. I was there. I saw it happen. It was very quick. I doubt he even knew about it.'

His words were like hammer blows. A cold wave of numbness crept over Ricky's body. He stared uncomprehendingly at Zak, then suddenly staggered to his bathroom. Once inside, he stared in the mirror. He was shocked to see that his own face had taken on the same, haunted expression that Zak's had displayed. He closed his eyes. Felix? *Dead?* It didn't make sense. He had only spoken to him a few hours ago . . .

He felt tears coming. He wiped them away just as there was a knocking on the door. Zak's voice: 'We don't have much time.'

Ricky took a deep breath and suppressed a surge of anger. How could this guy be so calm, when such terrible things had happened? He spun on his heel and marched back out of the door, his chin jutting out, ready for an argument.

Back in the main room, Zak had one hand up, palm outwards. A mollifying gesture. He seemed to be expecting Ricky's anger. 'I know how you feel,' he said. 'Whoever shot Felix shot my handler, Michael, at the same time.'

Ricky felt as though the wind had been taken out of his sails. 'I don't understand.'

'You need to listen carefully. Things are moving fast, and we have to move faster. They'll soon realize I've sent them on a wild-goose chase, and when they do, they'll be straight back here.'

'Who's "they"?' Ricky whispered.

'The Agency,' Zak said. 'The people we work for. I had a two a.m. RV with a guy called Calaca. He was once the henchman of someone called Cruz Martinez, a young Mexican drug lord who likes to

think of himself as my enemy. Calaca is in prison –
at least he was, until I turned up. He escaped when I
was there. At the same time, my Guardian Angels,
Raf and Gabs, were abducted from the place where
we live. The Agency thinks I helped Calaca escape,
and that I was involved in the disappearance of Raf
and Gabs. They think I've gone bad. They probably
even think I'm in league with Cruz. And I don't want
to sound cocky or anything, but if they think *that*,
they'll take the whole world apart trying to find
me. I guess they'd do the same to you, if *you* went
missing – don't worry, I'm not asking you to do
that. But Felix was about to help me go off the
grid until Michael got it sorted out.' A frown
creased his forehead. He looked like he was
remembering something terrible. 'They didn't get
a chance,' he said.

– *How do we know he's telling the truth? How do we
know he* hasn't *gone bad?*

Zak smiled. Something in Ricky's expression had
obviously told him what he was thinking. 'If I was
going to hurt you, Ricky, you'd already be hurt,' he
said quietly.

There was a silence.

'Why don't you just let the Agency capture you,
and explain to them what you just explained to me?'

Zak shook his head. 'If Michael thought this was

serious enough to take both me and Felix out of
action, the Agency must be very certain that I'm
working for the other side. My guess is they're not in
the mood to be persuaded otherwise.' He looked
down. 'It probably didn't help that some passers-by
saw me rummaging through our handlers' clothes.'
He looked slightly apologetic. 'I needed to find
Felix's phone to get in touch with you.'

Another silence.

'So who *did* kill Felix and Michael?' Ricky asked
finally. 'If it was this Cruz guy, why didn't he kill
you too?'

'I'm not sure,' said Zak. 'I guess that's one of
the things we need to find out. Cruz is . . . *crazy*.
He's also rich. And he really, *really* hates me.' He
sighed. 'Well, he hates someone he knows as Harry
Gold.'

'Why?'

'Long story.' Zak glanced nervously towards the
window, then towards the front door. 'Look,' he said,
'it won't be long before the Agency distributes my
picture to law enforcement, and as soon as that
happens, every policeman in London will be looking
for my face.'

'So you thought you'd come and hang out at my
place? Thanks a million.'

Zak gave him a serious look. 'If I hadn't come,

you'd never have known what happened to Felix.'

Ricky stared at him for a moment. 'What about your Guardian Angels? Do you think they're still alive?'

'I don't know,' Zak said, and for the first time his voice sounded slightly weak.

Ricky nodded. 'How can I help?' he asked.

'Thank you,' Zak said quietly. He put his hand in his pocket and pulled out a small USB data stick. 'I think there might be some answers on here. Calaca put it in my hand when he escaped. I need to use your computer. Then I'm out of your life.'

'In the bedroom.'

'Show me.'

Ricky was still numb as he led Zak to his laptop. In the absence of his own parents, Felix had been like a father to him. A strict, sarcastic, demanding father, but a father nonetheless. If what Zak had just told him was true, there was suddenly a massive hole in Ricky's strange life.

The laptop was set up at a table in the bedroom. Zak sat in front of it, but didn't yet plug in the USB stick. Instead, he disconnected the laptop from the wireless network.

'What are you doing?' Ricky asked.

'If the Agency's watching you, they'll be monitoring your internet traffic,' Zak said. He pulled another mobile phone from his pocket and tethered it wirelessly to the laptop.

'How do you know they're not monitoring your mobiles?' Ricky asked.

'They're not mine,' Zak said. 'I stole them from some passers-by.' He gave Ricky a sidelong glance. 'You're not the only one who can pick pockets, you know.'

Once the new internet connection was up and running, Zak plugged in the USB stick. Watching the screen, Ricky saw that it contained a single document. Zak opened it up. They were presented with a web link. Zak clicked it.

A web page came onto the screen. At its centre was a Quicktime window.

Zak clicked 'play'.

8

THE CRADLE WILL ROCK

At first there was nothing. Just a black screen. Zak felt sick to the pit of his stomach. He'd been relying on this data stick. Calaca had surely pressed it into his hand for a reason. But as the seconds passed, and nothing appeared on the screen, he felt his hope draining away.

Suddenly, however, there was a flicker. A face appeared. Zak's sickness turned into something else – halfway between fear and anger. It was Cruz Martinez.

Cruz had changed since their last meeting. His face was leaner and his hair longer – almost shoulder length. His eyes were cold and hard.

'Who's that?' Ricky breathed.

'Cruz,' Zak said quietly. 'Shhh . . .'

'If you're watching this, Harry Gold, and everything

has gone according to plan, you will have suffered this morning.'

'Who's Harry Gold?' Ricky asked.

'Me,' Zak told him. 'It's one of my cover names.'

'If everything has happened the way I hope, my most loyal employee is on his way back to me, your handler is dead and your friends Raphael and Gabriella will be under my control.' Cruz smiled. *'I'd like to say that they are being well looked after, but we both know it would be a lie and I won't insult your intelligence. By now, I kind of imagine they're wishing they'd never been born.'*

'He's a real charmer, isn't he?' Ricky said.

Zak stared hard at the screen. Awful images of what Raf and Gabs were undergoing spun through his mind.

'I imagine your employers think you were involved in the jail break. So, you will be watching this by yourself. Be assured that as soon as you have finished watching this video, the link will no longer work. There will be no benefit in delivering it to your employers to prove your innocence.'

Another smile. Cruz seemed very pleased with himself.

'I thought we might play a little game, Harry.'

'Why do I get the feeling,' Ricky cut in, 'that he isn't thinking Buckaroo?'

'*I'm taking your friends to a secret location. If you fail to locate them by midnight on* el Día de Reyes, *I'll kill them, just like that witch Gabriella killed my father.*' His eyes narrowed unpleasantly. '*The feast for the King of Kings. A day to bring me a special gift –* yourself. *If you do find them, but it appears that you have had – how can I put this – adult supervision, I'll also kill them. But if you turn up alone, I'll spare their lives.*' Cruz leaned further in towards the camera. '*I'm not making any promises about* your *life, though, Harry.*' He leaned back again. '*I am taking them to a place between yesterday and tomorrow. From time to time I might upload some footage of your friends, just to keep you focused.*' A third unpleasant smile. '*I hope you've got a strong stomach. My next message might be a bit of a video nasty.*'

Cruz lowered his head, and the video ended.

Zak's mouth was dry, his skin tingling with hate and panic. He tried to play the video again. But when he clicked, it didn't work.

'*El Día de Reyes?* The king of kings?' he said, puzzled.

'Epiphany,' said Ricky. 'Sixth of January.' He bit his lip. 'Foster parents, once,' he added. 'Knew all that kind of stuff, crammed it into me and I guess some of it stuck.'

Zak looked at his watch and made a quick

calculation. It was 8:45 a.m. That gave him just shy of eighty-seven hours to find his Guardian Angels. And they could be anywhere in the world.

Silence in the room. He could feel Ricky looking at him, sense the waves of sympathy coming from him. For some reason that made him even angrier. He didn't want sympathy.

He wanted to get his Guardian Angels back.

'I don't understand what he was on about,' Ricky said. 'How can a place be between yesterday and tomorrow? It doesn't make sense.'

'It'll make sense,' Zak said grimly. 'We just haven't worked it out yet.' He looked around the flat. 'I shouldn't have come here,' he said. 'I've put you in danger. I'll go now. I know what I have to do.' He removed the USB stick and stood up.

'Where do you think you're going?' Ricky said.

'To find Raf and Gabs.'

'Not on your own.'

Zak narrowed his eyes. 'It's a trap, Ricky. Can't you see that? Cruz thinks I'll do anything to save them, and he's right. He's forcing me to go to him so that he can kill me. And if you're by my side, he'll kill you too.'

Ricky shook his head. 'I don't think so. From what you've said, he's had two opportunities to kill you this morning. Why didn't he?'

Zak didn't have an answer for that. But his mind was made up. He was doing this alone. 'I'm sorry, Ricky. I know this has been as bad a morning for you as it has for me. But this is my mission, not yours.'

Ricky's eyes flashed. 'He killed Felix. That makes me involved. End of.'

'Forget it,' Zak said bluntly. 'I'm leaving. Alone.' He stood up and headed to the exit. But when he was three metres from the door, he stopped.

He'd heard something. A scratching noise on the other side of the door. Instinct took over. He strode towards it and peered through the spy hole. His pulse rose at what he saw: four men in full combat gear – helmets, flak jackets and assault rifles. They were clearly preparing to enter.

Zak turned sharply to Ricky, who was just behind him. 'Hold them as long as you can,' he mouthed. 'And remember, you never saw me . . .' He pushed quickly past his fellow agent and back into the main room of the flat. His eyes picked out the line of baseball caps on the wall. He grabbed a lime-green one and ran to the open window. He could already hear shouts coming from behind the door as he looked out.

His stomach turned.

The window-cleaning cradle that he had used to scale the building was still empty, but now it was moving downwards. Vertical distance between Zak and it: fifteen metres. And the distance was increasing with every second. It was blowing and rattling precariously in the wind . . .

There was the sound of a heavy fist banging on the door. Zak looked over his shoulder, then back out of the window. He knew he had no option.

He took a deep breath, then climbed through the open window, trying to stop his brain focusing on the terrifying drop from here to the ground – the very thought of which made the strength drain from his muscles. *Concentrate on the cradle*, he told himself. *Concentrate on the cable.*

He heard the door burst open. He looked down. The cradle had descended another five metres. He couldn't wait.

He pushed himself out and, still clutching the baseball cap, let his body fall.

Zak kept his arms by his side and his legs straight as he tried to ignore the horrible rushing sound in his ears. The drop seemed to take an age. He tried to look straight down – to keep his eyes on the landing zone of the cradle – but he couldn't stop himself from looking further afield and seeing the awful vertical distance he'd fall if he missed his target . . .

Suddenly, with a great clatter, he hit the cradle. He bent his knees as his feet made contact, as though he were landing after a parachute drop, and let his body fall to the floor. The whole cradle juddered and rocked with the impact. Zak, sweating profusely, found he was still holding his breath, waiting to feel if the cradle was still safely descending.

It was.

Zak rolled over onto his back and looked up. There was a chance that the armed men in Ricky's flat would check the window. If that happened, he needed to know, because it would mean a welcoming party when he reached the ground. But as the cradle descended, nobody appeared at the window.

It took five minutes to descend. Bizarrely, the nursery rhyme 'Rock-a-bye Baby' started whizzing around his head. *When the wind blows, the cradle will rock.* The wind *was* blowing, and the cradle *was* rocking. Zak lay very still, moving only to pull the lime-green baseball cap back onto his head. As the cradle touched the ground, Zak prepared himself for an argument. Whoever was operating the cradle would be less than pleased to see a teenager walking out of it. He pulled the peak of the baseball cap over his eyes, and stood up.

He was right to expect a commotion. Standing next to the cradle were two middle-aged men, one of them slightly balding. To the side, where the over-ride controls for the cradle were situated, was a third man. They were all looking at Zak with expressions of outrage.

'What's your game, son?' said the bald man. 'This thing ain't a toy, you know?'

Zak quickly looked from each man to the other. Which of them had the kindest face? He selected the guy next to the bald man. He looked like the oldest of the three. There was something about his eyes that told Zak he'd be sympathetic. Zak put on what he hoped was a scared face, and addressed this older man directly. 'They were chasing me,' he said. 'These big guys – five of them. They beat my friend up and they were going to do the same to me, and steal my wallet, and . . .'

'All right, lad, all right,' said the man. 'Now you just climb out of the cradle and tell us what these fellas looked like.'

Zak nimbly did as he was told. 'Don't make me grass them up,' he said. 'If they find out, they'll come after me. I'm really sorry about the cradle, I know I shouldn't have done it, I just couldn't think of anything else . . .'

The three window cleaners exchanged a look.

'Go on,' said the balding guy. 'Get out of here.'

Zak gave him a grateful look and immediately edged away from them. 'And don't do it again!' the bald guy shouted after him.

He wanted to run. To sprint away from Ricky's apartment block as quickly as possible. But he knew that would just attract attention to himself. So he set a steady pace, skirting round the edge of the plaza, his shoulders hunched and his head down.

Zak had practically forgotten the drama of jumping into the cradle. That was in the past, and his mind was firmly set on the future. He had less than four days to find Raf and Gabs. Four days, and almost nothing to go on. As he headed towards the nearest underground station, he repeated Cruz's sinister words in his head. *I am taking them to a place between yesterday and tomorrow.* It didn't make any sense. *Today* was between yesterday and tomorrow, but 'today' was a time, not a place.

He continued to struggle with the riddle as he bought himself a ticket and, checking around to see that nobody was watching him, headed through the barrier, down the escalator and then – almost as a reflex – back up it to check nobody was following. He hoped Ricky was dealing with the armed response unit OK. He seemed like a good guy. A bit under-cooked, maybe – but he *had* just lost Felix in the middle of his training. Zak made his way onto the westbound platform. He took a seat at the far end and continued to think. He knew that if Raf and Gabs were here, they'd tell him not to take Cruz's bait. But he also knew that if the shoe was on the other foot, nothing would stop them from hunting him down and getting him home.

A cool breeze from the other end of the platform told Zak that a train was approaching. A wave of fatigue crashed over him as he stood up and moved to the edge of the platform. It had been a physically and emotionally exhausting morning. He wished he was back in bed on St Peter's Crag and then, with a jolt, realized there was a good chance he'd never see that place again.

The train arrived and the door hissed open. Zak stepped into the carriage. It was only half full and he easily found a seat. As he sat down, another passenger took the seat next to him. A young guy wearing a blue baseball cap.

Zak swore under his breath. Either he was too tired, or too preoccupied, or he was losing his edge.

He turned to look at his neighbour, who smiled. 'You're not the *only* one who can creep up on people,' said Ricky.

9

ALAS

Ricky couldn't work Zak out. Half an hour ago he had needed his help. Now, as they sat side by side on the underground, he seemed furious to be in Ricky's company. He put it down to the stress of the morning. Ricky felt it too.

They didn't speak. Both of them knew to keep quiet in public. At Piccadilly Circus, Zak got off the train and Ricky followed. Only when they were out in the street, walking north through Golden Square, did Ricky strike up a conversation.

'So where are we going?'

'I'm going this way,' Zak said. 'I don't know about you – you just seem to be tagging along.'

Something snapped inside Ricky. He grabbed Zak's left forearm. Zak suddenly spun through a quarter-circle, with the speed and deftness of a cat, his right arm raised and ready to strike. It was the reflex action of someone prepared to fight. Zak's movement, however, was precisely matched by Ricky, who had raised his left arm, ready to block the blow.

They stared at each other, then carefully lowered their arms.

'Listen, mate,' said Ricky. 'I know you've been in this job for longer than me, but I just slipped away from four heavily armed men who were looking for you, and now they'll be looking for me too. So spare me the sulks and tell me: where are you going?'

They stood almost like statues for a moment.

Then Zak sighed.

'I'm sorry,' he said. 'A lot has happened in the past few hours. I'm not thinking straight.'

Ricky grinned at him. 'Two heads are better than one.'

'Yeah. And three heads are better than two. Cruz has set us a puzzle, and there's a guy I know who's very good at puzzles. Just a kid. He lives on Lexington Street, just up here.'

They started walking again.

'So who is this guy?' Ricky asked.

'His name's Malcolm.'

'Is he an agent?'

'Nope.'

'Is he trained?'

'God, no.'

'Do you trust him?'

Zak stopped, seemed to think about it for a minute, then put his hand up and wobbled it slightly, as if to say, 'Sort of.'

'You're not filling me with confidence, mate.'

'Malcolm's all right. We've been on a couple of missions together. I've seen him do seriously amazing things with computers. One time, he took over the whole of Twitter. Then another time, in Africa, he reverse-engineered the whole mobile phone network.' The corner of Zak's mouth turned upward. 'He's pretty good at crosswords too.'

'So how come you know about him and the Agency doesn't?'

'It's complicated. Michael put him up in a flat in Soho, but he kept it quiet from the Agency. There are a lot of people in our line of work who'd like to get their hands on him – not all of them friendly. We kind of had a feeling he might come in useful one day. I guess today's that day.'

'I bet it's a pretty dodgy place,' Ricky said.

'How do you know?'

'I used to have this landlord who let me live underage in one of his rooms. The fact that I didn't want anyone asking questions meant he didn't need to worry too much about making sure it was fit for human habitation.'

They took a right-hand turn, past warm, inviting cafés that were full of punters, then left into Lexington, where they stopped outside a tall, rather shabby terraced building, with a black front door. Zak sniffed. 'Don't take this the wrong way,' he said, 'but Malcolm's a bit of a weirdo. He gets nervous around strange faces. Best to let me do the talking.'

Ricky shrugged.

There was an intercom by the door. Zak pressed the button.

No answer.

'Maybe he's gone out,' Ricky said.

'To be honest, Malcolm's not the "going out" kind.'

'You're really bigging him up, you know that?'

As Ricky spoke, there was a noise above them. They both looked up. A window had opened three floors up. A boy about their age had poked his head out. He had a thin face, greasy brown hair and brown glasses. He stared at them for about five seconds, then disappeared back into the building.

'Is that him?' Ricky asked.

'Yeah, that's him.' Zak raised his hand to ring the buzzer again, but there was a small tinkling sound as a key fell onto the pavement. Ricky picked it up and handed it to Zak, who opened the front door and let them in.

It was dark inside, and it didn't smell too fresh. They closed the door behind them and felt their way up a steep, creaking, rickety staircase. There were apartments off the first- and second-floor landings, both of which had music blaring from them – Taylor Swift from the first floor, old-school drum and bass from the second. The third-floor landing, however, was silent. The number 3 had been roughly painted on the door, which was firmly shut.

Zak knocked.

No answer.

'Malcolm, mate. It's me. You need to open up.'

'How do I know you're not going to kill me?' came a muffled voice from behind the door.

'Why does everyone think I'm going to kill them?' Zak muttered in a slightly exasperated voice. 'I've *never* killed anyone.'

'It's probably just the way you look,' Ricky whispered. 'Look, mate, are you sure about this guy? He sounds more than weird.'

Zak ignored that. 'Malcolm, how many times have I saved your life? Come on, buddy, open up.'

'Michael told me not to open the door to anyone.'

Zak and Ricky exchanged a look. 'I'm sorry, Malcolm,' Zak said in a quiet voice. 'Michael's dead.'

Silence.

Then, from the other side of the door, the sound of several locks being unfastened. It took a full thirty seconds before the door swung open.

Malcolm looked pale and unhealthy. His eyes – behind the thick lenses of his glasses – were darting around nervously. He made no attempt to invite them over the threshold.

'Er, Happy New Year, Malcolm. Now can we come in?' Zak asked.

Malcolm blinked, and looked slightly surprised by the request. But he stepped aside while Ricky and Zak entered. As soon as they were through the door, Malcolm started locking it again – Ricky saw that there were three separate mortice locks, and a steel bar that crossed the entire door. He looked around the rest of the room.

– *Zak's not wrong*, said the voice in his head. *The guy is a weirdo. Look at this place.*

Malcolm's apartment was a single large room, with a small kitchen area in one corner and a door leading to what Ricky assumed was a bathroom. The floor vibrated from the music playing below. A wooden broom was leaning against one corner, but a quick glance at the floor told Ricky it hadn't been used very often. Every inch of one of the walls was plastered with crossword puzzles, meticulously filled in. On another wall was a collection of closed-circuit TV camera pictures, blurry and indistinct. They all seemed to contain one person. As Ricky peered a bit more closely, he realized that it was Zak – getting in and out of cars, ducking down into subways, running round street corners. Zak had obviously noticed this too. He was staring at the pictures with a slightly stressed look on his face.

'Been keeping an eye on me, Malcolm?'

Malcolm clearly didn't get the irony. He stared straight at Zak. 'Of course,' he said.

Ricky looked over at the kitchen area. He saw ten boxes of cornflakes, meticulously piled up. Next to them, packets of chocolate biscuits. In the middle of the room was a large table with five computer screens in a circle. Cables trailed all over the floor, and in one corner, piled just as neatly as the cornflakes, were seven iMacs, all boxed up.

'Why is Michael dead?' Malcolm asked directly.

'Somebody shot him,' Zak said. He spoke slowly and carefully, as if to a small child. 'It was very quick.'

'Why did somebody shoot him?'

'I don't know. I think it was something to do with me.'

'Why didn't they shoot *you*, then? Wouldn't that have been better?'

If Zak was offended, he didn't show it. 'Doesn't the guy downstairs ever turn his music off?' The thumping bass had just got louder, and the floor was vibrating.

'I think he's a drug addict.'

'Because he plays loud music?'

'No. I've seen him buying things on the street corner.' Malcolm pointed towards the window.

Zak nodded. 'Sit down, Malcolm,' he said. 'We need to talk.'

There was only one place to sit – a workstation chair at one of the computer screens. Zak let Malcolm use it and, over the next few minutes, told him the story of what had happened that morning just as he had told it to Ricky – only this time he spoke very simply. Ricky watched Malcolm's face closely. It was completely expressionless. Ricky couldn't tell what he was thinking, and he found that very un-nerving.

Once Zak had finished talking, Malcolm sat in silence for a moment.

'I always hated Cruz Martinez,' he finally said. 'Now I hate him even more.'

'You've got good reason, buddy,' Zak said.

Ricky looked from one to the other. 'Something I should know about?' he asked.

Zak nodded. 'Cruz killed someone very close to Malcolm. In cold blood. In front of him.'

'My cousin,' Malcolm said. 'She was the only person who ever looked after me.' He frowned. 'Apart from Michael and Zak.'

Ricky was suddenly struck by the look of pain in Malcolm's strange eyes. He felt a pang of sympathy. 'I'm sorry,' he said.

Malcolm stared into the middle distance for a moment, then appeared to shrug it off. 'Between yesterday and tomorrow. What does that mean?'

'I was hoping you could help us out with that,' Zak said.

Malcolm blinked heavily and fast. 'Give me the data stick,' he said.

'There's no point, Malcolm. The link's dead.'

'Give it to me.' And then, as an afterthought: 'Please.'

Zak shrugged, put his hand in his pocket and gave Malcolm the data stick. Malcolm plugged it into the back of his computer and faced the screen. He clicked on the data stick icon, and his hands rested lightly on the keyboard. But before he could even type anything, a new video window popped up.

'The opening frame's different,' Ricky said immediately. 'It's not all black – it looks like the camera's pointing at the sun, or something. It's a different video.'

'Play it,' Zak said. 'And try to capture the video so we can watch it again.'

Malcolm fingers flew over the keyboard, then he clicked on the screen. The juddery video footage started to play.

Ricky could immediately tell that it *was* the sun, being shot through the window of an aircraft. He caught a glimpse of the plane's wing as the camera panned round to reveal the interior of the aircraft.

– *Small plane*, said the voice in Ricky's head. *I'm thinking private jet. Very luxurious . . . Oh my God . . .*

The camera was now focused on a person sitting in one of the seats. It was a woman. She had blonde, shoulder-length hair, and a face that had obviously been beautiful before she'd been captured. Now, though, it was a mess. Her nose had been broken, there was a huge swelling on her right cheek. Her face was streaked with blood, and her lip was split. She was blinking very fast, as though she had something in her eye. Ricky thought he recognized her from his last mission. He glanced at Zak. His expression was grimmer than Ricky had ever seen it. 'That's Gabs, isn't it?' he asked.

Zak nodded.

The camera panned left. It stopped on another figure, also blond, but male. If anything, he was in a worse state. His whole face was bruised and bleeding, and his left eye was so swollen that he couldn't open it.

The video footage stopped.

'Did you capture it?' Zak asked in a thick voice.

Malcolm began typing again. The video started to replay.

'They were abducted this morning, so that must be the rising sun,' Zak said. He continued to scrutinize the screen. 'Pause it,' he said suddenly. Malcolm tapped the keyboard. 'Look.' Zak pointed at the screen. 'I think that's the door to the cockpit. The sun was shining through the rear starboard window. So they're heading . . .'

'North-west,' Ricky said. 'That means that if they left the UK this morning, they must be crossing the Atlantic.' He gave Zak a sympathetic look. 'I'm sorry, mate – I don't know how we're going to follow them if we have to get through passport control and the Agency's looking out for—'

'Play it again,' Zak interrupted, as though Ricky hadn't spoken. Malcolm tapped the keyboard. The footage rolled. They saw Gabs, her face brutalized, blinking erratically. 'Slow it down,' Zak said.

Malcolm clicked his mouse on the left-hand side of the screen. The footage moved to half speed. 'Why is she blinking so much?' Ricky asked.

Zak shook his head. 'She's not blinking,' he said. 'She's sending us a message. Morse code.'

Ricky's own eyes widened. He'd been taught Morse code, and now Zak had pointed it out, it seemed obvious that Gabs was giving a series of short and long blinks – dots and dashes. He followed them carefully.

Dot dash.

Dot dash dot dot.

Dot dash.

Dot dot dot.

'A – L – A – S . . .' he said slowly as he deciphered each letter, before the camera panned away from Gabs. Malcolm stopped the footage.

'Alas?' Ricky said. 'That's what you say when something's going really badly, isn't it? It doesn't make any sense. Why would she go to all that trouble, just to say "alas"? Maybe she meant to sign "alias" or something.'

'No,' Zak said. 'If she signed "alas", she meant "alas". But she's trying to tell us something else.'

'What?'

'I don't know. Malcolm, play the footage again.'

But Malcolm didn't move. He was staring at the screen, his own eyes blinking almost as fast as Gabs's had been.

'*Malcolm!*'

Malcolm ignored them. He swung away from the computer terminal and moved over to one of the others, where he started typing furiously. Ricky could see the screen reflected in his glasses. Lines of code were scrolling up very quickly.

Suddenly he stopped typing and lowered his head. When he raised it again, a mysterious smile played across his lips.

'What is it, Malcolm,' Zak asked, his voice tense.

'Two things,' said Malcolm. 'First thing, that video was uploaded from coordinates 60.985520, 41.646348. That's about fifty miles off the coast of Greenland. I hacked into the global satellite communications network and triangulated the three satellites that received the signal.'

Ricky gave a low whistle. 'You can do that?'

Malcolm looked genuinely puzzled. 'Can't you?' he asked.

'Leave it,' Zak said in a low voice to his fellow

agent. 'And what's the second thing, Malcolm?' he asked.

'Oh, that,' said Malcolm. His smile became broader, and his glasses slipped down his nose a little. 'I know where they're going,' he said.

10

BRAINIAC

Zak and Ricky stared at Malcolm. Ten seconds passed and Malcolm said nothing.

'OK, brainiac,' Zak urged him. 'Where?' He'd forgotten how frustrating his strange friend could sometimes be.

'It's obvious, isn't it? We only saw the first four letters of Gabs's message before the camera moved away from her. She wasn't saying "alas". She was saying "Alaska".'

There was an uncomfortable silence. The very word made Zak feel chilled.

'We can't be sure of that,' he said. 'The message could have meant all sorts of—'

'We *can* be sure,' said Malcolm. 'One hundred per cent.' He pointed at his screen. Zak and Ricky walked round to look at it. Malcolm had brought up a satellite map. There was an expanse of water, with a peninsula of snow-covered land on either side. In the middle of the water, about the same distance from both peninsulas, were two islands, very close together: a small one on the east, a larger one on the west.

'What are we looking at?' Zak demanded.

Malcolm pointed at the expanse of water. 'The Bering Straits,' he said. 'It's a body of water that separates—'

'America from Russia,' Zak filled in. 'They're off the north-west coast of Alaska. But why do you think that's where they're going?'

Malcolm pointed at the two islands. 'These islands are called Big Diomede and Little Diomede. Big Diomede is Russian, Little Diomede is American – just off the Alaskan coast. They're both in the middle of the Bering Straits. The International Date Line passes between the two islands. That means that, even though they're very close, Big Diomede is twenty-one hours ahead of Little Diomede. And *that* means that for twenty-one hours a day, it's a different day on each. They call Big Diomede "Tomorrow Island" and Little Diomede "Yesterday Island".'

'*Between tomorrow and yesterday*,' Zak heard Ricky murmur. 'Kind of makes sense . . . Hey, Zak, you were right – Malcolm *is* good at puzzles . . .'

Zak barely heard him. His body felt numb, but his mind was turning somersaults. They might have solved one puzzle, but there were much bigger puzzles outstanding. Such as: why was Cruz luring Zak out like this? If he'd wanted him dead, why hadn't he just killed him when he shot Michael and Felix? None of it made any sense.

'What's the time difference between here and there?' he said.

'On this side of the date line,' Malcolm said, 'nine hours.'

Zak looked at his watch and did a quick calculation. 'That gives us a few hours' breathing space,' he said. 'Ninety-seven hours until midnight on Epiphany.'

'Maybe we should go to the police,' Ricky said. 'There's no way we can follow them that far.'

At the word 'police', Malcolm visibly started. He wheeled his chair back. His pale face had gone even whiter.

Zak flicked Ricky an irritated look. '*Dear Mister Policeman*,' he said, a note of sarcasm in his voice, '*we're secret agents and our friends have been kidnapped and taken to the Bering Straits. We've only got ninety-seven hours to save them. You do believe us, don't you?*'

Ricky frowned. 'No need to be like that,' he said.

'Sorry. Long morning. What else do you know about these islands, Malcolm?'

Malcolm still seemed nervous, and he spoke hesitantly. 'Um . . . Big Diomede was a Russian military base during the Cold War. There's a tiny population of indigenous people on Little Diomede, and in the winter months it's possible to walk across the ice pack from one island to the other. Dangerous, though, and illegal . . .'

'But if you wanted to meet *between* yesterday and tomorrow, that's what you'd have to do, right?'

'Right.'

Zak thought for a moment. Then he stuck his hand into his back pocket and pulled out the passport in the name of Harry Gold that he'd brought along with him. He handed it to Malcolm. 'Can you get me on a flight to . . . I don't know, somewhere close to Alaska? Using my Harry Gold identity?'

Malcolm looked at the passport, then up at Zak as though he was a simpleton. 'Of course,' he said. 'But—'

'Do it,' Zak said. Malcolm raised an eyebrow. 'Please?' he added. Then, remembering that Malcolm didn't much care about pleases and thank-yous: 'What?'

'Obvious, isn't it?' Ricky cut in. 'If the Agency's watching you, they'll know the very second Harry

Gold – or any other alias you use – is booked on a plane. They'll be at the gate, waiting for you.' Malcolm nodded in agreement.

'I can deal with the Agency,' Zak said grimly.

Ricky looked at him warily, as though he wasn't sure how Zak would react to what he had to say. 'Mate,' he said, 'I'm not saying you aren't good. You *are* good. But we've already slipped through their fingers once. They're not going to let it happen again.'

Zak felt himself sneering. But deep down, he knew Ricky was right. He'd be walking into a trap of his own making. He felt another surge of anger pass through his blood. Cruz's cold face flashed in front of his eyes. If his enemy was here now, in front of him, he didn't know how he'd react . . .

'I've got a better idea,' said Malcolm.

Zak snapped out of his reverie. 'What?'

'I said, I've got a—'

'I mean, what's your idea?'

'I hack into the UK passport service. Order a new passport in a new name. They'll deliver it here tomorrow, and I can put you on any flight you like.'

'You can do that?' Ricky said for a second time.

Malcolm looked affronted. 'Of course,' he said. 'How do you think I manage to stay in this place by myself? I can get you anything like that you want.'

'Do it,' Zak told him. He hesitated, and glanced over at Ricky. 'Get a second one for him. Any name will do.'

Within seconds, Malcolm had held up a smartphone to take their photographs. And in no time at all, his fingers were flying over the keyboard again.

The afternoon passed slowly, but not as slowly as the night. Zak paced the room like a caged animal. Each moment that passed was a moment closer to Cruz's deadline. They were wasting time, and it made him want to howl.

The noise of drum and bass from the flat below stopped at sunset, but the bustle from the Soho street outside continued into the small hours. Malcolm didn't offer them any food or a place to sleep. Zak and Ricky asked for neither. Grief and anxiety had chased away their appetite, and the idea of sleeping seemed crazy. Zak *thought* they were off the grid at Malcolm's, but he couldn't be entirely certain. Having hacked into the passport system, Malcolm had given his address away so that new passports could be delivered there the next morning. That meant there was a weak link in the chain.

And so, as night fell, Zak and Ricky sat facing the

locked door, while Malcolm typed incessantly at one of his workstations. Zak didn't bother asking what he was doing – he doubted he'd understand it anyway. But when, just before midnight, the sound of his fingers on the keyboard became too much, he said, 'Malcolm, what else do you know about these Diomede Islands?'

Malcolm looked up in surprise. It was almost as if he'd forgotten they were there. He blinked at them. 'I know lots,' he said. He nodded at his computer screen. 'I've been researching.'

Zak had to smile. 'Let's hear it then, mate,' he said.

'Little Diomede – the American one – is very remote. A helicopter tries to deliver supplies there regularly, but sometimes the weather is too bad and they can't get there. Right now they've gone a month without flights because it's too dangerous.'

'Great,' Zak muttered.

'It has a population of about one hundred and seventy Inuit islanders, who all live on the west side of the island, in the village of Diomede. Big Diomede is all military. When the Soviets were in charge of Russia, they moved all the islanders back to the mainland. It's still full of military units.'

'What's the best way to get there?' Ricky asked. 'When flights are working, I mean.'

'You need to get to a place in Alaska called Nome. That's where the flights go from—'

As Malcolm spoke, there was a knock on the door. Everyone fell silent.

'Expecting someone?' Zak breathed.

Malcolm looked terrified. 'I've never had a visitor,' he said.

There was a horrible silence in the room. Zak cursed himself for not having been more vigilant. He'd broken one of the fundamental rules: always have an escape route. They were three storeys up, and there was no window-cleaning cradle to save him this time. He and Ricky should never have stayed here . . .

He immediately looked around for something that might be used as a weapon, then grabbed the broom leaning up against the wall, while Ricky picked up a wireless keyboard from the desk and made a slicing motion through the air with it. As weapons went, they were pretty feeble – especially against an armed response unit.

Another knock. Harder this time. Impatient.

'Answer it,' Zak whispered.

'What if it's the Agency?' Malcolm said.

'Surely they wouldn't knock,' Ricky breathed. Zak wasn't so sure, and he gripped his broom handle a bit harder.

'Nobody's *ever* knocked on my door,' Malcolm said uncertainly.

'Just open it.'

Malcolm approached the door diffidently. He slowly undid all the locks as Zak and Ricky took up positions just behind him – the room was too small for them to pretend they weren't there.

The door opened.

A man. Early twenties. He had long, greasy hair and very grubby clothes. He hadn't shaved for days, and his eyes had a spaced-out, faraway look to them. His lips were twitching. His hands were behind his back, and Zak had long ago learned never to trust someone whose hands he couldn't see.

The man didn't even seem to see beyond Malcolm, whom he addressed in a vague tone of voice. 'Lend us some sugar, mate.'

'You're the person from downstairs,' said Malcolm.

'Give the boy a prize.' He was looking beyond all of them, at the computer equipment in the flat. 'About that sugar . . .'

'I don't like sugar,' said Malcolm.

The guy sneered. 'No need to be like that,' he said. He took a step forward. As he did so, his hands appeared with surprising speed from behind his back. He was holding a knife. Five inches. Sharp.

111

Zak and Ricky moved suddenly and in unison. Ricky grabbed Malcolm by the shoulder and pulled him back, away from the door. Zak slammed the broom pole hard against the man's wrist. There was a sickening cracking sound. The knife fell to the floor. Ricky kicked it away, then fronted up to the man.

'You heard him,' Ricky whispered. 'He doesn't like sugar. Probably best you go now.'

The stranger's spaced-out eyes had gone wild. He was clearly startled by the way he had been so suddenly disarmed. Clutching his wrist, he stared at Ricky, then Zak. He managed to look both shocked and angry. But he knew when he was beaten. He turned and scampered back down the stairs.

Zak watched as Ricky closed the door and bolted it again. He had to admit, they made a pretty good team.

Dawn came. Zak ached with tiredness. Dealing successfully with their midnight intruder hadn't made them any less anxious. Quite the opposite. The guy from downstairs had seen that Malcolm had possessions worth stealing. There was every chance that he could get some mates together and have another go at robbing him. Zak wasn't concerned about winning a fight. But fights could mean the police being called, and that was the last thing they wanted.

So it was a tense, irritable trio that waited for the post to arrive. At 9 a.m. Malcolm gave them bowls of cereal moistened with water from the tap – there was no milk – while Zak and Ricky took up positions at the window. They were watching for the post, but also for any other suspicious activity. Zak fixed the images of passers-by in his mind, so that he would recognize them if they passed a second time – a sure sign that Malcolm's flat was under surveillance. But he saw nothing that aroused his suspicions.

At nine-thirty, Zak noticed that Malcolm had fallen asleep at his terminal, his head lying on his folded hands.

'I feel bad about leaving him,' Ricky said quietly. 'He couldn't have dealt with that guy from down-stairs by himself. What if he comes back?'

'He's more capable than he seems,' Zak said. 'We were in Africa once and he got us out of a pretty tight situation. Listen, Ricky, there's something I need to tell you. It's not up for negotiation.'

'Go on.'

'Cruz Martinez and I used to be friends, kind of. Since then, he's done some terrible things. I've always thought he'd see the error of his ways. Always thought that maybe I could turn him back to the boy he used to be. Turns out I was wrong.' He looked down. 'When . . . *if* . . . we finally catch up with him, he's mine to deal with, OK?'

Ricky gave his companion a calm look. 'What if he deals with you first? You're walking into his trap, you know.'

'Of course I am. But it's a trap set for one person. And we're not going to be one person, are we?'

Zak was stopped from elaborating by a red post van pulling up outside. A postman got out, package in hand, and posted it through the door.

'I'll get it,' Ricky said quietly. Zak nodded his agreement.

Two minutes later, Ricky had returned, a brown Jiffy bag in his hand. He locked them back in, then opened up the envelope. He pulled out a fresh passport, checked the ID page and handed it to Zak. Zak gave it the once-over. It was a perfect, authentic passport, with Zak's photo but in the name of Charlie Fletcher. Out of the corner of his eye, he saw Ricky looking through his own passport.

Then he heard his companion cough meaningfully. Zak looked up. Ricky was holding open a third passport at the ID page. It had Malcolm's photograph on it.

'Either he's booked a holiday,' Ricky said, 'or he wants to come with us.'

The two boys looked towards Malcolm. He was still sleeping. In fact, he had just started to snore. Zak smiled. Ricky looked astonished. 'You *want* him to come with us?'

'Sure,' Zak said. 'But I didn't want to force him into it. It had to be his choice. That trap Cruz has set for one person will have to manage three. Gives us the upper hand, don't you think?' He walked over to Malcolm and shook him gently by the shoulder. 'Wakey-wakey, brainiac,' he said. 'It's time to go.'

11

VIDEO NASTY

— Money won't be a problem, then? Ziggy, the voice in Ricky's head, observed drily.

— Guess not.

Ricky's eyes widened at the contents of the three boxes Malcolm pulled out from under his sofa bed. They were cornflake boxes, just like the ones in his kitchenette. But they didn't contain breakfast cereal. They contained bank notes – fresh, crisp twenties. There had to be several thousand pounds there.

'Where d'you get all that cash?' Ricky asked. 'Wait, don't tell me, you hacked a cash machine.'

Malcolm blinked at him. 'Of course not,' he said.

'So what *did* you do?'

'I hacked the Bank of England mainframe,' Malcolm said with a perfectly straight face.

– OK, I'll admit it, I'm beginning to see why Zak thinks this guy is so useful . . .

– Useful when he's behind a screen, sure. But out in the field?

'We need to be careful how we carry it and how much we take,' Zak said. 'If we get stopped and searched at customs, it'll be suspicious if we're carrying massive amounts of cash. We don't want anyone to question us too closely. Malcolm, I'm taking it you have an untraceable credit card.'

'Of course,' Malcolm said. 'I told you – I can get anything I want.'

'Then I say you bring that, and we take a couple of hundred pounds each in our wallets. Everyone agreed?'

Ricky nodded, though he couldn't help his eyes lingering on the boxes of money. Old habits die hard. He pointed to the computer screen where Malcolm had been working for the past ten minutes. 'You sure you've got us onto the flights?' he asked. 'Just like that?'

He received another strange look from Malcolm, as though it was a rather stupid question. 'Of course,' Malcolm said, rather testily. 'We're on the 13:00 flight from Heathrow to Seattle, then the 20:45 from Seattle to Anchorage. I've altered the manifests on both flights and made it look as if the seats were booked seven weeks ago.'

Ricky turned to Zak. 'You're sure this is going to work?'

'Hope so,' said Zak. 'It's a hell of a long way to swim.' He pointed to the wall plastered with CCTV images of himself. 'Can you get into the government's facial recognition files?' he asked.

'Of course,' Malcolm said.

'My guess is that they'll have cameras at all the major borders, scanning for me and Ricky. Can you corrupt the files so that our faces don't trigger an alarm?'

Malcolm didn't reply. He just set to at his terminal again. Five minutes later he nodded. 'Done,' he said.

'Good,' Zak said. He drew a deep breath. 'Then let's go.'

Ricky saw threats everywhere. As they left the house in Lexington Street, two female police officers turned the corner and appeared to stare curiously at the three teenagers leaving the building together. As they walked back towards Piccadilly Circus, he glanced frequently at the windows of the shops they passed, and in the side mirrors of any parked cars, checking that they weren't being followed. When a middle-aged man in a tweed jacket who he'd seen in Lexington Street reappeared in Golden Square, he opened his mouth to warn Zak, but didn't get a chance to speak.

'I know,' Zak interrupted him. 'If we see him again, we'll take precautions.' The man didn't reappear.

As Ricky had predicted, Malcolm was a lot less useful on the street than he had been in front of a computer screen. He was the only one with any luggage – he had a bulky laptop case slung over his shoulder. He flinched almost every time someone passed, and hugged the laptop close. His obvious nervousness clearly attracted attention.

On Piccadilly, they ducked into a chemist, where Zak bought two pairs of thick-framed reading glasses. They were very weak, and didn't spoil Ricky's eyesight too badly. He was glad to have them. Malcolm might have been able to fool any computers that were trying to recognize them, but humans were harder. If their photos had been circulated, they needed to disguise themselves as best they could.

The Piccadilly line train took them straight to Heathrow airport. The last time Ricky had been there was during his days as a thief, picking the pockets of tourists sleeping around the terminals as they waited for connecting flights. He'd been on the lookout for security guards then, just as he was now.

As they stood in a line on the travellator that took them towards the terminal, his eyes lingered on the numerous armed airport security guards. Was it him, or were there more than usual?

'Stay close,' Zak murmured. 'They'll be looking for two people together. If we look like a group of three, we've a better chance of being ignored.'

They left the travellator in a huddle. The terminal was swarming with people. Before heading to the check-in desk, they went shopping. 'It's midwinter,' Zak said. 'The Alaskan terrain will be brutally cold.' Each of them selected a sturdy rucksack, which they stuffed full of foul-weather gear: windproof jackets, base layers, fleeces, hats and gloves. Malcolm paid for them with his credit card. Then they went to the Bureau de Change to change their notes into dollars. Only then did they move to the check-in desk for the flight to Seattle. Malcolm handed them each a slip of paper.

Zak checked his, then swore under his breath. 'What's up?' Ricky asked him.

'Look at it.'

Ricky examined the slip of paper in his hand. He immediately saw what was wrong, and groaned inwardly. He looked at Malcolm. 'You put us in first class, mate?'

Malcolm blinked. 'Yes?'

'Leave it,' Zak muttered. Ricky silently agreed that there was no point giving Malcolm a hard time.

He had the impression that their computer genius friend wouldn't understand that three teenagers in expensive first-class seats were more likely to attract attention than if they were sitting in economy class. And there was nothing they could do about it now. Wordlessly, they headed for the first-class desk. 'If anyone asks,' Zak said, 'we're cousins, visiting our grandparents for a few days before term starts. Got it?'

There was no queue here. Zak went first, Malcolm immediately after. Ricky kept watching them, looking to see if either of his companions were getting any trouble. But he himself was called fifteen seconds later. Heart pumping, he approached the desk and handed over his passport.

The check-in assistant scrutinized it closely.

— *I think she just frowned.*

— *You're paranoid.*

— *And I haven't got good reason?*

Ricky tried to look casual as she scanned his passport, then double-checked the likeness of his photo.

'One minute, sir,' she said. She stood up from her desk and walked over to one of her colleagues.

Ricky's stomach hit the floor. He told himself that he needed to keep looking casual and relaxed, but he couldn't help glancing around to see what his exit options were.

– You should run. Now.

– If I do that, I'll just draw attention to myself.

– If you don't, you're done for. Why's she talking to that guy?

Ricky didn't know the answer. But he decided that it was better to stand here and see how the situation evolved than to run and risk having to answer some uncomfortable questions if he was caught.

The check-in assistant was walking back now. Her face was unreadable. Ricky felt a bead of nervous sweat trickling down the side of his face.

'Sorry about that, sir. Random checks.' She smiled at him, then handed over a boarding card. 'Enjoy your flight,' she said with a smile.

Fat chance, Ricky thought, breathing deeply to stop himself shaking. But he nodded, pushed his glasses further up the bridge of his nose, and walked back out onto the concourse where Zak and Malcolm were waiting for them.

He was halfway over to them when he felt a tap on his shoulder.

He froze. His eyes quickly picked out the nearest exit – fifty metres away below a yellow sign saying 'Taxis'. He drew a deep breath, then turned.

A young woman with brown hair pulled tightly back into a bun was standing there, carrying a clipboard. 'Excuse me, sir, I'm doing a short survey about airport facilities. I wonder if—'

'Sorry,' Ricky said, relief crashing over him, 'I'm going to miss my flight . . .'

His tension mounted as they passed through the security checkpoint and then passport control. At any moment he expected to feel a hand on his shoulder, or a line of armed guards approaching. But it seemed that they were just three faces in the crowd. Whatever Malcolm had done to keep them anonymous, he had done it well.

At 12:30 precisely, Ricky was sitting in a comfortable first-class seat in the nose of an Airbus, waiting for takeoff, his seat belt clipped round his waist. He knew he should be alert. He knew he should be keeping an eye out for threats. But now the plane was moving, and for the next nine and a half hours he wasn't going anywhere. He hadn't slept for more than twenty-four hours. He was physically and emotionally drained. And the seat was, after all, very comfortable . . .

He was asleep before the wheels left the ground.

Ricky was awoken by Zak shaking his shoulder. He sat up with a start, and for a moment he couldn't work out where he was. Then he felt the hum of the aircraft's engines, and the horror of the past twenty-four hours hit him – Felix dead, Cruz Martinez's diabolical videos.

'We need to talk,' Zak said.

Ricky unclipped himself from his seat and followed Zak along the aisle. At the head of the plane there was a lounge bar. A few passengers were sitting around with drinks, but there was one table, close to a window, that was free. They took a seat there, and Zak ordered a Coke for each of them. Ricky looked through the window. Below, there was icy terrain as far as he could see.

'Greenland,' Zak said, speaking quietly so only Ricky could hear him. 'We're over the northern Atlantic. Harsh terrain down there. But not as harsh as what we can expect when we hit Alaska. Did Felix ever give you any instruction in cold weather survival?'

Ricky shook his head. All his training had been done on the streets of London. The idea of being activated on terrain that wasn't covered with tarmac was anathema to him. 'None,' he said. 'You?'

'A little. If we find ourselves out in the open, we'll need to be vigilant about hypothermia, frostbite and snow blindness. If we sweat too much, the moisture can freeze on our skin. And it'll be hard to find food it we don't take sufficient supplies with us.' Zak glanced across the cabin. They could just make out

Malcolm, fast asleep, his glasses halfway down his nose. 'He'll find it difficult,' he said.

'I think you made a mistake, letting him come.'

Zak's face was expressionless. 'Maybe,' he said. 'Maybe not. I have a feeling Malcolm will have more of a part to play by the end of this.'

There was a short silence before Ricky brought up something that had been bothering him. 'If we find this Cruz guy, and if everything you've told me about him is true, he won't let Raf and Gabs go once you've handed yourself over. You know that, right?'

'Of course,' Zak said. 'But what else can I do? I'm not going to leave my Guardian Angels to rot. I owe them too much for that.'

'Your only chance of finding them will be to force their location out of Cruz.'

'You mean, torture him?'

'It's as good a word as any. Do you think you'd be up to it? Would you have the stomach?'

Zak turned and stared out of the window, an unreadable look on his face. 'I know *how* to kill,' he said quietly, 'but I've never done it. I've undergone resistance to interrogation training, but I've never put anyone else through the same horrors. If my Guardian Angels were here, they'd do everything they could to stop me from crossing either of those lines. But they're not here.' He turned back to Ricky, and his face suddenly looked older. 'The Agency recruited us because we were kids,' he said. 'But we can't stay kids for ever. Most children have – what do they call it, a rite of passage? A life-changing moment that marks the point when they become adults. Maybe this is ours.' He gave a grim smile. 'Or mine, at least. You don't have to do anything you don't want to. All I know is that this isn't the first time Cruz Martinez has tried to get to me by endangering Raf and Gabs. But it *is* going to be the last.'

Ricky didn't reply. There was something in Zak's voice that chilled him. He'd only met the guy once before yesterday, but he could tell that Zak had changed. He didn't know if it was for the better or for the worse. All he knew was this: next time Zak Darke and Cruz Martinez met face to face, only one of them was walking away.

Zak looked at his watch. 'We land in three hours,' he said. 'We should follow Malcolm's lead and get some more sleep. I've got a feeling we're going to need it.' He frowned. 'This is all going too smoothly,' he muttered, almost to himself. 'It can't last.'

He stood up and walked back to his seat, leaving Ricky to stare out over the frozen wastes of the north.

* * *

It was a cavernous space. Metal walls. Metal roof. Concrete floor. Harsh strip lighting flickering high overhead.

And cold. The kind of cold that saps everything from you. That makes your joints feel so solid you can barely move them. The kind of cold that hurts. There was frost on the walls and icicles hanging, in places, from the ceiling. The only blessing was that the interior was protected from the harsh wind outside.

There were four figures in this space. Two of them – both men – were standing. The other two – a man and a woman – were sprawled on the floor with their hands tied between their backs.

The two men standing spoke in Spanish. Clouds of frosty condensation billowed around them with each word. One of them had only a single eye. The missing one was covered over by a pale layer of skin. 'The Russians want them dead,' he said.

'The Russians, Calaca, can wait,' said the second figure. He was much younger than Calaca, but his eyes were even colder than the icy air. 'They are still useful to us.' He looked down at their two prisoners. They were a pitiful sight, shivering almost un-controllably. The bleeding wounds on their faces had frosted over in the cold, and it was all they could do to keep their eyes open – as if their bodies were trying to shut down, but they were forcing themselves to stay awake, just a minute at a time. A helicopter had put them down on the water's edge, and they had been forced to follow a difficult path to get here. It had been hard enough for the two able-bodied men. For their prisoners, it had been torture – only their high level of fitness had made it possible for them to get through the journey at all.

The young man crouched down to look at them. 'You think,' he said in English, 'that your boy wonder is coming to rescue you?'

The prisoners stared at him, but they seemed incapable of responding.

The young man suddenly lashed out, swiping the woman harshly round the side of her face. 'When I speak to you,' he hissed, 'you answer.'

The woman's glazed eyes rolled as a fresh trickle of blood dripped from her nostril. 'Whatever . . . you . . . say . . . sweetie,' she whispered.

'If I was in his shoes,' the young man spat, 'I would leave you here to rot, or freeze.'

'If you were in his shoes, sweetie,' whispered the woman, wincing with every word, 'you'd find they wouldn't fit.'

Calaca bent down now. 'If I cut out her tongue,' he said, 'it would put an end to her smart remarks.'

The young man shook his head. 'No, my friend,'

he said. 'She'll be needing her tongue. They both will. It's time for them to send our precious Agent 21 another video. Maybe this time I'll let them talk to him. It would be a shame for him to lose interest.' He grinned nastily at his prisoners. 'I've been meaning to ask you,' he said. 'After my Russian friends have extracted everything they need from Zak, and they've handed him back to me to dispose of in whatever way I see fit, what will your people do? Employ number 22? Or can't your kids count that high?'

He laughed at his own joke, but only for a few seconds. There was something in the cool gaze the woman gave him that he didn't find funny. He looked at Calaca. 'You have the camera?' he asked.

'Of course.'

'Start filming. And hand me your knife.'

The blade which Calaca handed him was long, narrow and very sharp. The flickering strip light reflected off the metal, which made it look like a shard of ice. The young man's thin, cold face had a greedy expression as he held it up, with Calaca filming him on a handheld GoPro camera. He approached his female prisoner first, held the blade lightly against her bruised, swollen right cheek, then gently sliced the skin. Her eyes widened slightly, but she gave no other indication that she was in pain. The young man pulled his hand away to reveal a knife wound, no wider than a paper cut but at least ten centimetres long. Blood streaked down the woman's pale skin as the young man moved over to his male prisoner, whose cheek he sliced in exactly the same way.

He stepped back to admire his handiwork. Both faces looked suitably gruesome: bruised, exhausted and smeared with blood, new and old.

'Go ahead,' the young man said. 'Give your boy wonder a message. Make it count. It might be the last time you ever speak to him.'

12

ANCHORAGE AWAY

21:00 Pacific Time Zone

'Would you like some headphones?'

Zak blinked at the heavily made-up stewardess who was holding out a set of inflight headphones in a clear plastic bag. 'Thanks,' he said quietly. 'Whatever.'

Their landing at Seattle-Tacoma International Airport had been choppy, but not nearly as choppy as their takeoff two hours later. The aircraft taking them north-west to the Alaskan town of Anchorage was an elderly twin-prop, easily buffeted by the high winds that screamed across the runway. It was almost as if someone was warning them not to travel north, but Zak put that thought from his mind. They needed to rely on logic, facts and skill. Not superstition.

It was a very bumpy flight. As the light started to fail, Zak just had time to see that the terrain below was turning white again, before his view was obscured by thick, grey, swirling cloud. And as the aircraft descended through that cloud bank, the lights flashing at the end of the wings illuminated thick sheets of heavy snow, which was falling almost sideways thanks to the howling winds. This wasn't picturesque, Christmas-card snow. It was harsh, violent and strangely alien. Zak closed his eyes, trying to ignore the fact that even the cabin crew looked scared, and attempting to put the violent shaking of the aircraft from his mind. He'd flown a light aircraft before, and even been involved in a dramatic crash landing. But that didn't make it any easier.

The tyres screamed as they touched down. Zak realized he was sweating. Through the aircraft windows he could see snow-shifting vehicles along the side of the runway, their neon lights flashing in the frosty night. As they queued up to leave the aircraft, he saw that both Ricky and Malcolm had faces that were as white as the snow drifting outside. They were obviously as glad as he was to be back down on solid ground.

'You OK?' Zak asked Malcolm quietly. Malcolm nodded a bit unconvincingly. 'Cousins, remember,' Zak breathed. He wasn't sure Malcolm was listening.

As they stepped out of the aircraft onto the landing steps, the cold air made Zak gasp as it hit his chest. The swirling snow bit into his face. From the top of the landing steps, he surveyed the surrounding airfield. There were a lot of flashing lights, but he couldn't tell what kind of vehicles they were coming from because visibility through the snow was so poor. Somehow that made him even more anxious than the bumpy flight had.

Ricky drew up behind him as they walked down the steps. He was shivering. 'What next?' he asked.

'We clear passport control, then we find out about flights to Nome, and then on to Little Diomede. And we get online. We need to see if there's anything else from Cruz.'

Having successfully cleared immigration at Seattle, getting through passport control at this smaller, more out-of-the-way airport was somehow less nerve-racking. They encountered no difficulties. In the immigration hall, Ricky's eyes picked out a couple of US army personnel. He saw that they each had a badge on their sleeve showing a picture of a ferocious polar bear, and figured that had to be the insignia of the Alaskan branch of the army. He kept his head down, and didn't catch their eye.

It was just past 11 p.m. as Zak, Ricky and Malcolm

walked out onto the airport concourse. At this time of night, very few of the airport shops were open. Just a café, and a stall selling postcards and cheap Alaskan souvenirs. They used a few of their dollars to buy hot coffee and chocolate bars. Zak left Ricky and Malcolm to refuel, then approached the one ticketing booth that seemed to be open.

It was manned by a broad-shouldered guy in his late sixties. He wore a baseball cap with a picture of a brown bear embroidered on it, and a scowl that was about as welcoming as the weather outside. He was reading a slim paperback book, and pretended not to see Zak at first. When he did finally – and reluctantly – lower his book, Zak gave him what he hoped was a winning smile. 'I need to know about flights to Nome,' he said.

The guy raised his book again. 'You're not from around here,' he said in a lazy American drawl.

A hint of steel entered Zak's eyes. 'That's why I'm asking you,' he said.

'You can forget about flying north, son. Ain't been no flights out of here for the past two days with these blizzards. Ain't going to be none for two days coming, neither. Probably longer.' He licked one finger, and made a point of carefully turning the page of his book.

Zak narrowed his eyes, but he could tell there was

no point arguing. He turned and strode back to the café where Ricky and Malcolm were sitting. Ricky had both hands wrapped round his hot cup of coffee. Malcolm had his laptop out. 'Weak wireless,' he said. 'But I'm on it.'

'Have you hidden your IP address?' Zak asked.

Malcolm looked at him in such a way that it was clear he thought that a very stupid question. He continued to type, then a sharp look crossed his face. 'There's another video,' he said quietly.

Zak looked around to check they weren't being observed. Then he took a seat next to Malcolm. 'Play it,' he said. 'Keep the volume down so we're not overheard.'

Malcolm clicked his trackpad as the three of them leaned in towards the laptop. The video started.

It was shaky to start with. The footage seemed to show a starkly lit open space – maybe a warehouse or a hangar – with metal walls and concrete floor. As the camera steadied, it fixed on two figures sitting on the ground, hands tied behind their backs. Zak instantly recognized Raf and Gabs. They looked worse than before. Their faces were more bruised. Their eyes rolled. They shivered.

Another figure entered the scene. He had his back to the camera, but Zak instantly recognized Cruz's thin frame and dark, lank hair. And he caught a glimpse of the cruel-looking knife he was holding. He watched, in frozen horror, as Cruz bent over and sliced Gabs's cheek, and then Raf's. The worst thing wasn't the blood. It was the tightness about their eyes. Zak, who knew them so well, could tell that they were in pain, but were doing what was necessary to stop themselves showing it.

He felt a hand on his shoulder. Ricky. 'You all right, mate?'

Zak nodded. Cruz spoke. *'Go ahead. Give your boy wonder a message. Make it count. It might be the last time you ever speak to him.'*

The camera focused in on Raf. He lifted his head with difficulty. And when he spoke, his words were slurred, almost as though he was drunk. *'Remember the first thing I ever taught you – that your first duty is to stay alive.'*

He drew a deep breath. Even over the tinny laptop speakers, Zak thought he could hear his lungs rattling. He coughed weakly, then spoke again. *'That means you have to stay on the . . . on the right side of the track . . .'* His voice petered away. Zak clenched his jaw. His Guardian Angel was barely making sense.

The shaky camera footage moved over to Gabs. She looked monstrous close up: puffy, bruised skin, blue lips and blood streaming from the fresh cut on her face. But she managed to stare straight into the camera, and even let the beginnings of an odd smile flicker at the corner of her mouth. Zak concentrated on her bloodshot eyes, trying to see if she was blinking him another message. Sure enough, her eyelids were flickering.

'You getting it?' he asked Ricky.

'F – I – N – D – M – O—'

Zak held up one hand to stop him reciting the letters out loud. Still blinking, Gabs spoke. Her words were as incomprehensible as Raf's had been. '*Be careful . . . of hangers-on, eh, sweetie?*'

Cruz's voice. Harsh. Angry. '*Switch off the camera. Do it!*'

The screen went black.

The three teenagers sat in silence. Zak struggled to keep his breathing steady. Malcolm started typing again.

'What was the Morse code message?' Zak breathed. He'd been concentrating too hard on what Gabs had been saying out loud.

'I think she said: *Find Moriarty*. But who's that? Is it someone you know?'

Zak shook his head. The only Moriarty he'd ever heard of had been in a Sherlock Holmes book.

'What was all that stuff about hangers-on?' Ricky asked. 'More secret messages?'

'I don't think so,' Zak said.

'So what did she mean by it? Is she talking about us? Me and Malcolm?' Ricky sounded a bit offended.

Zak shook his head. 'They sounded delirious, that's all. They're in a bad state.' His voice cracked as he spoke.

'She was able to blink a message and speak at the same time,' Ricky pointed out. 'I don't think she was *that* delirious.'

'You're right,' Zak said. 'Gabs is tough. And clever. So we've just got to figure out what she was trying to tell us.' He looked around. 'But we have to get there first. And there are no flights to Nome. We need to find another way.' He frowned. 'Either that, or we need to find someone called Moriarty.'

Ricky stared at him. 'Mate,' he said. 'I don't want to put a damper on things, but it's five hundred miles to Nome, it's the middle of winter, and there are no roads to take us in that direction. We wouldn't make it in five weeks, let alone five days. Flying's our only option.'

'Be quiet,' Malcolm said suddenly.

Zak and Ricky turned to look at him. 'What?' Zak asked.

'I'm on the UK passport system. They know they've been hacked.' He was blinking very fast. 'They've identified the three fake passports. The details were supplied to Interpol and immigration agencies twenty-eight minutes ago.' He looked up from his screen. 'The Agency knows we're here,' he said.

Zak felt his body tense up. He immediately started to scan the terminal concourse. It was not busy at this time of night – there were maybe a hundred passengers milling around, and only a handful of airport staff. But even as he looked, at a distance of fifty metres, just by the entrance to airport security, he saw three uniformed police officers, all armed, speaking urgently to each other and examining a smartphone screen.

'We've got three . . .'

'I see them,' Ricky breathed. 'We need to get out of here. Malcolm, pack up your laptop.'

But as Ricky spoke, another four officers seemed to appear from nowhere. They were by the ticketing office, and were speaking to the surly man with the paperback book. He was a lot livelier now – as they showed him another smartphone screen, he nodded vigorously and started looking around the concourse.

'We've got about thirty seconds to get out of here,' Zak said. 'Move.'

The ticket guy was still scanning the area. One of the police officers was speaking into his radio.

'*Move!*' Zak hissed.

Malcolm was still closing up his laptop, but there was no time for that. 'Leave it,' Zak hissed. Malcolm started to object, but Zak grabbed him by the arm, pulled him to his feet and pushed him towards the exit, which was thirty metres away with a bright yellow sign over a revolving door. As Ricky, his rucksack over one shoulder, hurried their companion in that direction, Zak grabbed both his and Malcolm's rucksacks and marched after them. They didn't run – that would draw attention to themselves – but they walked very fast.

Malcolm was the problem. He practically stumbled all the way to the revolving doors, saved from falling only by Ricky, who kept stabilizing him with one arm. As they hit the exit, Zak looked over his shoulder. The armed officers had moved no closer, but the three by the security entrance were jogging towards their colleagues. The ticketing guy continued to survey the concourse.

They were no more than three metres from the exit when his eyes locked with Zak's. He grabbed one of the officers by the arm and shook him vigorously while pointing in their direction. Zak cursed himself for letting the guy see his face, but there was no time to regret it. A second later he heard a loud American voice shouting from behind them.

'STOP! STOP OR WE SHOOT!'

'They won't fire in a crowded area,' Zak hissed as they slammed into the revolving door. It took an agonizing three seconds to spit them out of the terminal building. Once again, Zak found the air shockingly icy. He inhaled noisily as he surveyed the scene in front of him. A one-way vehicle lane ran the length of the terminal building. It was clearly a drop-off area – a line of fifteen vehicles were parked along the kerb. The area was covered, but Zak could tell it was snowing because the vehicles had a layer of snow over their bodywork. Their lights glowed in the night, and their exhaust fumes billowed in the freezing air. Passengers were hauling luggage out of open trunks, and in a few instances, money was changing hands with cab drivers.

Zak looked up. He immediately saw three security cameras covering the area. Then he turned his attention back to the vehicles. One of them, ten metres away, was a dark-green people carrier, with good, sturdy snow tyres. It was obviously a cab because the passengers were handing over some money to the driver.

'This way,' he hissed to the others and, grabbing Malcolm by the elbow, pulled him towards the people carrier. The driver was a shabby guy, with a pinched, lined face and hair greying at the temples.

He raised an eyebrow at these three young people sprinting towards him. Zak didn't like the look of him – not one bit – but their choices were limited. They *had* to get out of sight. 'Can you take us downtown?' he asked breathlessly.

'Sure can, kid,' said the driver, sliding open the side door of the vehicle. 'Jump on in.'

Zak, Ricky and Malcolm tumbled into the back of the people carrier, slamming the side door shut. Zak caught a strong whiff of tobacco and, maybe, alcohol as the driver got behind the wheel and pulled away. Not a moment too soon. Through the tinted window of the vehicle, Zak saw three of the armed guards burst out of the terminal building.

'I think that's what they call a close thing,' Ricky breathed.

Zak didn't answer. He was too busy wiping the sweat from his brow. But he did notice the look the cab driver gave them in the rear-view mirror. It was sharp. Calculating. The friendliness had somehow fallen away. Zak scanned the front of the vehicle, looking for some sign that this was an official cab. There was none.

'Looks like someone's in trouble,' the driver drawled. He sounded almost pleased about it.

A beat. Zak and Ricky exchanged a glance. A glance that said: 'What the hell do we do?'

Ricky suddenly put his hand in his pocket and pulled out all the dollars he had. He held them up so the driver could see them. 'These are yours,' he said, 'if you get us out of here without running into the police.'

The driver licked his lips and grabbed the notes. 'You're in luck, kid,' he said. 'Turns out that avoiding the police is something I'm pretty good at.'

Zak felt a small surge from the engine as the vehicle accelerated away from the airport.

13

ORDINARY KIDS

Ricky was drenched in sweat, despite the cold. As the car swung away from the terminal building, his attention was divided between the armed guards and the driver. He didn't know which one he feared the most. The guards had just threatened to shoot them. But the driver had a look on his face that Ricky recognized from his time scavenging on the streets of London: the look of a man who'd do anything for a pay day. It also meant that this was not a man they should trust.

'Don't drive too fast,' Zak said, his voice very tense. 'It'll be too suspicious.'

'What you do?' the driver asked. 'Steal a bag of candy from one of the shops?'

Ricky and Zak exchanged another glance. 'Yeah,' Ricky said. 'Something like that.' He turned to

Malcolm, who was looking unusually anxious and digging his fingernails into his palm. 'You all right?' he asked.

'My laptop,' Malcolm muttered, his voice slightly wild. 'What if they find it? What if they hack into it? What am I supposed to do *without* it?'

Ricky had no answer. They fell into an uncomfortable silence.

They trundled down a slip road. The vehicle stank of cigarettes – Ricky saw a packet of Lucky Strikes and a pale red disposable lighter on the dashboard. 'You saw the security cameras?' he murmured to Zak. Zak nodded. They both knew what those cameras meant: it was only a matter of time before the Agency saw footage of them getting into the green people carrier, whose registration number they'd also be able to view. They couldn't stay in this car for long.

The snow was very heavy – a billowing, twisting blizzard. Ricky could barely see anything through the window.

– *The snow might be a good thing*, said the voice in Ricky's head. *If it's harder to make out individual cars, we'll have a better chance of slipping past any police patrols.*

– *Maybe. But something tells me police patrols aren't our only problem.*

He glanced towards the front of the vehicle again. The driver's eyes were flicking regularly between the road ahead and the rear-view mirror.

– *He's planning something.*

– *Tell me about it.*

The driver swung onto a turnpike. Squinting through the swirling snow, Ricky saw a brightly lit overhead sign. He could just make out the word 'Downtown'. Ricky had examined a tourist map of Anchorage on the plane, so he knew that meant they were heading north. Even as he read it, the driver indicated left. He pulled off the turnpike and down another slip road.

'Where are we going?' Ricky asked.

'Short cut,' said the driver. 'Less traffic. Won't be no police, this way.'

– *He kept looking straight ahead as he spoke to you. He was trying to avoid eye contact. He's lying.*

– *Keep your bearings. We're heading east now . . .*

They continued driving for five minutes. There were few cars here. The road was lined with tall, snow-laden fir trees, and more snow had drifted in high piles along the sides. The road itself was clear – maybe it had been well salted – but off road, the conditions were extreme.

Suddenly, Ricky's heart almost stopped. He saw flashing blue neon in the rear-view mirror. It was hard to make out the distance, but maybe 100 metres.

Almost immediately, the driver swung left again. They turned down a much smaller road, which immediately wound round to the left, taking them out of sight of the bigger road. 'Ain't no police going to follow us down here, kids,' the driver said.

Somehow that wasn't a comfort. Ricky could see Zak eyeing the doors and the locks, and sizing up Malcolm, as if trying to establish if he was capable of making a sudden run for it. Not for the first time, Ricky wondered if they'd made a massive mistake, bringing Zak's strange friend with them.

'Where are we going, pal?' Zak said. His voice was tense and wary.

'Like I told you, short cut.'

The snow was falling even more heavily now. For the next five minutes, the road twisted and turned. It was almost impossible to work out their direction, but when the road finally straightened out a little, Ricky decided they were still heading east. The going was icier here, but the people carrier's snow tyres were up to the job.

It was obvious to Ricky, however, that with each passing mile, they were heading further from civilization.

'Stop the car,' Zak said suddenly.

The trace of a smile passed the driver's lips. 'Well,

you know,' he said, 'I might just do that.' He didn't stop immediately, but continued for another twenty metres before pulling over on the side of the road and killing the engine.

There was a deep, muffled silence. The driver looked straight ahead. Ricky could hear the tense, shallow breathing of his companions.

'We're paying you,' Ricky said. 'Now you need to keep your end of the bargain.'

That smile again. There was no humour in it. 'Well, here's the thing, kiddo,' the driver said, still staring straight through the window at the blizzard outside. 'Three things, actually. First thing: I'm pretty sure there's a whole lot more of the green stuff where that came from. Second thing: storm like this, out in the wilds like we are, you ain't getting no place without my help. And third thing: I don't know why you're on the run from the police, but I'm guessing you probably don't want to make a big deal about someone like me helping themselves to your riches. Am I right, or am I right?'

– Maybe we can overpower him. Take control of the vehicle, use it to get back to the main road.

It looked to Ricky as though Zak was having the same thoughts. Malcolm, on the other hand, had gone paler than usual and was sinking back into his seat.

'Oh,' the driver said. 'There was one other thing I forgot.' He turned to look over his shoulder. 'This part of the world, most everyone carries a gun.'

He raised his right arm. Ricky's skin prickled as he saw the driver firmly holding a grey handgun.

'Not a big deal, to get the better of three ordinary kids. And you might as well know that if I bury you in the snow, nobody's going to find you till next spring. So let's not make this any longer or uglier than it has to be.' The driver pointed the gun from Ricky to Zak – he had obviously identified the two of them as his greatest threats. 'Collect your bags, get out of the vehicle and keep your hands where I can see them. Try to run and I'll pick you off like a god-damn grizzly.'

'Look, mate,' Zak said, 'you've got the wrong idea. We don't want any trouble. We're just here to visit our grandparents—'

'*Get out of the car!*'

A tense silence.

'Do it,' Zak said.

Ricky slid the door open. The three of them climbed out. Ricky instantly felt himself sink into about thirty centimetres of snow.

'Move round to the front of the car. And hands where I can see them!' the driver barked. Ricky, Zak and Malcolm all raised their hands above their heads as they skirted round the vehicle – Malcolm standing about three metres away from the engine, then Zak, then Ricky. The swirling snow bit into their faces, and within seconds, Ricky could feel his body temperature plummet. He watched the figure of the driver shuffle round the front of the people carrier, then approach them, his weapon pointing directly at their chests. He stopped just half a metre in front of Zak. 'OK, kids,' he said. 'Open up your packs. Let's see what you've got.'

None of them moved.

'I said, open up your packs!'

'Sure,' Zak said quietly. 'But before we do, *I've* got three things to tell *you*.'

The driver looked almost amused as snow started settling on his clothes. 'Oh yeah?' he said. 'Well, make it quick, son. I'm getting cold.'

– Zak's distracting him. He's getting him to lower his guard. You understand that, right?

– Right.

'First thing: we've got nothing to give you.'

'We'll see about that, kid, just as soon as you've emptied out your pack.'

'Second thing: I've got a feeling *you* don't want to talk to the police any more than we do.'

The driver sneered. 'And the third thing?'

'Oh yeah,' said Zak. 'The third thing. That's the most important.' He leaned forward slightly, and as he did so, the driver mirrored his action. 'The third thing is that we're *not* ordinary kids . . .'

– *NOW!*

Ricky didn't have to be told. His right arm shot out as a look of puzzlement crossed the driver's face, cracking against the man's gun wrist. A fraction of a second later, Zak had grabbed the gun, pointed it over his left shoulder and slammed his heel straight into the pit of the driver's stomach.

The driver doubled over, spluttering and cursing badly. He still had his hands wrapped round the gun, but as Zak held his arm, he wasn't in control of its direction. There was a sudden crack as the gun went off – it was surprisingly loud and sent such a shock through Ricky's body that for a moment he thought he'd been hit – but then there was the sound of glass shattering. A round had slammed into the windscreen, and the glass had burst inward.

Zak and the driver were struggling, their feet sliding over the icy road. As they slipped towards the middle of the road, a second round exploded from the gun. It slammed into the side of the car, and petrol started glugging out. Ricky jumped forward to help Zak. He wrapped his arm around the driver's neck and squeezed hard, as Zak wrenched the firearm from his fist then aimed a solid kick at the man's ankles. Disarmed, he collapsed to the ground.

Zak was holding the gun with two hands. He was aiming it at the driver and had a fierce look in his eyes. Ricky held his breath. He found himself remembering Zak's words: *I know how to kill but I've never done it . . . Most people have a rite of passage . . . Maybe this is ours . . .*

Surely Zak wasn't going to shoot this guy in cold blood.

Snow swirled around them. The driver looked up at Zak, terrified.

Zak lowered the gun. Without even looking at it, he removed the magazine and chucked the remaining rounds out of sight into the distance, where they would sink into the snow. The driver scrambled to his feet. With a quick glance at his vehicle – which was obviously un-driveable – he scrambled back down the road. He disappeared into the gloom in the direction they had come from.

Silence. Malcolm was shivering by the side of the road. Zak stalked round the car, taking in the damage, the fire still burning in his eyes. Ricky stood still, his heart pumping, peering into the darkness. 'What do we do?' he asked tensely.

Zak joined him. 'We can't stay here,' he said.

'That driver won't leave his vehicle to get covered in snow. He'll bring someone as quickly as possible to remove it. Maybe even the police. We need to get away from here.'

'We can't use the road,' Ricky said. 'Not if people are out looking for us. It means going cross-country.'

Zak frowned for a moment and looked up. Ricky realized he was trying to see the stars, to help him navigate. But there was nothing visible except the thick, swirling snowflakes. Going cross-country was not an attractive option. Especially as they now only had forty-seven hours until the deadline.

'I think this road runs east–west,' Ricky said. 'We need to get back to the city. That's the only place we've got a chance of getting transport to the Bering Straits. Anchorage is to the north-west. That way.' He pointed in what he thought was a north-westerly direction. It looked no different to any other direction.

'Agreed,' Zak said. He peered into the icy darkness, then gave Malcolm – who was still shivering by the side of the road – a slightly worried look. 'It could be slow going, and dangerous in the snow. We need to be prepared.' He looked over at the car, then back at Ricky. 'Help me,' he said.

* * *

Cruz Martinez stood over his captives. They were lying on the floor, unconscious, their hands still tied behind their backs, their ankles bound. Their breath formed clouds of condensation, but their breathing was shallow and the clouds were small. The gashes Cruz had inflicted on their faces had stopped bleeding, but now they were white and puffy. If anything, they looked more alarming.

Cruz was holding a handgun. He walked up to his prisoners and placed the gun less than a metre from the woman's head, with the barrel pointing down to the floor. He fired. The retort of the weapon was deafeningly loud. The round it fired shot a crack in the concrete floor of the hangar. The prisoners' eyes immediately opened, and their bodies shuddered as if they themselves had been shot. It was a brutal way to wake them. You could see the stress and terror in their faces. But that was exactly what Cruz had intended.

'I thought you'd like to know,' Cruz said, 'that Agent 21 has landed in Anchorage.'

The woman's eyes tightened. 'How . . . do you know?' she asked. It was clearly difficult for her to speak with her bleeding lip.

'We have our contacts. The Alaskan police are in

pursuit, but they seem to have lost him. You taught him well. Running away is clearly a speciality of his.'

The woman looked him in the eye. 'You should . . . let us go,' she said. 'Better for you . . . long run.'

Cruz smiled. 'I'm very touched that you're so concerned for my welfare. No, I won't be letting you go. I'm looking forward to seeing what kind of state he's in, if he makes it this far alive. The Alaskan wilderness can be deadly at this time of year.' He crouched down so that he was at eye level with the prisoners. 'I almost forgot,' he said. 'Our sources tell me he's not travelling alone. I did make it very clear to him what would happen to you if he failed to follow my instructions.'

The barrel of the gun was still warm. He placed it against the woman's cheekbone. She inhaled sharply, but didn't take her fierce eyes off him as his fore-finger caressed the trigger.

Time stood still.

Then Cruz started to laugh, very quietly. 'He's got two little helpers,' he whispered. 'Kids. I don't think we need to worry about them, do we? Three little kids for the Three Kings Day.' He gave a hollow laugh.

The woman said nothing. But there was a strange expression on her face. It was almost like triumph. Cruz Martinez didn't notice it. He lowered his gun, stood up and, still laughing softly, left the ice-cold hangar that he had converted into a prison.

14

FIRE-STARTER

01:00 hrs

The cold was biting and deep. They had only been standing still a couple of minutes, and already the heat of the fight had seeped out of Zak's body. In its place, a profound and sinister chill. Before doing anything else, they needed to pull on the snow gear they'd bought at Heathrow.

As they stripped out of their ordinary clothes, Zak felt his body temperature plummet even further. All three of them scrambled into their cold weather gear. 'Make sure you put on your base layer,' Zak told the others. 'It'll wick the sweat away and stop the liquid freezing on your skin.' He noticed how Malcolm's thin body was juddering even more than his and Ricky's, and had to help him get his fleece over his head. 'You OK, buddy?' he asked quietly. Malcolm didn't reply.

'What do we do with our old clothes?' Ricky asked.

'Dump them. We're going to need the room in our rucksacks.'

Once they were fully dressed, Zak and Ricky got to work on the vehicle. There were precious resources here. It was worth risking a little time to gather them.

In the glove compartment, they found a metallic water canteen, a powerful torch and a sharp hunting knife. 'Maybe we should fill the canteen with whatever fuel we can still get out of the tank,' Ricky said. 'We could use it if we need to make a fire to warm up.'

Zak shook his head. 'We'll need water,' he said.

'Mate,' Ricky objected. 'There's snow all around. Can't we just eat that? Get fluids that way?'

'No way.' Zak had been well drilled in cold weather survival by his Guardian Angels. 'It can hurt your mouth and lips, and dehydrate you even further. Plus, if you're already cold, eating snow will just make you colder. Better to melt it first.' His forehead creased. 'But you're right, we might need to make a fire at some point.' He slashed the driver's seat with the hunting knife and started pulling out the spongy stuffing. 'Soak that in petrol, then try and find a bag to seal it in. It'll be good fire-starting material. But make sure you get any petrol off your skin. It has a lower melting point than water so can damage you if it freezes.'

While Ricky did as he was told, Zak cut into one of the tyres and started ripping off strips of rubber, which he knew would burn fast and easily. He stowed these strips in his pack. Malcolm watched, shivering as a layer of snow settled on his clothes. 'You keeping warm, buddy?' Zak asked him quietly.

'No,' Malcolm said. 'And I'm not strong like you. I don't think I'll manage out there.' He pointed vaguely into the snow-filled darkness.

'You'll be fine once you get moving.' Zak tried to inject some fight into Malcolm. Continuing his search of the vehicle, he found the manual and stowed it with the rubber strips – the paper would also be good for fire-starting, and out here he reckoned they'd need all the help they could get. Opening up the bonnet, he considered removing the battery and taking that to create sparks, but figured it would just be too heavy. And anyway, he had pocketed the driver's cigarette lighter. Instead, he settled for tearing an old rag he found in the back of the car and dipping it into the oil reservoir. The strips came out thick, greasy and stinking, so he found an empty pocket in his rucksack and carefully stowed them away.

He turned his attention to the vehicle's wing mirror. It was solid and heavy, and would be difficult to get off. But Zak judged that it was worth it: the mirror could be used for signalling if they needed to attract someone's attention. He used all his strength to wrench the mirror from the body of the car, then cut through the cables that attached it using their stolen hunting knife.

By the time Zak had removed the mirror, Ricky had found an old plastic bag in the back of the vehicle and stuffed it full of petrol-soaked seat-stuffing. Malcolm was still loitering by the car, looking helpless. Zak felt another twinge of doubt about the wisdom of having brought him, but then reminded himself that without Malcolm, they'd have been caught at Anchorage airport, or even stuck back in the UK.

'Malcolm,' he said, deciding that he needed a job to keep him active. 'There are some rubber foot mats in the front and the back. Why don't you roll them up and get them into your pack?'

'What for?' Malcolm asked.

'They'll do as sleeping mats if we have to make a camp,' Zak explained. 'Better than lying on the snow. Mind the shattered glass in the front. You'll cut yourself easily.' And as he said that, he helped himself to one of the larger shards. It had a wickedly sharp point, and would do as a tool or a weapon if the situation demanded it.

'Look what I found!' Ricky called from the back of the vehicle. He sounded pretty pleased with himself. As he walked round to Zak and Malcolm, he was carrying a silver space blanket, neatly folded up, in one hand. In the other was an entrenching tool – a kind of lightweight, folded-up shovel. It figured that the driver had carried a good insulating sheet for emergencies, and something to dig him out of drifting snow.

It had taken them ten minutes to strip down the car. Now Zak called them all together. They huddled in a group, absorbing some of the residual heat from the car's engine while they could. Zak looked up to the sky, where the snow was coming down even more furiously than before. 'The snowfall will cover our tracks a little, but not completely. Anyone following us will be better equipped for the weather, and there will be more of them. So we have to move fast, and we have to move smart. Understood?'

Pale-faced nods all round.

'With a bit of luck we'll find a back route into Anchorage within a couple of hours. But if we don't, our worst enemies are going to be wind and water. Our winter gear should help with that, but we need to keep our hoods up and the drawstrings closed.

Don't remove your gloves, and look out for numbness in any part of your body – it could be the first signs of frostnip. If any of us starts to feel sleepy, we need to say so – it's the first sign of hypothermia. Don't try to be brave about it – it'll hinder us much more if we don't deal with it immediately. Be very careful where you step. If there's running water, there might be a thin layer of ice with snow on top. Trust me, you don't want to get wet in this cold weather. At this temperature it'll knock the air from your lungs, you'll curl up into a little ball and your muscles will seize up . . .'

'What happens then?' Malcolm asked anxiously.

Zak sniffed. 'We'll deal with that if we come to it. And anyway, with any luck we'll hit Anchorage in a couple of hours.' He peered into the distance. 'Order of march: Ricky, then Malcolm, then me. Let's move.'

With their backpacks on and their hoods drawn tightly around their heads, they trudged across the road. It was icy underfoot, but at the road's edge Zak felt his feet sink into a good sixty centimetres of powdery snow. Malcolm was three metres ahead of him, Ricky three metres ahead of that. Zak's eyes were drawn to the footprints his companions were leaving in the snow. They were deep and obvious. Even though the snow was falling heavily, it would take several hours for it to cover those footprints. It would be the simplest thing in the world for anyone to follow them. Anxiously, he looked back over his shoulder. They'd only been marching for forty-five seconds and already the vehicle was lost among the swirling snow and the darkness.

Zak stopped. He had a sudden hit of panic. This was foolishness. They had no means of navigating properly – no compass, or sight of the stars, or visible landmarks. They were walking blindly into a hostile environment none of them had any experience of. Perhaps they would be safer keeping to the roads after all . . .

These thoughts festered in his head for perhaps two minutes before he hissed quietly to Ricky, 'Stop!'

Ricky halted, but Malcolm continued to walk – he clearly hadn't heard Zak, who shuffled up to him and grabbed him by the shoulder.

'What's wrong?' Ricky said. He sounded very tense.

Zak looked back, watching their clear footprints disappear back the way they'd come. He was about to suggest that they retrace their steps, when a noise drifted across the night air. It was very faint – distant – but there was no doubting what it was: a car engine.

Zak quickly turned back to Ricky, who seemed to understand his unspoken worry. 'If we get lost,' Ricky said, 'we'll have a few hours to retrace our steps before the snow covers them up. I say we keep going, before anyone has a chance to catch up.'

'Agreed,' Zak said. 'Let's pick up our pace. Keep going.'

The way was slow and difficult. As they continued into the snowscape, the wind above them began to howl, and they felt it swirling around their bodies along with the snow. It was an invisible, icy whip. The powdery snow whirled all around them. There was nothing to distinguish one moment from the next. It was almost like walking on a treadmill – constant movement, but nothing to show for it.

The temperature started to drop. The high-pitched whistling of the wind grew stronger. Zak realized he was in a kind of trance, unaware of exactly how much time had passed. An hour? Perhaps more? He forced himself to snap out of it.

Just in time.

Malcolm was only a couple of metres ahead when he stumbled. He fell knee deep into the snow. Zak called to Ricky to stop marching, then hurried up to help his friend. Malcolm was shaking badly, and there was something worrying in his gaze. He was staring into the middle distance, as if he didn't know where he was or what was happening.

'Get to your feet, buddy,' Zak said. Malcolm nodded, and allowed Zak to pull him up. 'How many fingers?' Zak asked, holding up three.

Malcolm squinted. 'Three,' he whispered.

Ricky grabbed Zak by the arm. 'We should *be* somewhere by now,' he said. 'The outskirts of Anchorage, or somewhere. But we haven't seen a road or a building in an hour.' He frowned, and Zak saw that snow had settled on his eyebrows. 'I think we're lost.' He nodded his head towards Malcolm. 'And he needs to warm up,' he said. 'We all do.'

Zak reckoned Ricky was right. They'd made a bad call. Zak looked back along the trail of footprints. They weren't too late to follow their path back to the road. But what if someone was on their tail? They'd walk right into them. If they went static now, and lit a fire to warm up, they'd be sitting ducks . . .

'We need to walk a loop,' he said.

Ricky looked confused. 'What do you mean?'

'We can't go static without knowing if someone's following us. If we loop back on ourselves, we can see the footprints of anyone following, then bug off in a different direction. If there are no footprints, we can find somewhere out of the wind and rest up for a bit.'

Ricky nodded. 'Let's do it,' he said.

They veered to the right and started trudging a large loop, several hundred metres in diameter. Zak could see Malcolm's knees trembling as they walked. He knew it was only a matter of time before he collapsed again. Ten minutes passed. Visibility: five metres. Their pace was slowing because of Malcolm. The slower they went, the colder they grew. Zak heard a strange howling noise, but told himself it was only the wind. Any minute now, they'd reach the trail and would be able to take a rest, maybe even light a fire . . .

Ricky stopped and raised one hand to indicate that the others should do the same. He was staring at the snow, and Zak could tell something was wrong. He hurried past Malcolm to join his other companion.

He immediately saw what was troubling Ricky.

The tracks they'd left had been slightly covered by the snowfall, but they were still distinct. Alongside them, however, was another set of tracks. They were larger, broader – and obviously not human.

'What is it?' Ricky breathed. 'What's following us?'

Zak stepped towards the fresh tracks and bent down to examine them. Each print was just over thirty centimetres long and half that much wide. There were five toes, each with a distinct claw mark.

He stood up, his jaw clenched and his heart pumping hard. 'A bear,' he said.

15

FROZEN

Ricky froze. It was nothing to do with the cold.

'I thought bears hibernated at this time of year,' he said quietly. His teeth chattered as he spoke.

Zak shook his head. 'They'd be lured out of hibernation if they were very hungry, or if they knew there was easy food nearby.'

There was a sudden screaming gust that blew a flurry of snow up from the ground. Riding on the wind was another noise. Distant, and yet somehow very close. A low, heart-stopping roar.

– *What was that?* snapped the voice in Ricky's head.

– *You really need to ask?*

Ricky saw that Zak was spinning round. He'd obviously heard it too, and was trying to work out what direction the noise had come from.

'Options?' Ricky asked tensely. He looked at Malcolm, who didn't appear to have registered the roar. He was hugging himself warm, and his teeth were chattering. The fact of a bear in the vicinity didn't appear to be worrying him. But as Ricky was fast learning, with Malcolm you could never tell.

Zak pointed at their footprints. Their paths made the shape of a T where their current trail had hit the original one at right angles. 'If we retrace our steps,' he said quickly, 'we'll be doubling up on our scent. The animal will be bound to follow us. I say we head straight on. If it reaches this junction, there'll only be a one-in-three chance of it following our trail.'

Ricky was about to agree, when another roar reached them on the wind. It was still impossible to tell what direction it came from, but it sounded closer this time.

'*Run!*' he hissed.

It was an unspoken thing. Ricky and Zak both grabbed one of Malcolm's arms and started hurrying him along with them. It meant they could move slightly more quickly than before, but Ricky could tell from the lethargic way Malcolm was stumbling, and the way his body felt so heavy, that he was tiring quickly. He heard Zak say, 'You can do it, buddy.' But he wasn't so sure that Malcolm could.

And suddenly, Ricky wasn't sure that *he* could

carry on much further either. A weird lassitude had suddenly crept over him. It didn't make sense. Half of his brain was panicking – the sort of panic he'd only experienced in a dream when he knew he was being chased but couldn't move his legs fast enough to run. The other half felt like it was falling asleep. His limbs were heavy and reluctant. He wanted nothing more than to curl up in the snow and close his eyes . . .

Somewhere in an active corner of his brain, he remembered what Zak had said before they'd set out from the car. *If any of us starts to feel sleepy, we need to say so – it's the first sign of hypothermia . . .*

'Sleepy . . .' Ricky muttered, even as they rushed through the snow. 'Feeling . . . sleepy . . .'

They stopped. Ricky felt his knees buckling, just like Malcolm's had. He was vaguely aware of Zak walking round to stand in front of him. He felt Zak pulling back his hood, exposing Ricky's head to the elements. Then . . .

Whack!

Zak slapped him hard across the side of the face. Ricky sucked in a lungful of cold air as a sharp, stinging sensation spread across his cheek. The lassitude immediately fell away. He saw Zak looking at him, head cocked, as if sizing him up. His companion raised his hand again to hit him for a second time, but as he took the swing, Ricky caught Zak's wrist in mid-air.

'I'm good,' he said, catching his breath. 'Seriously . . . I'm good . . .' The sleepiness had gone. Ricky watched as Zak moved over to Malcolm and appeared to size him up for a slap as well, but then seemed to think better of it.

'We'll up our speed,' Zak said. 'It'll keep you warm.'

They half ran, half walked, barely daring to look back, slipping and sliding through the snow. Ricky was sweating under his clothes, and he started to feel very thirsty. But they couldn't stop. Whenever Ricky did glance over his shoulder, he saw nothing but snow and darkness. Every few minutes, however, over the howling wind, he heard the same roar. Sometimes it was nearer. Sometimes it was further away. But each time he heard it, it struck an icy fear into his heart far colder than anything the Alaskan winter could throw at him.

– Whatever it is, it sounds hungry.

That one thought was enough to make Ricky up his pace.

Ten terrifying minutes passed. Fifteen. Gradually, up ahead, Ricky thought he could make out something different to the swirling mass of blackness that his eyes had grown used to. Tall silhouettes, lurking high in the distance, maybe fifty metres away, maybe a hundred.

'Trees,' Zak confirmed curtly.

They stopped moving.

'Do we move towards the forest?' Ricky asked. 'It'll be more sheltered there, but isn't that where bears are more likely to be hibernating?'

Zak nodded. 'Let's veer in the other direction,' he said.

They altered their bearing by forty-five degrees. Malcolm seemed to have regained some of his strength. After they'd travelled just a few paces, he released himself from their grip and started hurrying through the snow unaided. It was a relief. In the panic, Ricky hadn't realized how exhausting it had been holding him up. Now that they were running separately, their speed increased. Ricky took the lead again, with Zak holding up the rear, so that Malcolm wouldn't lag behind. They moved surprisingly fast. Fear was a good accelerator.

For three minutes they heard no roaring. But every ten paces, Ricky found himself looking around, trying to spot some movement he thought he'd seen at the edge of his vision. But when he tried to pick it out, there was nothing but the falling snow.

The wind quietened, and for a moment the moon appeared from behind the clouds. It lit up the snowscape all around, which was much more undulating than Ricky had thought. He looked over his shoulder, once more trying to see whatever was on the edge of his senses. But there was nothing, except the treetops perhaps one klick away.

– You're imagining it. There's nothing there . . .

Then the moon disappeared again, plunging them back into darkness.

'STOP!' Zak bellowed.

Ricky skidded to a halt. But he was a millisecond too late. There was a cracking, splintering sound under his right foot. He felt his leg sinking into cold water. He heard Zak shouting – 'Ricky!' But even as he heard the word, he lost his balance completely, toppled forward and fell. The cracking sound was much louder this time. In a corner of his brain, Ricky knew what was happening. He'd stepped onto the thin ice of a hidden river crossing their path. He was suddenly underwater.

Ricky had never known cold like it. He was completely submerged. The water felt ten times colder than the snowy air, and the difference in temperature knocked the air from his lungs as though someone had punched him hard in the guts. He felt his body curling up into a ball, and had to fight the desire to suck in a lungful of air, knowing that he would only inhale icy water. Within seconds his body went entirely numb. He couldn't feel the cold any more, but he couldn't feel anything else either. He was simply floating under the ice, and the lassitude he'd felt before Zak had slapped him had returned tenfold.

— *Your body's shutting down.*

— *I don't care.*

— *Move! Do something!*

— *It doesn't matter. It's over—*

The conversation in his head was suddenly interrupted. He felt strong arms on his shoulders. He was being yanked back through the surface of the water, then dragged away from the hole in the ice.

Zak's voice. Calm but urgent. 'Listen carefully. I'm going to roll you in the snow. It will act as a sponge and absorb some of the water. Don't fight it.'

Ricky didn't have the strength to fight anything. The coldness had returned, and it felt as though his bones had turned to ice. He could hear Zak's heavy breathing as he forced Ricky out of his foetus position and then started rolling him through the powdery snow. His extremities started to hurt badly, and his limbs shook more violently than he had ever known them to.

— *That's a good sign. Your body's trying to warm itself up . . .*

But for how long? Ricky had no energy. He wasn't even sure if he could stand . . .

Zak was pulling him up. His face was fierce, his eyes bright. 'Ricky, can you hear me?' His voice sounded slurred and slightly distant. Ricky's eyes went in and out of focus. He nodded.

'We have to get you to that forest. We need a fire to dry you out and warm you up. Can you walk?'

Ricky tried to speak. He wanted to say 'bear', but the sound that came from his mouth was indistinct. Zak seemed to know what he was trying to say, however. 'Don't worry about that now. This is more important.' And through his wooziness, Ricky could hear the urgency in his companion's voice. He knew what it meant. This was life and death.

Zak put Ricky's arm round his neck and supported him as they started moving through the snow. Ricky's uncontrollably shaking limbs made it incredibly difficult to walk, and he felt his feet dragging through the powder. Ricky had no sense of where Malcolm was at first, but gradually became aware of him walking just over his shoulder. He hoped Zak was keeping an eye on him too . . .

Minutes passed. Or maybe it was hours. Ricky felt only semi-conscious. He blacked out for seconds at a time. When he came to again, Zak was practically dragging the dead weight of his barely-standing body through the snow. And with each minute that passed, the feeling in his limbs was replaced by a sinister numbness, and the violent trembling subsided slightly as his body burned up what energy was left in an attempt to keep itself warm.

Above it all was Zak's voice. Constant. Encouraging. 'Stay awake, buddy.' 'You can do it.' 'Keep with me.' 'We're almost there.'

Above that was the howling of the wind, which bit harshly into his wet clothes.

And above *that*, dipping in and out of his consciousness, the occasional howl.

He didn't know how long it was before he realized they had stopped. All he knew was that his back was propped up against the trunk of a tree. His rucksack was no longer on his back, and he was sitting on one of the rubber floor mats from the car. He was panting desperately, as if his body needed to get oxygen inside it, but simply didn't have the energy to take a deep enough breath. He looked through half-closed eyes, trying to make out his companions, but he couldn't see them.

In a tiny active corner of his mind, he felt sudden panic. Where were they? Had they just left him here? Or had something happened to them? He tried to muster enough strength to push himself to his feet, but there was nothing there. He simply slid to the side, and blacked out again in the snow.

Someone was shaking him. It was Malcolm. He was speaking, but now Ricky's brain was too slow even to make any sense of the words. Perhaps he'd heard him say 'firewood', but the voice was too blurred and confused to be sure.

Malcolm helped him to sit up again. He was aware of activity in front of him. Another figure, presumably Zak, was removing something from Ricky's rucksack. The pungent smell of petrol hit Ricky's weakened senses, and he saw the spark of a cigarette lighter, followed by a glowing flame. By the dim light of that flame, he saw Zak's silhouette hunched over the fledgling fire. He was feeding strips of ripped car tyre into the car-stuffing tinder. A worse smell filled the air. Burning rubber. Foul though it was, Ricky tried to gulp it in. In his confused mind, he thought the smoke might warm him up. And the stench reminded him that he was still alive.

The flames grew bigger. Ricky realized that Zak was slowly piling dead branches onto the fire. Small ones first, then slightly larger ones as the fire grew bigger. The active corner of his brain wondered how Zak had managed to find firewood amid the snow, and he noticed how the fuel smoked and sizzled as it started to burn. But most of all, he felt the warmth. It was like life itself, seeping into his blood, defrosting his limbs and drying him out.

He tried to shuffle closer, but suddenly Zak was there, gently holding him back. 'Don't get too close,' he said quietly. 'You'll burn yourself.' His voice no longer sounded blurred.

Zak moved round to the other side of the fire. Ricky saw that he and Malcolm had made a little frame out of branches. They were hanging the silver space blanket over the frame. It was clearly a strategy to reflect the heat of the fire back towards Ricky, but would also have the added advantage of shielding some of the light spill from anyone following, or from any predators.

Predators.

'The bear,' he said hoarsely.

Zak looked over his shoulder from the other side of the fire. 'Don't worry about it. Chances are, it'll avoid the fire.'

'But if it's hungry . . .' Malcolm said weakly.

'We have to get Ricky warm and dry, mate. We don't have a choice about that.'

Ricky didn't have the energy to argue. He stayed huddled by the fire. Malcolm joined him, but Zak took the entrenching tool and started digging a protective wall out of the snow on the other side of the fire. 'It'll shield us from the wind,' he said, but Ricky knew it was also another way of camouflaging their position. He cursed himself for his stupidity in falling in that river. Thanks to him, their situation had just got ten times worse.

As his body warmed up, so did his senses. He looked around. They were in a small clearing. The snow was not quite so deep here, but the trees were heavily laden. 'How far back from the tree line are we?' he whispered.

'About twenty metres,' Zak said. 'With a bit of luck, that's enough to stop anyone seeing the fire, but we shouldn't let it get too big. How are you feeling?'

Ricky was just about to reply with a sarcastic 'On top of the world', when yet another strange sound cut through the air. It was more high-pitched than the roar of the bear they'd heard, and it came from more than one animal. The sound sucked some of the newly acquired warmth from Ricky's body.

'Did you hear that?' Malcolm shouted, jumping to his feet. '*Did you hear it?*'

Zak stopped digging. They all looked around, trying to work out which direction the sound had come from.

'What was it?' Ricky breathed, even though he knew what the answer would be.

Zak's face, sweaty from the exertion and the fire, creased into a frown. 'You really want to know?'

'Damn right I want to know.'

'Wolves,' said Zak.

16

GRIZZLY

'Wolves,' Zak said. He had a sinking feeling in his stomach.

He bent over and started digging again, but could see Ricky and Malcolm exchanging an anxious look. 'You don't seem very worried,' Ricky said.

Zak gave him a slightly forced smile. 'Feeling better enough to argue with me? That's a good sign.'

'You shouldn't be arguing,' Malcolm said. 'You *shouldn't* be. What if there *are* wolves nearby? What if they attack us?'

'Just because we can hear them, it doesn't mean we're going to see them. Packs rarely attack, unless they're very sure that they've got easy meat.'

'I feel like easy meat right now,' Ricky said with a slightly rueful look on his face.

'Just stay close to the fire. Most animals are afraid of it. There aren't many animals that'll be brave enough to approach.' Zak hoped he sounded convincing. The truth was, they weren't in a state to run anywhere – and he hadn't forgotten about the bear tracks they'd seen.

He continued digging his trench and wall around them. The scraping sound of his entrenching tool was dull and monotonous. He was glad to hear Ricky talking. He'd given them a scare back there. In conditions like this, contact with icy water could bring about death in a matter of minutes if you didn't act correctly in the few golden moments you had. In a way, Zak was thankful that it had been Ricky not Malcolm who'd fallen in – he doubted that Malcolm would have been able to survive that. He was also thankful that Raf and Gabs had thoroughly briefed him in cold-weather survival techniques back at St Peter's Crag.

He felt a pang. In the struggle to escape their pursuers and keep alive, he'd almost forgotten about his Guardian Angels. They were the whole reason the three of them were here, on the run in this inhospitable Alaskan backwater, with no idea of how they were going to travel hundreds of miles across the frozen state. He felt his lip curling bitterly. Things were looking bad. They were lost, and a very long way from where they needed to be.

But he wasn't going to give up. He'd crawl the length and breadth of Alaska rather than give up now—

He looked up suddenly. Had he seen something move from the corner of his eye, away to his eleven o'clock? He squinted into the darkness, trying to pick it out.

Nothing.

Zak took a deep breath, trying to ease the sudden pumping of his heart. He looked over his shoulder. Neither Ricky nor Malcolm showed any sign of having seen anything.

He drew Malcolm to one side. 'Listen, mate,' he said in a low voice. 'You need to keep an eye on Ricky. Watch his movements carefully. If he speaks, listen to his words. Any sign of slowness or slurring, you tell me, right? It could be a sign that hypothermia is setting in.'

Malcolm nodded while Zak went back to his digging.

It took thirty minutes to finish building up the wall. He looked at the pile of wood he and Malcolm had collected while Ricky had been semi-conscious. He estimated that, if they kept the fire low, it would be enough for another two to three hours. It meant they'd need to collect more before sunrise. But he didn't want to leave Ricky just yet. He joined the other two by the fire.

'What's the plan?' Ricky asked. His words were clear. No slurring.

'We stay here till dawn,' Zak said. 'There's no point moving around at night now that we've lost our bearings. When the sun comes up, we can use it to orientate ourselves. Maybe even see some physical landmarks to help us get back into Anchorage.'

'And then?'

'Then we find a way of getting to the Bering Straits.' As Zak spoke, there was a sudden, more vigorous flurry of snow, as if someone was telling him that this would be impossible. He looked over at Malcolm. He was huddled by the fire, staring deep into its embers. 'You OK, buddy?'

Malcolm opened his mouth to answer. But he was interrupted by Ricky. '*What was that?*'

'What?'

'I saw something move. That direction.' Ricky pointed to nine o'clock.

Zak looked. He saw nothing but snow and night. He was about to say as much when he heard it. A deep-throated roar. A bear's roar. Identical to the one they'd heard above the wind.

But louder. Which meant closer.

All three of them jumped to their feet. They

circled the fire, with their backs to it. Zak's heart was pumping brutally again. He could feel the blood moving around his veins as he tried to work out which direction the roar had come from, and how far away it was. Eleven o'clock, and maybe thirty metres, he decided – but he knew it could easily be closer.

'*Make a loud noise!*' Zak shouted.

'What?'

'*We can't fight a bear! If we make a loud enough noise, we might spook it and drive it away. SHOUT!*' He started to shout at the top of his voice – short, aggressive barks. Ricky joined him, bellowing into the darkness. Malcolm tried to do the same, but his shouts were much quieter.

Still yelling into the darkness, Zak turned to the pile of wood. He grabbed three sturdy branches and placed them so that the end of each branch was nestling in the hottest part of the fire. Then he took another two branches, held them over his head and started banging them together to make even more noise.

Another roar. Twice as loud. Twice as aggressive. Either their new companion was getting angrier, or it was getting closer. Or both.

'It's not working!' Ricky shouted, his voice edged in panic. 'What do we do?'

'Keep making a noise!' Zak urged. But Ricky was

right. They weren't scaring the animal away . . . Zak glanced down at the branches he'd placed in the fire. They weren't burning yet. His mind was frantically whirring. He looked behind him at the nearest trees. They were ten metres away. Should they try to climb them? He knew bears could also climb trees, but if they each took a different one, at least two of them would be safe. But the trunks were tall and smooth – almost impossible to climb freestyle. In any case, that would be retreating, and as Raf and Gabs had told him a hundred times, you can never win a defensive fight. Stuck up those trees, the bear could pick them off at his leisure.

Still shouting and clacking his branches noisily, he looked back in the direction of the roar and his blood turned to ice. He could just make out a shape on the edge of the clearing. Distance: approximately twenty metres. Size: *massive*. Brown bear? Black bear? Grizzly bear? Zak didn't know. But now it had launched itself onto its hind legs, and Zak reckoned it was well over two metres tall.

A third roar. It seemed to echo through the trees. The dark silhouette of the bear fell down onto all four paws, then began to lumber towards them.

'Get to the far side of the fire!' Zak shouted. '*Now!*'

Quickly, Zak, Ricky and Malcolm circled round

their tiny fire, so that it stood between them and the approaching bear. Zak checked the branches again. The ends in the fire were beginning to smoulder, but they were not yet flaming.

The bear stopped five metres beyond the snow barrier that Zak had dug. It reared up on its hind legs again. Zak had underestimated its height. It was easily three metres high, and almost as broad. Its paws were enormous, its eyes mean and hungry. And when it roared yet again, the noise seemed like it was going straight through Zak's body. The bear thumped down onto all four paws once again, slamming into the wall of snow that Zak had built and slipping down into the trench beneath it. This seemed to enrage it even more. It swiped a front paw aggressively at the space blanket that was still erected between it and the fire. It ended up in a crumpled heap five metres away. Snow spat up into the air and hissed as it landed on the fire. The glow of the embers dulled slightly. The bear started to pad heavily round the fire, clockwise towards them, growling ferociously.

Zak, Ricky and Malcolm also circled the fire clockwise, in an attempt to keep that burning barrier between them and the snarling bear. Distance between it and them: barely four metres.

'We should run,' Malcolm whispered.

'Run and you're dead,' Zak said bluntly. 'It'll chase

you down in seconds.' An image of three badly mauled teenagers flashed across his brain. They were face down and surrounded by blood-streaked snow . . .

Zak checked out the branches he'd laid in the fire. Their ends were burning now. He bent and grabbed two of them with trembling hands, before handing them to Ricky and Malcolm to hold like swords. Then he bent down again for the third branch. His fingers just touched the bark when the animal bared its teeth and took a sudden pace forward. Zak jumped back, out of reach of the burning branch. The bear was padding clockwise again. They had to do the same to keep the fire between them and it. Ricky and Malcolm waved their branches in the bear's direction. But Zak had no such weapon. He felt naked without it, and now it was out of reach, unless they performed another full circuit of the fire.

The bear stopped. It moved a little closer to the blaze again. Zak could sense that it was feeling braver. The fire was becoming less effective as a barrier. And when the animal kicked up another shower of snow that fizzed and hissed on the flames, Zak had an instinct that the animal knew what it was doing. In which case, they wouldn't have the fire for much longer.

They continued to stalk around the circle. A

quarter-turn . . . a half-turn. Zak was sweating badly, but also shivering. The trio continued to move about the fire in this terrifying game of round and round.

Ten seconds later, he was alongside his burning branch. He stepped forward to pick it up. But as he lifted it from the fire, he heard a whimper from behind him. He glanced back. Malcolm's branch had gone out. He let it fall to the snow. He was staggering backwards, terror etched on his face.

'Stay with us,' Zak hissed, trying to keep himself sounding and looking as unruffled as possible. Not easy. 'Just stay with us!'

But Malcolm was still retreating.

Zak knew it was coming. So, clearly, did Ricky who, still waving his burning branch in the direction of the bear, shouted: '*Stop!*' But Malcolm ignored them. He turned tail, then ran into the darkness.

Zak's stomach plunged as the bear, with more agility than he would have thought possible from such a large animal, gave yet another roar, then lolloped away, curving round to intercept Malcolm.

'*NO!*'

Neither Zak nor Ricky hesitated for a second. Brandishing their burning branches, they sprinted through the snow after their friend. They didn't have to run far, because he had slipped and fallen fifteen metres from the fire. He was splayed out in the snow.

The bear had moved fast. It was just five metres from him.

It launched itself up on its hind legs, front paws outstretched, ready to strike. Another great roar cracked through the air.

Zak's muscles burned as, with Ricky alongside him, he sprinted the final few metres through the snow to position himself in the space between Malcolm and the bear. Shouting loudly, they waved their burning branches at the beast. It seemed to flinch backward. It landed heavily back on all four paws, but it was still snarling and Zak could smell a rotten stench on its breath now he was only a couple of metres away . . .

'Get back to the fire!' he yelled at Malcolm, thrusting the burning branch, sword-like, in short jabs towards the bear.

No movement from behind. He looked over his shoulder. Malcolm was still lying there. Maybe he was frozen with terror. Maybe he was unconscious. Zak couldn't tell. All he knew was that if Malcolm couldn't move, none of them could retreat. And the only things stopping the bear attacking them all were two burning branches. Zak and Ricky held them aloft, waving them at the snarling bear. But . . .

'*They're going out!*' Ricky shouted. His voice was high-pitched with stress.

He was right. The flaming ends of the branches were flickering. Tendrils of thick smoke were curling up from them.

'*Malcolm!*' Zak yelled. '*Get up! Get back to the fire!*'

But there was no reply, and no movement.

Zak's was the first branch to go out completely. It was as though someone had blown out a birthday candle – a sudden rush of smoke, then nothing but a charred stump.

'*Get behind me!*' Ricky said.

Zak didn't like retreating, but he knew he had no choice. While Ricky continued to wave his barely smouldering branch at the bear, Zak jumped backwards towards Malcolm. The bear roared shockingly as Zak bent down and, with a great effort that made him realize how weakened he was by the cold, scooped Malcolm up in his arms and hauled him over his shoulder in a fireman's lift. '*Walk backwards to the fire!*' he shouted at Ricky. But his companion was already doing this. With a sudden surge of hope, Zak saw that the bear itself was staying put.

They retreated ten paces. The end of Ricky's branch flickered weakly. It was little more than a glowing stump now, but it seemed to be doing the job. The bear was still snarling, but it wasn't moving forward. Perhaps they'd done enough to discourage it . . .

Zak looked back. They were halfway to the waning fire. He looked forward again.

His heart stopped.

Ricky's branch had gone out.

The bear had noticed this too. It had started to lumber forward. Ricky was staggering back. 'Run!' Zak bellowed. *'Run!'*

Too late. The beast was building up speed. Ricky had turned to sprint back to the fire, but it was clear he wasn't going to make it. Zak lowered Malcolm back down onto the snow, then sprinted towards his other companion, not quite knowing how he was going to help him ward off the bear's attack, but realizing that he had to do *something* . . .

The bear was three metres from Ricky when it reared up onto its hind legs once again. It loomed alarmingly over him . . .

It roared.

Time slowed down.

There were no screams or shouts of alarm. The bear made no sound as it raised both its enormous front paws and prepared to go in for the kill. Ricky didn't scream. There was a horrible, dread silence.

But the silence was suddenly broken by a loud,

echoing, cracking sound that caused Zak's ears to ring and snow to fall from the treetops.

He knew immediately what it was.

Gunshot.

He looked down at himself to see if he'd been hit.

17

TASHA

— *This is it*, said the voice in Ricky's head. *This is the moment you die.*

He felt like his whole body was screaming as the bear drew itself up to its full height above him. As the seconds flashed by, he had a premonition of those ugly claws ripping into his flesh. He could almost feel the bear tear open his abdomen to scavenge his soft organs.

He tried to scamper further back to the fire, but his legs weren't doing what his brain was telling them to . . .

Crack!

Ricky knew it was a gunshot. Had the authorities found them? Were they firing on Zak and maybe even on Ricky and Malcolm?

But then another strange sound hit his ears. An

angry whimper, and it was coming from the bear. By the flickering orange light of the fire, he saw a flash of dark liquid streak across the snow. The bear toppled and fell to its side, no more than four metres from where Ricky was standing.

Silence. He looked around to see where the gunshot had come from.

The great beast roared again. The sound was filled with pain.

'*Get back!*' Zak hissed from behind him. '*It's dangerous when wounded . . .*'

'But who just shot—'

'It doesn't matter. *Get back!*'

As if confirming Zak's fear, the bear suddenly lashed out a single paw that missed Ricky by only a few centimetres. Ricky jumped away, and was preparing to sprint back to the fire when another shot rang out.

The bear's whole body juddered. There was another spatter of dark liquid across the snow. Then it fell still.

'*Hit the floor!*' Zak hissed. But Ricky was already dropping. Whoever had just shot the bear was still armed. There was nothing to say that the three teenagers weren't next in the firing line.

'We need to get out of here,' Ricky whispered, panicked sweat dripping down the nape of his neck.

Zak was lying a metre behind him. Just beyond Zak, Malcolm – immobile.

'Not without Malcolm,' Zak said. He squinted beyond the bear to the far side of the clearing. 'Look,' he breathed.

Ricky followed his gaze. Through the darkness and the still-swirling snow, he could just make out the silhouette of a person and a dog. The person wasn't particularly tall, nor did they move very fast. But they were definitely walking in this direction – distance about fifty metres – with the dog trotting calmly by their side. Ricky could just see the outline of a gun barrel slung across the person's chest. Ricky found he was holding his breath as he kept his eyes firmly fixed on these strange figures emerging from the darkness. With a sick feeling, he wondered if it was the driver from earlier, here to finish them off. But the driver had been taller than this person, and his gait was very different.

A great deal of blood was oozing from the bear's two gunshot wounds. It melted the surrounding snow. Ricky felt a sudden pang of sadness that this amazing creature had lost its life, even though it had been on the point of killing him. But his real attention was on the figure, now twenty metres away. He could make the clothes out a bit better. Tey wore a fur over-coat, very similar to the pelt of the dead bear, and a heavy hat, covered in loose snow. The rifle that had just fired two rounds looked old, and was slung casually across the figure's front. The dog seemed to glow in the dark, brighter and whiter than the snow. Ricky squinted harder. It was definitely not the driver. And he didn't think it was the authorities, because surely there would be more than one of them and they'd have their weapons raised.

When the figure was ten metres away, and Ricky could see the face, he got another surprise. It was a girl, with black tendrils of hair tumbling out from under her hat, and a thin face with a pointed nose. It was hard to tell exactly how old she was, but Ricky didn't reckon she was much older than him. The dog looked like a husky, with shockingly white fur.

The girl walked up to the bear, which she kicked casually with one foot. Without looking at Ricky, Zak or Malcolm, she called out through the snow-filled air: 'You's lucky I was in the neighbourhood.' She spoke very slowly, with a pronounced American drawl. 'This ol' bear would've had ya.' The dog sat down obediently by her side as she pulled out a very large hunting knife. 'What you doin' in these parts, anyhow?' she asked, as she bent down and plunged the knife expertly into the bear's belly.

Ricky and Zak pushed themselves up to their feet. 'We, er, we got lost,' Ricky said carefully. He had the very distinct feeling that the dog would pounce if the girl told it to.

The girl gave a cynical snort. 'You bet you got lost,' she said, as she sliced carefully up the dead bear's belly.

'We're, er . . . we're trying to visit our grand-parents.'

Their cover story sounded pretty unconvincing here in the middle of nowhere, and it was met with a disbelieving look from the girl. She glanced over at Malcolm. 'What 'bout that one? He dead?'

Her words were like an electric shock. Ricky and Zak rushed over to where Malcolm was lying. Zak checked his pulse, while Ricky put his hand an inch above his mouth to check for breath. As he did so, Malcolm's eyes opened. 'Cold,' he whispered.

'Get him to the fire,' Zak instructed. They grabbed their friend, one end each, and quickly hauled him over to where their small fire was rapidly fading. They laid him on the ground, then Ricky carefully started adding more fuel to the fire, while Zak tried to get Malcolm to sit up. All the while, the strange, fur-clad girl continued her quiet, efficient butchery of the bear.

After a couple of minutes she walked over to them, the dog trotting along beside her. She was holding something in both hands. Only when she was close to the fire, and lit up by its orange light, did Ricky see that it was a glistening, bleeding organ. Her hands and furs were smeared in blood. She held it out, as though she was presenting a gift.

'What is it?' Ricky asked.

'Liver.'

'Not a fan, to be honest.'

'Then you ain't never been hungry before.' The girl looked around at the drifting snow. 'Weather like this,' she said, 'you gotta eat. Hold it.' Without waiting for a reply, she handed the liver to Ricky. It was heavier than he expected, and his skin crept away from the warm, wet flesh. The girl examined what remained of their firewood, then pulled her hunting knife from inside her furs and expertly whittled away three thin sticks. Each was very straight, about thirty centimetres long, and two had a forked end. She dug these into the snow right next to the fire, forked end pointing upwards, then balanced the remaining stick between them to make a small spit. As Ricky held the liver, she started to cut thin slices off it. Once she had six, she threaded them onto the stick. Blood dripped from the slices onto the ground, and the meat began to sizzle.

'Give my dog the rest of that liver, you got a friend for life,' the girl said.

Ricky laid the remaining liver down in the snow,

before wiping his bloodied hands on his clothes.

'OK, Snow,' the girl said. Snow was obviously the dog's name. He trotted over to the fresh liver, dragged it a few metres away from their position and started to eat. Ricky caught sight of some extremely sharp teeth.

'What's your name?' Ricky asked.

She gave him a suspicious look. 'What does it matter?'

'It doesn't. I'm just asking.'

She sniffed. 'Tasha,' she said.

'I'm Ricky. This is Zak and Malcolm.' He glanced over at Zak, half expecting to be reprimanded for giving their real names. But Zak didn't seem bothered. There was hardly any point out here, and they really needed this girl's help. 'Er . . . thanks for saving our lives back there, Tasha.'

'Yo' lives ain't saved yet,' Tasha said. She picked up the skewer of liver pieces and handed them round. 'You want to make it through the night? Eat.' She crammed her pieces of cooked liver into her mouth. Ricky did the same. Instantly, he wanted to gag. The meat was only just warmed through – he felt like he was chewing a mouthful of jellied blood, and the taste was intense and high. He saw Zak swallowing his food, but it was too much for Malcolm, who spat his out. Tasha looked at him, then shrugged, as if to say: 'That's your problem.'

'What are you doing out here at night?' Zak asked.

Tasha sneered. 'Could ask you the same question.' But when Zak didn't reply, she said, 'Huntin' that bear. Been prowlin' round where my family live. Causin' damage. Beast had to go. Pops told me he hasn't seen a grizzly walking around in winter since he was a boy. Can't have him hanging around our livin' quarters. Brothers went north and south. I went west.'

She spoke in a weirdly adult fashion. 'You're a bit young to be out hunting bears, aren't you?' Ricky said.

'An' you's a bit young to be killed by one,' she shot back. She looked over towards the bear's corpse. 'Wolves in these forests,' she said.

'We heard them.'

'Bet you did. They'll soon sniff out that dead beast. You don't want to be here when they do. Trust me 'bout that. They get the taste for blood, they don't care much whether their meal's livin' or dead. That's why I won't be taking no meat from the beast back home.' She stood up, nodded to them, and made a clicking sound at the back of her mouth. Snow trotted obediently up to her. Ricky noticed that the dog had different coloured eyes – one orange, one green. Snow followed Tasha as she walked away from the fire, back in the direction from which she'd come. As she passed the bear, she glanced at it slightly regretfully.

Ricky and Zak looked at each other. An unspoken question passed between them. Ricky knew what Zak would be thinking: that they only had forty-something hours until Cruz's deadline, and they still had half a continent to cross. Things were looking very bad. But they couldn't stay out here unprotected and with no shelter. It would be suicide. They nodded at each other. 'Tasha,' Ricky called. 'Wait up.'

She stopped and turned.

'You live near here?'

She gave her characteristic shrug. 'Kinda.'

'In a village? A town?'

Tasha sneered. 'No way. My family don't live among other people. We live in the wild. Build our own houses, hunt our own food, live by our own rules.'

'Look, we need shelter. Just for the rest of the night. We can pay you.'

It was the word 'pay' that did it. Tasha's eyes lit up. 'How much?'

'We'll talk about that when we get to your place.'

Tasha turned her back on them and continued to trudge through the snow. 'Well, if you's gonna come, you's better come.' And as they spoke, they heard, for the second time that night, the chilling sound of a wolf's howl floating above the wind. It sounded closer than before.

Ricky quickly started getting their gear together. He gave a moment's thought to packing up the snow blanket, but it was splashed with blood. 'Leave it,' Tasha said. 'Blood'll attract wolves like nothing else.'

Zak shovelled snow over their fire to extinguish it, before speaking urgently yet reassuringly to Malcolm, who managed to push himself to his feet. It didn't take them much more than thirty seconds, but by that time Tasha was already at the far end of the clearing. They were rapidly losing sight of her.

Hunching their shoulders, they battled quickly through the heavy snow. Ricky glanced down at the dead bear as they passed it. Once more, he felt a pang of sympathy for the beast. Its stomach was split open and its insides had spilled out all over the snow. There was a foul, fetid smell as they passed.

As they reached the far edge of the clearing, he saw that Tasha and Snow had disappeared behind the tree line. They upped their pace. Another wolf howl pierced the air. Tasha was waiting for them under a tall fir tree. Snow's ears were pricked up and alert, and he was smelling the wind. Tasha said nothing as they came into view, but simply turned and headed further into the forest. Ricky watched her carefully. There was something peculiar about the way she walked. It was almost as if she would have been more comfortable on all fours, like the bear she had just shot. Her weapon was now slung over her back, and as she occasionally looked back, there was something wild in her eyes.

They trudged through the forest for what seemed like hours. There were many noises. Strange shufflings and the cracking of twigs in the distance. Ricky started every time he heard them. But Tasha seemed unconcerned, and her dog was relaxed. He took some comfort from that.

Exhaustion overcame him. Every part of his body shrieked at him to stop and rest, but he knew he had to keep going. Every time he looked at Zak and Malcolm, he could see that they were in the same state. Their eyes were rolling and their gait was unsteady. At least, here among the trees, they were protected from the wind. Although Ricky was incredibly cold, he didn't feel his body was in danger of shutting down. And Malcolm was keeping up, just. Often, he saw Zak supporting him as they moved through the snow, a look of grim determination on his face. It was obvious to Ricky how desperate Zak was to find his friends. His own thoughts drifted towards Felix. Ricky still couldn't quite believe he was dead. The thought of catching the guy responsible gave him a little extra momentum as they tried to keep up with the strange, wild Tasha.

He didn't know how long they'd been walking when the trees started to thin again. It seemed like all night, though in truth it had probably not been much more than a couple of hours. He caught a glimpse of light in the distance. It was obscured by the trees, but it was a warming sight. They walked for a couple more minutes until they came to the edge of the forest. There, standing alone about thirty metres from the tree line, was a house – more of a large shack, really. It was made of logs, its low roof covered in snow. The light came from two small windows, one on either side of the door. Ricky could tell by its flickering nature, and by the smoke curling from the chimney, that there was a fire burning inside. Half of him thought it seemed very risky, burning a fire in a log cabin. The other half wanted nothing more than to get warm. He took an involuntary step forward.

'Wait,' Tasha hissed.

Ricky froze.

'I'll go first. Tell 'em you're coming. Otherwise . . .' She left it hanging.

Ricky, Zak and Malcolm stood by the tree line

and watched her walk towards, and into, the shack, with Snow at her side. They were too tired and cold to speak. Even Ziggy's voice in Ricky's head sounded slow and slurred.

– *I'm not sure this is a good idea.*

– *We don't have a choice. If we stay out in the snow, we'll die.*

The door of the shack opened again. Two figures appeared. They were much taller than Tasha. One of them carried a hunting rifle, the other a handgun. They were pointing their weapons towards the trees. There was no sign of the girl or her dog.

'Get your hands above your heads,' one of them called in a deeply unfriendly voice, 'before we fill you with holes and leave you for the animals . . .'

18

THE SHACK

If someone has a gun pointing in your direction, you'd better have a good reason for not doing what they tell you. Zak raised his arms. Ricky and Malcolm did the same. Zak took a step forward.

'Stay back! You's think we're stupid? You's think you punks can make friends with lil' Tasha, then come rob us? What are you, drug addicts?'

'We're not here to rob you,' Ricky called out. 'We'll pay you to give us some shelter. Maybe some help.'

The guy with the handgun wiped his nose with the back of his hand while still holding up his weapon. Zak noticed that he seemed to have painted the body of the weapon in a blood-red colour. 'Oh yeah?' he called.

'We have money,' Ricky said.

The gunman licked his lips. 'Well . . . let's see the colour of it, kid.'

Zak stepped forward again. This time, the gunmen didn't object. He loosened his backpack, dropped it into the snow and then pulled out all his dollars. He waved them in the direction of the gunmen. They nodded. The guy with the red-painted handgun lowered his weapon. Zak approached. As he got closer, he saw that these two guys were very lean, probably in their early twenties, and looked extremely similar. Tasha's brothers, presumably? They wore jeans and heavy, checked lumberjack shirts, and they had sharp, suspicious eyes and weather-beaten faces. He handed the notes to the man who had lowered his gun. The man examined them closely, then shoved them in a pocket. 'All right, kid,' he said. 'Get your friends and come inside.'

The two brothers – Zak was now sure that they *were* brothers – turned back into the shack. Zak waved at Ricky and Malcolm to follow him in.

The inside of the shack comprised one big room. It was a poor place. It looked like it had been built from the discarded parts of twenty other houses. The windows – two at the front, two at the back – were different shapes and sizes. There was a large wood-burning stove in the middle. It had a battered saucepan resting on the top, and an unmatching metal chimney protruding from the back and up through the roof of the shack. Snow the dog was curled up in front of it, but his mismatched eyes were still open and alert. There were odd, shabby sofas and a selection of tired mattresses on the floor. Haunches of cured meat hung from the ceiling, alongside bunches of dried leaves. It was dark. The only light came from the stove, and from a large yellow candle that smoked in one corner, casting flickering shadows on the walls.

Sitting on one of the sofas were a much older man and woman. The man had a messy grey beard, wore a red bandanna and had the same sharp, suspicious eyes as the two brothers. The woman had Tasha's pointed nose, and a face that was as cold and unfriendly as the snow outside. Tasha herself was sitting cross-legged on one of the mattresses, her rifle lying across her lap. She was humming tunelessly to herself. Nobody else spoke as Zak, Ricky and Malcolm traipsed in, closing the door on the howling weather outside.

They stood there in silence for a full thirty seconds before the old man spoke. 'You's from that drug place?' he demanded.

'What drug place?' Zak asked.

Tasha pointed in what Zak thought was a north-easterly direction. 'Couple miles over there. Dealers moved into an old deserted farmstead thataways. They made a big score in the city. Word is, they're sitting it out with their cash till the heat dies down. Tyler and Travis thought you was some of them. I told them straight, you looked like newcomers to these parts, but . . .'

She pointed at her brothers in turn as she said this. Tyler – who had the painted gun – was the taller of the two. He had wispy stubble and a pointed chin. Travis was clean-shaven, and one of his front teeth was missing. They both looked like they could use a decent meal.

'Wherever you's from,' the old man said, 'I'm guessing you's a long way from home.' His voice was low and gravelly.

'We only need a few hours' shelter,' Zak said. 'Then we'll be on our way.'

The old man gave them an unpleasant grin that showed half his teeth missing. 'Who you runnin' from, kid?'

'We're not running from anyone. We're looking for some friends.'

'Right,' said the old man. 'Friends.' He clearly didn't believe them. 'Tyler, Travis, dust 'em down. Check they ain't packing.'

It took a couple of minutes for the two brothers to satisfy themselves that apart from the hunting knife Zak carried their guests had no weapons, either on their person or in their packs. Just rags of oil-soaked fabric, and the rest of what remained from their looting of the vehicle.

'They're clean, Pop,' Tyler said. ''Cept for this knife here.' He tossed it from hand to hand. 'I'll be holdin' onto this,' he said, looking at Zak, 'whilst you in our home.'

The old man stared at them. Zak could tell he was deciding whether or not to let them stay. Snow the dog suddenly got to his feet. He trotted over to where Ricky was standing and rubbed his thick fur against Ricky's trouser leg. The dog's approval seemed to satisfy the old man a little. He pointed to a far corner of the shack where there was nothing but hard floor. 'You can lie down there, get some shut-eye. But we don't have no food to spare, and I want you out of here when the sun comes up. Strangers don't welcome us, and we don't welcome strangers.'

They moved to the corner of the shack and set down their bags under the watchful eyes of this strange family. Zak didn't trust them not to rob them while they rested – he reminded himself that even Tasha had only offered to help once they'd brought up the subject of money. One of them needed to stay awake. 'You sleep first,' he muttered to Ricky. 'I'll wake you when I can't stay up any longer.'

Ricky nodded. The three of them lay down, using their backpacks as pillows, under the mistrustful eyes of Tasha and her family. Malcolm was instantly snoring. Ricky seemed more twitchy, but after five minutes Zak heard the slow, steady breathing that told him he too had fallen asleep.

Zak lay on his side, keeping watch on the shack. The others had taken to their beds, apart from one of the brothers, who sat in a rickety armchair with his weapon across his lap. He didn't take his suspicious eyes off Zak.

It was uncomfortable on the floor, but it was warm. And although Zak knew he should be staying awake, he soon found his eyes and limbs getting heavy. The flickering of the candle almost hypnotized him. A tiny voice in the corner of his mind urged him to stay awake. But the exhaustion was too great. The flickering shadows in the room receded into darkness as he fell asleep.

'Where is it? *WHERE IS IT?*'

Zak woke with a start. It was light in the shack. Tyler was leaning over him, and his thin face was furious.

'Wh-what are you talking about?'

'My gun – the red one – it's missing. *Where is it, kid?*'

Zak sat bolt upright, cursing himself for having fallen asleep. Ricky and Malcolm were still sleeping beside him. He looked at his watch. It was 8:30 a.m. Panic surged through him. He had slept too long. There was just under forty hours until Cruz's deadline, and they were no nearer to Little Diomede Island than they had been the night before.

Tyler was very agitated. He pulled Zak roughly to his feet, then dragged him across the shack, opened the door and hurled him outside. The snow had obviously been falling heavily while he'd been sleeping, because there was no sign of their tracks from the night before. And the weather was still foul. Tasha and her family were standing ten metres away by a small fire, obviously arguing. They fell silent as Zak tumbled into the snow. They stared at him in a very unfriendly manner – except Tasha herself, who looked slightly apologetic. Snow, as always, was by her side.

Tyler loomed above him. 'He stole my gun!'

'I didn't steal anything,' Zak snapped back. 'Search me if you like. Search my friends. Search the packs.'

His offer silenced Tyler momentarily. 'I will,' he said. But he didn't turn back into the shack.

'Maybe you dropped it in the snow,' Zak said, trying to sound as calm as possible. 'I'll help you look.'

'What do you's think I am?' Tyler retorted. 'An idiot?'

'That's enough, son,' growled the father. 'We'll find the weapon soon enough.' He looked at Zak. 'You's can't stay here,' he said. 'Those city folk don't like us living out here on our own. If they think we're harbouring good-for-nothings, they'll be out here, knocking down our house, messing with our way of life . . .'

Zak pushed himself up to his feet. He could feel the enmity coming from this strange, wild family. He needed to choose his words carefully. 'I haven't got much time,' he said. 'I really need your help.' He directed this towards Tasha, since she seemed the least hostile.

But this seemed to enrage the father all the more. He stormed up to Zak, his face red. 'I'm the head of this family. You speak to *me* . . .' he fumed.

Zak nodded. 'I apologize,' he said calmly. 'I need *your* help. I have to get to the Diomede Islands. It's incredibly important. Life or death. There are no planes from Anchorage, so I need to get there cross-country.'

The old man stared at him for a moment, his eyes narrowed as if he thought Zak was having him on. Then, slowly, he broke out into a mirthless laugh. He turned to his family. 'You's hear that?' he called.

'You's *hear* that? Kid's out in the snow for a couple of hours, almost gets mauled by a grizzly. Now he wants to cross Alaska off his own back in the middle of winter!'

The two brothers started laughing too. Tasha and her mother, however, didn't even break a smile. The old man walked back to his family, waving one arm in the air. 'Take my advice, kid. Pack your bags, take your friends and get the hell back to the city. You ain't cut out for the wild life.'

Zak didn't move. He kept his gaze on the old man as he stomped back to the fire and held his hands out to warm them. When he saw that Zak was still staring at him, a shadow crossed his face. 'I said, get out of here, kid!' he barked.

'I'll pay the rest of the money we have to the person who gets me to Diomede,' Zak said.

Travis walked up to him. 'You heard of the Kuskokwim mountains?' he asked.

Zak shook his head.

'They lie between here and where you want to get to. No roads. No one living there. Impassable in winter. Pop's right. You's best to forget it. Only way to head north-west is by plane. And weather like this, only a fool's gonna put one of them in the air.'

As he spoke, he glanced over at the rest of the family. Something seemed to pass between them.

'You're not telling me something,' Zak said. 'What is it?'

'Forget it, kid,' the old man ignored him. 'You're heading home. Go wake the others. My boys will put you on the right path, but I want you out of here.'

Zak strode up to him. 'Listen to me,' he said. 'If someone came out here and killed you, what would you expect your family to do?'

The old man's face creased up menacingly. 'Don't go thinking of anything stupid, kid . . .'

'Just answer the question,' Zak said.

The father licked his dry old lips. 'I'd expect my boys to run them down like the dogs that they are.' He glanced over at Tasha. 'My girl too.'

'Two days ago,' Zak said, 'the man who was like a father to me was killed. My brother and sister – as good as – were kidnapped. I'm chasing the guy who did it. If you don't help me, I *will* walk across those mountains to find them. I don't care how high they are, or if I die doing it.'

'That's your funeral, kid,' said the old man, turning back to the fire. But Zak could sense that something had changed; there was a note almost of respect in the man's voice now.

Tasha cleared her throat. 'I'll take them, Pop,' she said quietly.

The old man frowned at her. 'Hold your tongue, Tasha.'

'It's not far,' she said. 'Only a day's walk. An' if it earns us some money—'

'*What's* not far?' Zak said.

'Moriarty,' Tasha said.

Zak caught his breath; he didn't want to let on that he'd heard this name before. 'Who's Moriarty?' he said carefully.

Tyler stepped forward. He seemed – for now – to have forgotten about his gun. He kept a careful eye on his fuming father, but spoke before he could be interrupted. 'He's just some guy, lived in these parts best of ten years now. Lives out in the wilds like us. More so. Used to fly army planes, and has a plane of his own too. Heard it said, he'll put that plane in the air when no one else will.'

'But only for a price,' the father cut in. 'These kids ain't going to have the money to pay for that kind of trip. And even the airplane man won't fly in this kind of weather.'

'Take me to him,' Zak said. He was addressing Tasha and her brothers now. 'I'll pay you.'

'How much you got?' Tyler asked.

Zak totted up the money he thought they had left between them. Ricky had given his to the cab driver. Zak had given his to the brothers. Only Malcolm's money remained. 'Three hundred bucks,' he said weakly.

'Ain't gonna be enough, son,' the father cut in. 'Not to pay us *and* the pilot.' His sharp face suddenly had a hungry look. 'A thousand bucks will get you to the pilot, but no further.'

'It's all I have,' Zak stated. But then an idea dropped, fully formed, into his brain. 'The farmstead,' he said. 'Where the drug dealers are. How far did you say it was?'

'Couple of miles,' Tyler muttered.

'How many people live there?'

''Bout ten.'

'Tasha said they were sitting on cash they made in the city. What is it? Some kind of hideout?'

Tyler shrugged. 'Bad people come out here in the wintertime to lie low. They know people ain't so likely to follow them through the snows. Gives law-abiding folk like us a bad reputation.' His eyes widened slightly as he guessed what Zak was thinking about. 'You don't want to go messin' with them types, though. They know not to come harassing us – they know we give as good as we get – but anyone approaches their territory, they got plenty of guns to shoot 'em back. We've been trying to think of ways of chasin' them out of this neck of the woods, without involving them in a pitched battle.'

'We don't want their kind around here,' the father cut in.

Zak's mind was suddenly working fast. 'I know how to get rid of them,' he said. 'Lend me a couple of weapons, I'll make sure they never come back.' And when the father's eyes narrowed aggressively, he added: 'No bloodshed. That's a promise. I'll scare them away.'

The father's eyes narrowed. 'How?' he said.

'By thinking like a criminal. Where I was brought up, if a place gets robbed, chances are it'll get robbed again, because the thieves know how to break in, and that there's stuff there worth taking. Criminals know this. So if *they* get robbed, they move to a different location.'

The family were all watching him carefully now. 'You can't be planning on *robbing* them?' the father said incredulously.

'That's exactly what I'm planning.'

A pause. A conflicted look crossed the father's face. Tyler walked up to him. 'Think of the money, Pop,' he said. 'We *need* it. And taking it from folk like that ain't doing no wrong.'

The old man frowned. 'One of you three stays here, so we know you ain't just stealing our firearms,' he said.

Zak nodded his agreement. The way he saw it, his

plan meant everyone was a winner. Tasha's family wanted these drug dealers gone. But they would also certainly have cash with them. Zak wouldn't feel at all guilty about taking it from them. His need was greater. They just needed someone subtle enough and skilful enough to get on site and steal it.

Snow, who was looking towards the shack, inclined his head. It was an oddly friendly gesture. Zak glanced back to see what the dog was looking at. Ricky and Malcolm had woken, and they were standing outside the door. They both looked a lot better for a night's sleep. Zak focused on Ricky – Snow's new friend and the street kid who, if Zak had heard properly, could pick the pocket of the Artful Dodger himself . . .

19

THE PLAN

It seemed to Ricky that Zak's personality was changing hour by hour. The more desperate his situation grew and the closer they got to the dead line – the more determined he became. His eyes were like flint. It was sort of impressive. And sort of scary. Ricky couldn't stop wondering exactly what he intended to do when – *if* – they finally caught up with Cruz Martinez.

'This is the plan.' Zak, Ricky and Malcolm were back in the shack. Zak spoke urgently, and in a low whisper. 'Malcolm, you have to stay here.' He caught Ricky's eye, and Ricky wondered if he was thinking the same thing as him – that with no laptop and no internet, Malcolm's skills were no good to them. 'If we leave you with them,' Zak continued smoothly, 'they'll lend us some weapons.'

'Weapons?' Ricky breathed. 'What for? Mate, you're not thinking of—'

'I've already told you once,' Zak said. 'I don't kill people. The weapons are just a diversion.'

'And they definitely said this guy was called Moriarty?'

'Definitely.'

'Mate, it's pretty thin.'

'If you've got a better idea, now's the time to say.'

Ricky sighed and shook his head. There was no point arguing with Zak. 'No better ideas,' he said.

He listened carefully as Zak explained his plan.

– He's crazy. It's too dangerous. Ripping off a bunch of drug dealers in the middle of the Alaskan snows isn't the same as picking a pocket in a London side street.

– Like the guy said, have you got any better ideas?

The voice in Ricky's head fell silent. 'When do we do it?' he asked. His voice was shaking slightly.

'Tonight. After dark, when nobody can see us approaching.' He sniffed. 'We've got thirty-nine hours until Cruz's deadline runs out. That doesn't give us any time to waste.'

They spent the day in the wild family's shack. They were under the watchful eye of one of the brothers at all times. Travis didn't let go of his weapon. Tyler insisted on patting them down again and emptying out their packs in his search for his lost gun. He found nothing, of course, and had to concede that he must have misplaced it in the confusion of the night before.

But Ricky sensed that the attitude of this strange family had changed. They seemed a bit more respectful. It was as if they were grudgingly impressed by what they intended to do. That didn't make Ricky feel much better – it meant they thought it was very dangerous. And they were dead right. It crossed his mind that maybe Malcolm had the best role in Zak's impromptu plan . . .

Around midday, the mother handed round small bowls of stew. The meat was tough and strong-tasting. Ricky didn't know what it was, and he didn't ask. Snow gnawed on a bone in the corner of the shack.

As the sun set over the silent, snowy terrain, Zak and Ricky prepared themselves. Tyler gave Zak back the hunting knife, and the family also reluctantly supplied them with an old rifle, fully loaded. Zak checked it over – he was the one who'd be using it.

'We need a guide,' Zak told the family. 'Someone who can get us through the woods to the far side of the farmstead. It's important that our tracks don't make it look like we've approached from this direction.'

The two brothers looked at each other, then at Tasha. 'She moves quickest,' Tyler said, 'and knows all the back ways. Snow will take care of her.'

Ricky smiled as Snow allowed him to scratch his neck. 'Not sure this softy would be much good in a fight,' he said.

Tyler and Travis exchanged a meaningful look. 'Snow can take care of himself,' Tyler said. Then he walked across the shack to where Zak was standing. With their faces only a couple of inches apart, he said: 'Anything bad happens to *her*, something bad happens to *him* . . .' He pointed at Malcolm, who blinked heavily.

Ricky watched Zak give a determined nod. 'She'll be fine,' he said.

Ricky wasn't so sure.

It was 9 p.m. when they left the house. Twenty-six hours until the deadline. As he walked over the threshold, Ricky looked back over his shoulder. Malcolm was sitting on the floor, hugging his knees and looking frightened. 'You'll be OK, buddy,' Zak told him. 'We won't be long.'

Outside, the blizzard was at least as bad as the previous night. As Tasha and Snow led them quickly away from the shack, Ricky and Zak had to increase their pace to keep up with her. 'Use my footprints,' she called over her shoulder. 'Easier to walk in.'

It took them just a couple of minutes to get behind the tree line. Once there, Zak stopped them. 'Don't follow the perimeter of the forest,' he told Tasha. 'Go into the centre, then back out again. We want our trail to be as complicated as possible. It'll make it harder for them to trace it back to your house.'

'You really think this is going to work?' Tasha asked.

'Hope so,' Zak said.

'I hope so too. Pop won't admit it, but money's gettin' to be a problem.'

They continued silently through the trees. Ricky realized they were able to move much faster now Malcolm wasn't with them. He tried not to think of the previous night's bear attack, but he found himself listening hard for any sound of growling or roaring. So far, there was none.

They walked in what Ricky took to be a north-westerly direction for forty-five minutes. Then Tasha switched trajectory, and they headed north-east. It took another half-hour to get back to the edge of the forest. 'We's a couple of miles north of our house,' Tasha said as they peered out into the blizzard. 'Farmstead's a mile in that direction.' She pointed east.

'How can you tell where we are?' Ricky asked, staring out into the blinding blizzard.

'Same way you can find your way around a city,' she said. 'All those busy streets look the same to me. Also, I've got Snow. He can smell his way better than we can see our way.' She looked at Zak. 'What now?'

'We get back behind the tree line and move north for half a mile. Then we execute the plan.'

They continued to follow Tasha as she picked her way expertly through the snow and the trees. Ricky tried to engage her in conversation. 'Why do you live out here like this?' he asked. 'In that old shack, with everyone under one roof? It's a hard life. Why not move back to the city?'

Tasha shrugged. 'My pop says it's because we prefer the wild life. Truth is, though, we ain't got no money.'

'Wouldn't you prefer to live in the city?'

'Sure I would. We all would. But Pop's a proud man. He wouldn't take us back to the city to live like paupers. Out here, we can manage on not very much.'

Ricky didn't answer, but he saw Zak watching them with a strange expression. He wondered what that meant.

After another half-hour they stopped. Ricky realized his heart was pumping hard. He was very nervous.

'Are you ready?' Zak asked him.

He nodded.

'Tasha?' Zak said. 'Which direction is the farmstead?'

She pointed to the south-east.

'How far?'

She shrugged. 'Bit more'n a mile, thereabouts.'

Zak turned to Ricky. 'I'm going to give you thirty minutes,' he said. 'That should give you time to get to the farmstead. Then I'll fire several shots. With a bit of luck, that'll get the drug dealers moving this way to defend their territory. Then I'll move a hundred metres north and fire again. The different direction should confuse them and make them split up. It's an old military technique.'

'Ever done it before?' Ricky asked.

'There's a first time for everything,' Zak said. 'Do you think that'll give you enough time to search the farmstead and steal any money you find?'

'Guess it'll have to.' He gave Zak a rueful look.

'What is it?' Zak said.

'Nothing . . . It's just, Felix was always telling me I should think of myself as more than a petty thief. Dunno what he'd think about this.'

Zak clasped one hand on his shoulder. 'He'd tell you that making life difficult for a bunch of drug dealers is a sure way of making the world a better place. They cause a lot of misery. No second thoughts?'

Ricky shook his head.

'Good. Tasha, you stay here. Climb a tree if you have to. Only come down when Ricky or I give you the word.'

A cloud crossed Tasha's face. She obviously didn't like being told what to do. 'Snow won't let nothing happen to me,' she said.

'Snow's not a match for a bad guy with a gun,' Zak told her. 'Time check,' he said, looking at his watch. 'It's 2200 hours. I'll start the diversion at exactly 2245, OK? We meet back here. If there's anybody about, we skirt the perimeter of the forest north for five hundred metres. Now go.'

Ricky hesitated. There was something in Zak's demeanour that worried him. It was as if he was so desperate that he was being careless with his own personal safety. This all felt too rushed.

'*Go!*' Zak hissed.

– He can take care of himself. And Tasha can hide if she needs to. Get moving.

Ricky hurried off into the snow. He could hear his pulse thumping. Remembering how hard it had been to keep their bearings the previous night, he concentrated hard on moving in a straight line. There was very little wind tonight, which meant there was a strange and eerie silence all around. His heavy breathing sounded like thunder, and the snowfall stung his face.

The minutes passed quickly. At 22:32 exactly, he saw a shape emerging through the snow in the distance. The grey outline of a bulky, rectangular building. He hunched his shoulders and kept moving forward. A tiny glow appeared, maybe fifty metres away.

– A fire. People are there.

– Good. I'd hate us to be wasting my time.

The farmstead became clearer. There was one main building. It was about thirty metres wide but only a single storey high. It was surrounded by several outbuildings, all of which had snow drifting high up against their entrances. The orange glow came from one of the windows of the main building. Even from a distance, Ricky could tell that this was the only part of the farmstead that was occupied.

Ricky paused for a moment. His eyes picked out a particularly ramshackle outbuilding. It was the furthest from the main building and to the side. He figured it would be a good place to hide; as and when anybody exited the main building, they wouldn't see his tracks coming in from this direction.

Time check. 22:35. Ten minutes till Zak's diversion. When it came, Ricky could expect people to start spilling out of the main building, and slightly to its side. The roof was heavy with snow. He needed to be well camouflaged by then. He frowned. On the streets of London he knew how to blend into the background so completely that nobody would ever see him. But how could he do the same thing here, amid this thick blanket of endless snow?

– *Dig yourself in. It's the only way.*

Ricky hurried over to the outbuilding, positioned himself to one side of it, and started scooping out a hole in the snow. It took him three minutes to make it deep enough that he could climb in and hide. He jumped into the hole and scrunched himself up into a ball, ensuring that his head was beneath the snow line. He caught a whiff of petrol and could just hear the low grind of an engine. Probably an electricity generator, he thought.

He waited. Now that he was immobile, he started to shiver. Snow settled on his clothes. Anxiety coursed through his veins.

He checked his watch. 22:44. One minute to go.

It happened precisely on time. As Ricky's watch clicked on to 22:45, he heard three shots firing in quick succession. They were very clear, and sounded like they came from far closer than they actually did.

Ricky screwed up his eyes and listened hard. As the third shot died away, there was a moment's deathly silence. Then, from the direction of the main building, Ricky heard the sudden banging of a door. Several voices started shouting in the night. He opened his eyes. Looking up from the protection of his snow hole, he could see the beams of several torches cutting through the night air.

— Stay put. It's too early to move.

Three more shots rang out in the distance. They came from the same direction as the first three, but they seemed to Ricky to be perhaps a little closer. More shouting. He couldn't make out individual words, but he could tell from the general hubbub that the people living in the farmstead were organizing themselves to head in the direction of the shots. And although he couldn't see them, he was certain they would be armed. 'Be careful, Zak,' he found himself muttering. 'Be very careful . . .'

The shouts were dying away somewhat, as the occupants of the building hurried further towards the sound of the gunshots. Very slowly and carefully, Ricky eased his head up above the snow line to see what was going on. From his position by the ramshackle outbuilding, he could just see a line of grey figures disappearing into the snow. He looked at the main farmstead building. They had left the door open and there was no movement in that direction, nor any noise.

— It doesn't mean the building is empty. Sit it out for

a little while longer. See if anybody else emerges.

Even as the voice in Ricky's head made that suggestion, there was a third burst of gunfire. This time it came from a very different direction – further north. Zak had changed position. Ricky allowed himself a grim smile. There was no denying it. Agent 21 was sneaky. He heard more confused shouting. As he listened hard, his senses told him that the occupants of the farmstead had split up – some of them heading in the direction of the original bursts of fire, some of them in the new direction.

They were out of the way and confused by Zak's diversion.

That meant it was time for Ricky to move.

20

SNOW

Silently, stealthily, Ricky climbed out of his snow hole. Hugging the wall of the outbuilding, he moved in a straight line toward the main farmstead building. His hot breath steamed in the cold air, and his skin tingled with cold and nerves. He blinked frequently to keep the snow from settling in his eyes. The smell of petrol fumes grew stronger.

Distance to the main entrance: twenty metres. Ricky covered it in as many seconds. Breathlessly, he drew himself up alongside the open door. He pressed his back against the wall of the building, inhaled deeply, then carefully looked through the threshold.

Although the building itself seemed sound, the inside was a mess. The door opened straight into a large room. It clearly made up the whole building, and doubled up as sleeping quarters and a living area. There were old, stained wooden floorboards, and a large table in the middle with a gaudy yellow laminated tablecloth. It was covered with empty beer cans and cigarette packets. Against the far wall was a large fireplace – here, the fire Ricky had seen from a distance was burning. There was a sink against the left-hand wall, which was overflowing with dirty crockery. Ricky could smell its stench even from the doorway. Behind the sink was a window, its pane thick with snow. There was a second window on the back wall. Several mattresses lay on the floor, and there was a general air of neglect and decay.

– Get searching. Where would they be hiding their money?

All of a sudden, in his mind, Ricky was back in London, being tutored in the art of surveillance by Felix. *Divide the room into mental boxes*, Felix was telling him. *Search each box individually . . .*

Ricky got to work immediately. He started in the far left corner of the room, where there was an old kitchen unit. He opened the drawers and cupboards, and carefully checked through what was left of the crockery within. No money. He pulled out the drawers and examined their underside. Nothing. He moved left. There was another unit here, next to the sink. It was empty. The sink unit itself contained empty bottles of cleaning fluid, but no cash.

— *What if Zak's wrong? What if they're not hiding a stash of money here?*

— *Then we change our plan. Until then, we keep looking.*

Five minutes passed. Ricky diligently continued his search of the room.

No luck.

There was a sudden crackling sound. He started, and spun round. He exhaled slowly as he realized it was only the log fire spitting. He was about to get back to his search, however, when he heard another noise.

Voices. Outside.

— *Someone's coming back.*

— *How many?*

— *Sounds like at least two. Get out of here. Now!*

Ricky looked desperately at the remaining sections of the room that he had not yet searched. He badly wanted to continue the process. He *knew* there was money here. He could almost smell it.

But the voices were getting closer. They couldn't be more than twenty metres from the house.

There was an old metal bread bin on the side board. Ricky lifted the lid and looked inside. Nothing but a mouldy old loaf.

— *Get out of here!*

– What about the money?

– Forget the money! GET OUT OF HERE!

His eyes fell across the open door. He saw moving lights out there – torch beams, undoubtedly. And louder voices . . .

He hurried towards the window behind the sink. But as he reached it, a loose floorboard creaked under his foot. He paused.

– You haven't got time! Get through the window! They'll be here in seconds!

Ricky glanced at the door. The torch beams were brighter. They were falling inside the room itself.

He bent down and wormed his fingers in along the side of the loose floorboard. It lifted easily. A putrid smell of damp wafted up from underneath. But Ricky immediately saw that there was something there: a red plastic bag containing something bulky and wrapped round itself. He quickly lifted it out from under the floor and peeked inside. He caught his breath slightly as he saw several thick bundles of used notes.

He'd found what he was looking for.

Ricky quickly replaced the floorboard and got to his feet, clutching the bag of money. He stretched over the sink, brimful of dirty crockery, and unfastened the window. It took several good shoves to open it, because of the weight of the snow on the panes . . .

A voice. Very clear. Right outside the main door. *'Something ain't right. I reckon the others, they're off on a wild-goose chase . . .'*

'That's their problem. I say we take the cash. Get ourselves the hell out of here . . .'

Ricky's heart was in his throat. There was no time to clamber out of the window. He had to hide. He quickly dived towards the large table in the middle of the room and clambered under the laminated tablecloth. Not a moment too soon. There was only a couple of inches' space between the bottom of the tablecloth and the floor. So he could only hear – and not see – the feet that entered the room. He prayed that the new arrivals wouldn't notice the tablecloth flapping.

'You get the money,' said a voice. *'I'll check the others ain't on their way back.'*

'Wait! That window wasn't open when we left . . .'

Ricky's muscles froze. He held his breath as the two sets of footsteps moved past the table to the window.

Silence.

A scraping sound as one of the two men lifted the loose floorboard. *''S gone!'* he growled.

'*They must've escaped through the window. After them. Quick!*'

– *If they notice there's no tracks in the snow*, said the voice in Ricky's head, *you're finished*.

Ricky didn't need telling twice. His only option now was to escape through the front door and hope his own tracks got mixed up with those of the drug dealers. And he had only seconds in which to do it . . .

He listened hard. There was the chinking of crockery as the two guys clambered over the sink. One thud, then two, as they jumped through the window.

– *Now!*

Ricky scurried out from under the table and checked, with a single glance, that he was alone in the room. Then he sprinted to the main door and hurtled out into the snow. Still clutching the bag of money, he followed the tracks directly away from the house. He looked over his right shoulder to check he wasn't in the line of sight of the two men. No sign of them.

The snow was still heavy. By the time he was thirty metres from the house, he reckoned he was out of sight. He curled off to the right, doing his utmost to keep his bearings. He hoped he was heading north. If he continued in this direction, he would eventually find the tracks he'd left on his way towards the house. His heart thumped in his chest as he ran, and although it was cold, he was sweating heavily. His feet slipped occasionally in the snow, but he managed to stay upright.

After five minutes, he hit his own tracks. He allowed himself a moment to stop, regain his breath, and listen. He thought he could perhaps hear shouting on the wind, but it was very distant, and impossible to tell which direction it came from. He gulped down some more lungfuls of air, then started retracing his steps back to the forest.

It took ten minutes to reach the tree line again. He suddenly felt safer, but that feeling of security didn't last for more than thirty seconds. Because suddenly, as if from nowhere, he heard a sound he recognized from the previous night. A high-pitched howl that seemed to cut through him just as it cut through the air.

– *It's a wolf.*

– *Stay calm. Remember what Zak said. They don't attack unless they're desperate . . .*

Somehow, logic didn't help. 'Tasha!' he hissed. 'Zak! Where are you?'

Silence.

Ricky cursed under his breath. Where *were* they? He was, all of a sudden, shivering badly. He peered into the gloom of the forest, then out beyond the tree line. No sign of anyone.

Another howl. Closer this time. A second wolf answered the call. It was just as close, but coming from a different direction.

Ricky wanted to run with every ounce of his being. It took immense self-control to stay put. Zak's RV strategy was clear – Ricky was only to move north if this location was occupied.

He pressed himself up against a tree trunk just as a fourth howl cut through the air. He sensed movement to his eleven o'clock, deeper in the forest. Maybe twenty metres away, he wasn't sure. His heart was like a drum beating in his ears. He didn't even want to look in the direction of the movement.

But he couldn't help it.

He saw the eyes first. Cold, yellow eyes glinting through the darkness.

Ricky held his breath.

More movement.

The animal slinking towards him was thin and hungry-looking. It reminded Ricky of a cat stealthily stalking a mouse. Only this time, the mouse was him . . .

The wolf was fifteen metres away – and advancing – when Ricky saw movement from his nine o'clock.

There was a second beast, just as lean and ravenous-looking as the first . . .

Both animals were ten metres away. He could see them much more clearly now. These wolves didn't have the thick, luxurious coats he had seen in picture books. Their backs were covered with tufts of ragged fur, with occasional patches of piebald skin. They looked well used to fighting.

Nine metres . . .

– Shout out! Try to frighten them!

Ricky knew he should, but somehow he couldn't. He heard a low growl from the animals' throats. He hugged the bagful of money – as if *that* would do any good – and looked up into the branches of the tree against which his back was pressed. The lowest limb was three metres high. There was no way he could climb it.

Images of the wild bear from the previous night flashed through his mind. He remembered waving the burning branch at it. But tonight, he had no defence. And the wolves were still advancing.

Maybe he should run. But that would make the wolves' chase instinct kick in . . .

Eight metres . . .

Seven . . .

'Zak!' he managed to shout hoarsely. 'Tasha! *Help!*' His voice sounded deadened and dull against the thick white blanket all around. The wolves growled deeply, both at the same time. They paused for a moment, and something seemed to pass between them.

Then they pounced.

It all seemed to happen in slow motion. As the two wild animals lurched for him, there was a flash of white from his right-hand side. Ricky shouted out in alarm, but a fraction of a second later he realized what it was.

Snow.

Tasha's husky was all fur, teeth and growls. He was a different animal to the one who had let Ricky scratch his neck: alert, strong and aggressive. With a fast and lithe movement, he positioned himself in the five metres of open ground between Ricky and the wolves. The two wild animals stopped in their tracks, a cloud of white powder bursting up all around them.

They pawed the earth, but Snow stood his ground.

Five seconds passed. For a horrific moment, the intensely hungry look in the wolves' eyes made Ricky think they were going to attack the husky. But then Snow let out a low-throated growl, so deep that Ricky thought it might shake the snow from the trees. The two wolves scampered back a couple of metres.

Snow bounded forward. He growled again. One of the wolves howled – an empty but terrifying sound of frustration. Snow barked three times, then growled for a third time.

The wolves turned on their tails, and ran.

Someone whistled from further in the forest. Snow's ears pricked up, and he bounded over to where a slight figure was standing beneath a tree. It was Tasha. Snow sat obediently at her feet.

'Good dog,' Ricky heard her say. 'You's a good dog.'

Midnight.

Cruz Martinez's quarters were stark and military. Just like almost everywhere on Big Diomede island. It was a Russian military base, and such places are not known for their comfort. He had a room with a single bed, a desk and a sink with a mirror. Cruz was one of the wealthiest people in the world, but he was happy to live frugally.

As he stared in the mirror, he saw the face of someone who had not slept for many days. He hardly ever slept any more. Even when he did, he never felt refreshed. He had grown used to his reflection – those deep, black rings under the eyes of his thin face. He would stare at it for minutes at a time, vaguely wondering what had happened to the youthful features he once had. Not that he missed them.

Another figure appeared in the mirror. A broad-shouldered man in Russian military uniform. His nose was red from too much vodka, and his eyes were pale and watery. His name was Rostropovich, and he was not a man to cross.

'You don't know where he is, do you?' he said in stilted English from the doorway.

Cruz turned slowly. 'Of course I do.' His voice was icy. 'He is somewhere between Anchorage and here.'

'That covers a lot of space, Martinez. I don't like this plan of yours.'

'You don't like my plan?' Cruz asked very quietly. 'I fail to see how it could be any better. You want to get your hands on one of the British government's most secret assets. Because he is not yet an adult, you are too scared to abduct him yourself. You want to lure him to an obscure, secure piece of Russian territory of his own accord, without him even knowing that he is walking into the jaws of your trap. You want the British to suspect that he has defected to you, but that you have had no hand in it. That is exactly what is happening. Trust me: Harry Gold will stop at nothing to rescue those pathetic creatures in Hangar 1H. He will step right into your clutches. And I'm not even charging you for my trouble, Rostropovich. All I ask is the opportunity to kill his two friends in front of him when he has arrived. That will be ample payment for me.'

Rostropovich's eyes narrowed. 'What if he doesn't make it?'

Cruz walked towards him. 'Then, Rostropovich, he will most likely die a lonely death on the Alaskan ice. I, for one, will not mourn him. But he is stronger and more determined than, for example, you. Cleverer too, although *that* is not so hard. He will be here, and I will be able to hand over your precious British spy, to interrogate in whatever depraved way you have in mind. From the look of it, he might even be bringing a friend or two.' He gave a nasty kind of smile. 'Buy one, get one free.'

Rostropovich frowned. 'You'd better make sure this all works out,' he said.

Cruz didn't reply. He just turned his back on the Russian to indicate that the interview was over. He went back to looking in the mirror, pleased to see that the doorway was empty again. He stared into his own dark eyes. Were his doubts visible on his face? Would Rostropovich have known that Cruz had a nagging worry that even Agent 21 would find the difficulties involved in reaching this obscure corner of the earth insurmountable?

He shook his head and turned his back on the mirror. Harry Gold would find a way. He always did.

In twenty-four hours' time, midnight on his favourite festival of *el Día de Reyes*, they would be face to face. Agent 21 would be on Russian soil – or rather, Russian ice – and he would be under Cruz's control.

Cruz's father would be avenged.

And Harry Gold would be wishing that his life would come to an end very, very soon.

21

MORIARTY

It was almost dawn when Zak, Ricky and Tasha returned to the shack. The burning panic in Zak's gut had intensified. It was January the sixth already – Epiphany, the day of Cruz's deadline – but they were still hundreds of miles from their destination.

They had taken a roundabout route through the forest, looping back on themselves frequently to check they weren't being followed. And after his fright with the wolves, Ricky had moved a little slower than on the way out. Zak noticed that he kept very close to Snow.

The family were still awake. They all looked very relieved as Tasha and Snow entered. Malcolm looked even more relieved to see Zak and Ricky.

'What happened?' Travis asked immediately. 'Did you do it? Did you rip 'em off?'

Ricky held up the red plastic bag. His face looked drawn and tired. Hardly surprising, Zak thought, after the evening he'd had.

They carefully counted out the money. There was a massive amount – just shy of twenty thousand dollars in crumpled, used notes. The old man's eyes nearly popped out of his head.

'A deal's a deal,' he said. 'A thousand bucks to take you to Moriarty. Reckon he'll want another couple of thousand, if he agrees to the flight. Looks like you made yourself a good profit, kid.'

Zak felt a twinge of respect for the old guy. He was clearly a man of his word. He looked at Tasha and her brothers. He noticed again how lean they were. As hungry-looking as the wolves Snow had chased away. He counted out the two thousand dollars he needed, then pushed the rest of the money across the table. 'Tasha says you all want to move back to the city,' he said quietly. 'With this money, you can do it.'

Silence in the room. The rest of the family looked at the father. Zak couldn't be sure, but he thought he saw a tear in the watery eyes of that grizzled old face. He turned to Tyler and Travis. 'How long to get to Moriarty?' he asked. His voice was thick and gruff.

'Half a day,' Tyler said. He was looking at Zak

with a new expression. All the hostility had vanished from his voice. He walked up to Zak and shook him by the hand. 'We'll be happy to lead you there,' he said.

Zak looked at his watch. It was almost 5 a.m. They had nineteen hours until Cruz's deadline. 'We need to leave now,' he said.

Tyler nodded. Then he looked over at Malcolm. 'Ain't gonna lie to you,' he said. 'I'm not sure that one's fit enough to make the journey. We could . . . we could maybe look after him for a bit . . .' He looked around at his family to see if they agreed with the suggestion. Everyone nodded their agreement.

Zak walked over to where Malcolm was sitting. 'What do you reckon, buddy?' he said. 'Do you want to stay here, or come with us?'

Malcolm blinked heavily. 'I'm coming with you,' he said.

Zak hesitated for a moment, then nodded. He turned to the others. 'Let's get ready,' he said. 'We leave immediately.'

Their farewells were short. The mother and father – Zak realized he still didn't even know their names – stood alongside Tasha and Snow outside the hut. They shook hands. Zak had the impression that the old man gripped his hand a little harder than he needed to. He was clearly grateful for what Zak had done.

'Will you ever come back?' Tasha asked.

'I don't know,' Zak told her honestly. The truth was, he hadn't thought past his RV with Cruz Martinez. It was like a brick wall in his mind. He didn't know what was beyond it. Maybe nothing.

Tyler and Travis took the lead. They wore bear-skin clothes and boots. It made them look like something out of another century. Zak, Ricky and Malcolm followed in their more modern snow gear. It felt safer moving in the daytime. Even though their visibility was less than ten metres, the conditions felt less harsh than when they had been stumbling blindly through the night. Tyler and Travis seemed to have an unerring sense of direction, and led them confidently across the frozen landscape.

Every hour, they stopped for a cupful of water and a mouthful of the strong-tasting dried jerky the brothers had brought with them. Zak was glad of the sustenance as they trekked relentlessly in what the brothers insisted was a north-easterly direction. He had no choice but to assume they were right.

And they were.

It was just past midday when a bulky grey shape suddenly appeared in the distance. The little group of travellers stopped. It looked bleak and unwelcoming. Tyler and Travis turned to Zak.

'Moriarty,' Travis said.

'You need to leave us here,' Zak said.

'What if he turns you away?' Travis asked. 'Word is, he's a pretty weird old guy. And this weather . . .' He looked around meaningfully into the heavy snow.

'We'll just have to deal with it,' Zak said. 'Trust me, the less you can be linked with us, the safer you'll be. Get back home. Help your folks move back to the city. I've got a feeling this winter's only going to get harder.'

The two brothers nodded. Tyler shuffled slightly in the snow. 'I, er . . . I'm sorry I accused you of taking my gun. Must've just mislaid it, like you said.' He put his hand into his jacket and pulled out another firearm – a bulky old handgun that Zak could tell had seen better days. 'Use it for shootin' birds mostly,' Tyler said. 'But I reckon you could make use of it, wherever you're going.'

Zak carefully took the old handgun and stowed it away in his pack. He could feel Ricky's eyes burning into him, and he remembered the conversation they'd had on the plane. *The Agency recruited us because we were kids, but we can't stay kids for ever.*

He turned back to Tyler. 'Thank you,' he said shortly. 'I hope I won't need it.'

They all shook hands, then Zak, Ricky and Malcolm watched Tyler and Travis trudge back off into the distance.

Zak turned his attention to the grey building. There was no indication of any aircraft here, or even of any inhabitants. They pressed on apprehensively. The building grew clearer. It looked like an enormous barn, with a thick layer of snow over the roof. When they were twenty metres from it, Zak stopped.

'Can you hear that?' he said.

Ricky and Malcolm paused too.

'It's music,' Malcolm said. His eyes shone as he said it, and for the first time since they had arrived in Alaska he looked happy, despite the cold. And he was right. Coming from the building was the muffled, scratchy sound of old-fashioned dance music. A big band. Someone singing.

They edged forward. There was no visible entrance in the side of the barn they were approaching, so they skirted clockwise around it. At the left-hand end of the building were two enormous barn doors. Yellow light was escaping from around them, and the music was louder. It was definitely coming from inside.

Zak strode up to the doors. He clenched his fist and banged three times against them. They gave a huge, hollow echo.

Almost immediately, the music stopped.

There was a ghostly shriek of wind high above them. Zak and the others instinctively backed away from the doors as they heard footsteps. An ominous creaking sound as the door opened. The yellow light spilled out onto the snow . . .

Zak had never seen a more grizzled-looking person than the man who appeared in the doorway. Despite probably only being in his late-thirties, the lines on his face were deeply etched, and his skin was so tanned and tough it looked like leather. He had a straggly beard. His hair receded far enough to show an ugly scar that stretched from his forehead almost to the top of his scalp. He had a thin cigar smoking in the corner of his mouth. His eyes were a piercing blue – very bright, but deeply mistrustful. But at the same time, there was something incredibly familiar about him. Zak had the uncanny feeling that they'd met somewhere before.

He looked his visitors up and down. 'Who the hell are you?' he asked. His voice was gruff, cracked and unfriendly. Zak was surprised to hear that he had a very distinct British accent.

'We're looking for Moriarty,' Zak said.

The man's eyes narrowed. The end of his thin cigar glowed as he inhaled, before expelling a powerful jet of smoke from his nose. 'You'd better get inside,' he said. Zak blinked. This guy was definitely British, not Canadian or American. How come?

The man – presumably Moriarty – turned and walked back into the building. Zak, Ricky and Malcolm followed.

As soon as Zak entered, he realized that this was not so much a barn as an aircraft hangar. Parked up at the far end was a small light aircraft with a single propeller. The air was thick with the smell of fuel, and several panels on the underside of the plane were open. Moriarty had clearly been doing some running repairs. It looked to Zak as if he intended to ride out the winter here. There were many boxes of tinned food piled up in one corner of the hangar, and a small gas stove next to them. In another corner was a sleeping area – a single mattress with several thick blankets. A CD player sitting on an old table explained the music they had heard. A handful of discs were scattered around it and there were two large, very old, floor-standing speakers. One of the speakers had a half-drunk bottle of whiskey on it. The other had a VHF radio set sitting on top. But the thing that attracted most of Zak's attention was a photograph in a frame, next to the half-empty bottle. It showed a teenage girl. And Zak recognized her face.

'Gabs . . .' he breathed. His Guardian Angel looked much younger in the picture, but it was definitely her.

'What?' Moriarty barked. 'What did you say?'

'Nothing,' Zak replied. He was still trying to make sense of what he'd just seen.

There were a few fan heaters dotted around – Zak assumed there had to be a generator somewhere behind the hangar, powering them as well as the CD player and any other electricals. But the heaters had little effect on the temperature. It was extremely cold in here. The cold didn't seem to worry Moriarty. He wore jeans, regular trainers and a thick, checked lumberjack shirt. He watched the three of them carefully as they traipsed over the threshold in their snow gear, bringing loose snow with them. His face grew even more suspicious as they pulled back their hoods. 'So what is this?' he said. 'School trip?'

Zak ignored the sarcastic remark and got straight to the point. 'We need to get to Little Diomede Island,' he said. 'There are no commercial flights out of Anchorage. Someone told us you'll put a plane in the air when others won't.'

'Whoa, sunshine. Back up. You missed the bit that explains what three kids young enough to be my children are doing in the middle of the Alaskan snows, a day's march from anything resembling civilization.' Moriarty blew out a lungful of cigar smoke, then coughed noisily.

'Looking for you,' Zak replied.

'I haven't finished. You also missed the bit that explains why three kids are so keen to fly to the ends of the earth when no sane person is willing to put a plane in the sky.'

Zak gave him a level look. 'Can't help you with that one,' he said. 'You're just going to have to believe that we're not quite what we seem.' He glanced involuntarily at the picture of Gabs, then locked gaze back with the pilot. He didn't want to play that card until the right moment.

Moriarty gave a short, barking laugh. 'Right,' he said.

He wandered over to the CD player and was about to press 'play' when Zak spoke up again. 'Cessna 172 Turbo Skyhawk,' he said, pointing at the aircraft. 'Range, approximately a thousand nautical miles. That's, what, about eighteen hundred kilometres.'

The pilot stopped and looked at him curiously.

'Last time I was in a Cessna, we flew from Johannesburg to Dakar.'

'Impossible,' Moriarty cut in. 'Unless you had a . . .'

'. . . long-range tank, and a couple of refuelling stops.'

The pilot was looking at him curiously now. 'Doesn't sound like your average package holiday.'

'It wasn't,' Zak said. He looked around the hangar. 'What I'm wondering is, what's a skilled pilot like you doing miles from anywhere. It's almost as if you don't want anybody to find you.'

Moriarty took the cigar from his mouth, dropped it on the floor and stubbed it out with his foot. 'You think a lot, son,' he growled.

'Yep,' Zak said. 'And right now I'm thinking you're a former special forces pilot with a very good reason to stay under the radar.' He pointed to the corner of the hangar where the mattress and blankets were piled. Lying on the ground was a beige-coloured beret. Zak could just make out a badge on the front: the winged dagger insignia of the SAS. It was obviously precious to him. It really *meant* something. Why else would he have it lying by his bed?

'You're more observant than you look,' the pilot said with a dangerous edge to his voice.

Zak removed his pack from his back and started removing wads of money which he threw onto the floor at the pilot's feet. 'We'll pay you everything we have to make the journey,' he said. 'But that's not the real reason you'll do it.'

'Oh yeah?' Moriarty replied. He was trying to look dismissive, but Zak knew he had his attention.

'We're heading to the Bering Straits to rescue two people who the British government *really* want back.

We can't do it with the government's knowledge, because they think I'm a traitor. But believe me: if we pull this off, anybody who helped us will be welcomed back with open arms. Any past crimes forgotten about. A clean slate.'

Zak could see the effect his words were having on Moriarty. At first all his attention was on the money at his feet. But gradually he had stopped looking at that and fixed his gaze on Zak. At the words 'clean slate' he had spun on his heel and started walking towards the Cessna.

'You're a fast talker, son,' he called. 'I'll give you that.' Standing by the plane, he put one hand on the wing. It was a strangely affectionate gesture. 'Only a fool would put this old bird up in the sky in flying conditions like this,' he said with his back to them.

'A fool,' Zak countered, 'or an expert.'

Silence.

'You know who we are,' Zak said quietly. 'When you were in the SAS, you must have heard rumours. A government agency, working at the highest level of secrecy. As well trained as the SAS, but much more covert.'

Moriarty hunched his shoulders and turned. His gaze was sharp and piercing. 'Yeah,' he said. 'I heard rumours. None of them mentioned using kids.'

He seemed to be wavering. It was time for Zak to

play his trump card. 'You want to know who taught me so much about planes?' he asked. He turned, and pointed to the photograph sitting on Moriarty's speaker. 'She did.'

Moriarty gave him a sharp look. 'Impossible, son,' he said, with a strange edge to his voice. 'That's my baby sister Annabel. She died a long time ago.'

Zak felt a strange twist in his stomach. He'd never known Gabs's real name. To find it out now, here, in this way, was kind of disorientating. He shook his head. 'No she didn't,' he said, as kindly as he could. 'She works for the Agency, like me. I don't know much about her past. I've never even known her real name until now – I've always just called her Gabs. But I faked my own death when I joined. It wouldn't surprise me to learn that she did the same thing too.'

There were tears on the man's grizzled face. He turned his back on Zak. 'Shut up, son. It's not funny. You'd better leave. Go on! *Leave!*'

Zak gave him a level look and prepared to deliver his killer blow. 'She used to call you "sweetie", right?'

Silence.

Moriarty turned. His face was a mixture of horror and hope.

'Your little sister's in danger, Moriarty. She told us

to find you. She's obviously been keeping an eye on you for all these years. She knows where you are. And now she needs your help. If we don't get to Little Diomede Island before midnight, Gabs – I mean, Annabel – dies.'

Zak sensed that everyone in the room was holding their breath. Moriarty turned his back on them again. He walked towards the plane and stood by it for a moment, his shoulders hunched.

Silence.

'If we're going to go,' Moriarty called in a shaky, cracked voice, 'we need to go now. The wind's in the right direction for a takeoff. If it changes, we're stuck. Plus, the colder it gets, the greater the chance of ice on the wings. And if I'm reading the weather right, conditions are only going to get worse . . .'

22

TAKEOFF

Moriarty made Ricky very nervous. The moment he had finished sparring with Zak, he had turned his music back on. Scratchy old dance tunes filled the hangar as he went about finishing whatever maintenance he'd been doing to his plane. When Ricky asked if he could help, Moriarty had replied by saying, 'Yeah – sit down, shut up and keep out of my way.'

So Ricky, Zak and Malcolm hung back near the entrance to the hangar while Moriarty worked. 'You sure you trust him to get us there safely?' Ricky asked.

'Special forces pilots are the best in the world,' Zak said. 'If anyone can get us there in these conditions, he can.'

Ricky didn't like to point out that this wasn't *quite*

what he'd asked. 'Is he really Gabs's brother?' he said.

'I should have known the moment I saw him,' Zak replied. 'They look kind of similar.' He grinned. 'Apart from the beard, of course.'

Half an hour passed. Moriarty closed up all the open panels on the plane's body, then headed back to the other end of the hangar and sat down at his VHF radio set.

'What are you doing?' Zak said, his voice slightly aggressive.

'This isn't Africa, son. I can't just stick a plane in the air and hope the Americans won't notice. We need permission to follow your flight path to Little Diomede, or they'll shoot us out of the air quicker than you can say 9/11.' He almost smiled. 'Don't worry, I won't mention any of your names.'

'From what I've learned about this Cruz guy,' Ricky said as Moriarty made his call over the crackly radio connection, 'he'll know we're coming as soon as he learns there's a plane *en route* to Little Diomede.'

Zak sniffed. 'He knows we're coming anyway,' he said grimly.

Moriarty finished his call. 'Done,' he announced. 'Now help me get these doors open.'

Malcolm didn't move, but Ricky and Zak hurried

up to the far end of the hangar. The doors here, just beyond the Cessna, were several metres high, each one half the width of the hangar. The heavy bolts were locked by a chain and padlock. Moriarty unlocked them. He took the right door while Zak and Ricky took the left. Together they started pushing them open. A fierce blast of wind rushed through the crack between the doors. Hard pellets stung Ricky's face. While they'd been inside, the snow had turned to hail. It blasted in through the open doorway, clattering against the metal of the Cessna with a hard, percussive sound. It took all their strength to force the doors open against the power of the wind. They secured them against some stout wooden poles fixed in the ground for that purpose. Only then did Ricky properly look out beyond the hangar.

He could barely keep his eyes open on account of the wind and the hail. He could, however, make out a runway of sorts. It was probably no more than ten metres in width, but it was dead straight and stretched into the distance further than Ricky could see. The hail was settling lightly on the runway, but the snow was nowhere near as deep as it was on either side.

Moriarty ran up to them, his head bowed against the wind. 'I shovel salt onto it every other day!' he shouted in explanation. 'It keeps the snow from building up. But it's still pretty icy. We need to keep our weight as low as possible. Only bring what you absolutely need.' He looked towards the other end of the hangar where Malcolm was still sitting. 'That one over there seems like a dead weight. You should leave him here. There's enough food for him to—'

'He comes with us!' Zak shouted.

Moriarty looked like he was going to argue, but Zak immediately strode off towards Malcolm. Ricky followed. Together, they gathered their packs. Even at this end of the hangar, the wind was blowing chunks of ice towards them. As they hauled their rucksacks onto their backs, Ricky heard the sound of the aircraft's engines being started. He felt a lurch of anxiety in his gut.

— *This is madness. How can any aircraft take off in these conditions?*

'Surely the wind's too strong?' he shouted at Zak. 'We should wait till it's died down a bit.'

Zak shook his head. 'The strength of the wind is less important than its direction. Moriarty's right. At the moment it's blowing directly parallel to the runway. If we wait, we run the risk of it changing direction. It'd be much more dangerous to take off with a crosswind. It would blow us sideways across the icy runway. We'd crash before we even left the ground.' He grabbed Malcolm by the arm and encouraged him towards the aircraft. Malcolm looked terrified, but he seemed to trust Zak implicitly. 'Let's board,' Zak shouted.

Ricky's limbs were heavy with a kind of icy dread. He battled against the wind that was blowing into the hangar as they moved towards the aircraft. Half of him wanted to bail out – to tell Zak that this was crazy, that they were going to get themselves killed. His mind spun with the fear. But just as he was about to throw down his pack and refuse, he remembered something that Felix had once told him: *The time's going to come, Coco, when you'll have to be brave. Being brave isn't the same as being fearless. It's not an absence of fear – that would be stupid. It's the ability to master your fear. To keep it in a box and not let it get the better of you.*

Suddenly, it was almost as if Felix was right beside him. That feeling was like a knife in his stomach, carving out the fear. He remembered why he was here in the first place – to catch up with the guy who'd killed his friend and mentor. He set his jaw and upped his pace towards the Cessna.

It was cramped in the cockpit. Moriarty was already sitting in a leather seat by the control column. A bewildering array of dials and controls were lit up in front of him. There was a small rechargeable GPS unit, with a flashing blue light that indicated their location. The windscreen was being beaten and battered by the hail. It was deafening. Zak took his place next to the pilot. Ricky sat behind Moriarty, with Malcolm next to him behind Zak. They had their packs at their feet. Zak slammed his side door shut. The howling wind grew momentarily quieter, and Moriarty edged the aircraft forward, out of the hangar.

Ricky could tell the difference in the feeling of the wheels on the ground as soon as they moved from the hangar onto the icy runway. With less friction, everything felt much smoother. Once they were clear of the hangar doors, the pilot braked gently. Ricky wasn't sure, but he thought he felt the wheels gliding slightly before they came to a halt. Ricky's stomach glided with them.

Moriarty opened his side door. The screaming of the wind became louder again. He jumped out of the aircraft, closed the hangar doors and then re-embarked. Once the aircraft door was shut again, he turned to his passengers. His eyes were strangely bright, almost as if, in a wild kind of way, he was looking forward to this. It crossed Ricky's mind that Moriarty was just as crazy as the job they'd given him.

'Not too late to back out,' he said. 'We can while away the winter in the hangar. I could do with the company.' He grinned for the first time, and Ricky saw that he had several missing teeth. He struggled to put a lid on his panic.

'We don't have all winter,' Zak said. 'We've got less than twelve hours. If we're too late, your sister dies.'

Moriarty inclined his head. 'Then strap yourselves in, my friends,' he said. 'It's going to be a bumpy ride.'

They did as they were told. Ricky could sense that Malcolm was trembling, and he reminded himself that just because Malcolm hadn't spoken much, he still knew what was going on. 'It's going to be all right, mate,' he said. Malcolm just stared straight ahead.

The pilot accelerated. Immediately, Ricky felt the headwind buffeting the aircraft. He looked out of the window to his right. The wing tips were shaking alarmingly. He decided he didn't want to look at them. Instead, he stared directly out of the front windscreen. Bad idea. From this vantage point, he could see how badly the light aircraft was sliding on the runway as they sped forward. The hail formed a kind of vortex as it slammed against the cockpit – Ricky honestly expected the glass to break at any second. There was a terrible whining noise from the engine as they precariously gathered speed. The drifting snow on either side of the runway zoomed past in a blur. Ricky found himself praying that Moriarty knew where the end of the runway was – with such poor visibility, it would come at them out of nowhere . . .

'We're not getting enough speed!' Zak shouted suddenly. Ricky understood what he meant – the engines were shrieking badly, but Moriarty refused to pull back his steering column. The pilot said nothing, and Ricky stared at the back of his hunched shoulders, consumed with panic.

'*Stop!*' Ricky heard himself shouting suddenly. '*We're not going to make it! Stop!*'

'Uh-uh,' the pilot shouted, his voice very tense. 'We're too far gone. Either we take off, or we crash.'

'*Then take o—*'

Ricky inhaled suddenly. The aircraft had slipped and they were veering sharply to the left. The view through the windscreen was suddenly not one of the runway. It was of the drifting snow to its side. They were about to crash into it . . .

'*NO!*'

But as Ricky shouted, he suddenly felt a sensation of weightlessness. *They were off the ground.* He sucked in another lungful of air. The plane was badly wobbling. It banked sharply to the right. With a flash of insight, he realized Moriarty was trying to get them in line with the headwind again. But it was a struggle. Everything inside the plane seemed to be vibrating – including the pilot's hands on the control column. Through the windows, they could see nothing but pelting hail.

'*We need to get above the weather as quickly as possible,*' Moriarty shouted. '*Sit tight!*'

Ricky didn't think he *could* sit tighter. He was clutching his seat so hard, his knuckles had gone white. The engines suddenly shifted pitch again. The feeling of weightlessness returned as the aircraft quickly gained height. The plane was shuddering even worse now. Ricky heard himself shouting, though he doubted anyone else could hear over the immense noise of the engines and the weather.

Hail became cloud. Visibility: zero. Just a whiteout, all around. There was no way of telling if they were a hundred feet or a thousand feet above the ground. Horrific thoughts cruised through Ricky's head. What if they hit something? What if they collided with another aircraft that Moriarty simply couldn't see?

– Don't be stupid. Who else would be flying through this?

Ricky's lungs started to hurt, and he realized he'd been holding his breath ever since they'd entered the clouds. How long had that been? A minute? More?

But suddenly, they burst through the cloud line. Ricky realized it hadn't just been him holding his breath. Everyone in the plane explosively exhaled as the whiteout suddenly became a sharp, piercing blue. Ricky screwed his eyes shut. The sun, which they hadn't seen for so long, was throwing hot hammers into their eyes. He was vaguely aware of Moriarty pulling a pair of dark glasses from his top pocket so that he could fly safely. Ricky, Zak and Malcolm, however, had to settle for holding their hands over their eyes to shade themselves from the glare.

For a moment, nobody spoke.

Then Ricky cleared his throat. 'I, er . . . I'd say that went pretty well?' His voice sounded high-pitched and stressed.

Moriarty looked back at him over his shoulder. 'That was the easy bit, son,' he said. 'Landing in this weather? Now *that's* going to be a challenge, even for me.'

23

IMPACT

Zak's eyes ached. As afternoon became evening, the sun grew lower and redder. But they were heading in a north-westerly direction. With the sun setting in the west, the glare was almost straight ahead of them. He allowed himself to close his eyes and rest as the Cessna flew smoothly across the clouds.

His mind turned to Raf and Gabs. He couldn't get the image of them, battered and bleeding in Cruz's last video, out of his head. Anger burned through him. He knew Cruz was pulling him into a trap, and had no idea what was waiting for him when they landed. Even so, he was impatient to get back down on the ground. It was time to finish this, once and for all.

He glanced across at Moriarty. He had barely spoken since they'd broken through the cloud cover.

His attention seemed fully focused on controlling the plane, and keeping track of their position on the portable GPS screen.

Zak opened one eye. 'Tell me what happened,' he said quietly to Moriarty.

The pilot glanced at him. 'What are you talking about?'

'To make you run away and live in Alaska.'

At first, Zak thought Moriarty wasn't going to answer. 'You heard of Afghanistan?' he said finally.

'Of course,' Zak said.

'I was out there, in the early days of the war. I used to fly an Apache. It's an attack helicopter. Scary piece of kit. The order came through that I should launch a Hellfire missile at a deserted school where dangerous militants were hiding. So I did.' He breathed deeply. 'Turns out the intelligence was wrong. It wasn't a deserted school. It was an *actual* school. Thirty-five kids died, and two teachers.' Moriarty's jaw clenched. 'It was my fault.'

'No it wasn't,' Zak said. 'You said so yourself. The intelligence was wrong.'

Moriarty didn't seem to hear him. 'Before I fired the missile, I saw them. Three kids, playing with a ball outside the school building. I should have questioned the order, but . . .' His voice trailed off. 'I went a bit crazy after that. Couldn't handle what

I'd done, I guess. Couldn't handle the fact that those kids were dead because of me. I started disobeying orders for the hell of it. They turfed me out of the army soon afterwards. Dishonourable discharge.'

There was silence in the cockpit. Shielding his eyes, Zak looked at Moriarty. There was a tear on his weatherbeaten face. He wiped it roughly away, then turned to Zak. 'People don't know what it's like, taking a life,' he said. 'They think they can handle it. But every night, when you put your head on the pillow, you hear them. The screams of the ones you killed. And you can never escape them, even when you run to the ends of the earth.' He gave Zak a piercing look. 'Remember that, son, if you're ever tempted to put a bullet in someone.'

Zak turned away. It was time to change the subject. 'How long till we land?'

'*If* we land,' the pilot said. 'It'll be in about half an hour. It's going to be very rough getting back down through the clouds.'

'Have you landed on Little Diomede before?' Zak asked. 'Do you know the runway?'

Moriarty raised an eyebrow. 'Runway?' he said. 'There's no runway, son.'

Zak blinked. 'What do you mean, there's no runway?'

'The Little Diomede islanders carve a kind of makeshift runway into the ice in the winter. That's what we're heading for.' He flashed Zak a smile. 'Here's hoping we hit it, eh?'

'Yeah,' Zak breathed. 'Here's hoping.'

There was a pause. 'Tell me something about Annabel,' Moriarty said.

Zak looked out of the window. 'She's like a sister to me,' he said. 'She's been kidnapped, along with another good friend of mine, Raf. They're the best agents I know.' He turned to Moriarty. 'You'll see her soon,' he said.

The sky darkened as the blood-red sun dropped below the horizon. A few stars appeared in the inky sky. Zak shivered as he glanced towards the glowing screen of the GPS unit. He could see the crinkly coastline of western Alaska tracking across the screen.

Time check: 6:30 p.m. Five and a half hours to go.

Moriarty looked over his shoulder at Ricky and Malcolm. 'Strapped in?' he asked.

They nodded wordlessly.

'Then here goes nothing.'

Moriarty adjusted the steering column. Zak immediately felt the aircraft losing height. The cloud cover glowed slightly beneath them. It seemed somehow stormier now that night had come. More threatening . . .

The turbulence immediately got worse. Zak tried not to focus on the steering column, which was shaking in Moriarty's fist. The aircraft bumped and rattled its way down. After thirty seconds it felt like it was bouncing across the top of the clouds, like a stone skimming across lake. Zak put that image from his head, because he knew that all stones eventually would sink . . .

There was a collective hiss from the passengers as the clouds suddenly enveloped the aircraft. It felt as though someone – some*thing* – had grabbed the plane and started shaking it, like a baby shaking a rattle. Everyone in the cockpit juddered violently. If he hadn't been strapped in, Zak was sure the sudden convulsion would have thrown him up against the windscreen. He grabbed the edge of his seat and gasped for breath. Glancing at the pilot, he saw his face lit up by the glow of the cockpit controls. His creased forehead was sweating, his piercing blue eyes a picture of concentration.

Zak looked straight ahead again. There was nothing but blackness outside. No visibility. No nothing. Just the high-pitched whine of the plane's engines, and sudden spots of frozen moisture on the windscreen.

The intensity of the juddering increased. The sweat ran down Moriarty's face. Zak felt like he'd left his stomach several hundred metres away.

Then it happened.

The momentary weightlessness they had experienced during takeoff was nothing compared to this. Had they not been strapped in, they would literally be floating. There was no sound from the engines. The plane was in freefall.

'*What's happening?*' Zak screamed.

Not one sound from the pilot. Zak looked at him, to check he was still conscious and in control of the aircraft. It was some small relief to see that his eyes were open and his face fixed into an expression of fierce concentration.

'*I said, what's . . .*'

'*Button it, sunshine!*' Moriarty shouted. He yanked the control stick back with both hands. The aircraft lurched. Zak was thrown so savagely back in his seat that he felt the wind being knocked from his lungs.

He could see that Moriarty had some semblance of control over the aircraft. But it was tenuous. The control stick was still vibrating aggressively. The cockpit dials and controls were spinning. A yellow light was flashing, accompanied by a buzzing alert.

He heard Malcolm's voice from behind. It sounded

thin and terrified. 'If I'm going to die,' he said, 'I'm glad it's with my friends.'

Moriarty looked over his shoulder. His lip had curled and the sweat positively shone. 'We're not dead yet, my friend,' he growled. 'Not by a long shot.'

He turned forward again. Zak sensed him redoubling his efforts. It was still black outside. The plane was still shaking like a leaf in a gale. But Zak thought that maybe – *maybe* – Moriarty was controlling it more than the elements were controlling them.

'*Land!*' It was Ricky, shouting from the back of the cockpit. '*I saw it!*'

Zak looked sideways and squinted. Sure enough, for the briefest moment, he saw a glimpse of a white expanse somewhere below them. It was perhaps a hundred feet down, perhaps two hundred – hard to tell – and must have been reflecting an unseen moon.

Moriarty was concentrating harder than ever. His face was screwed up and still glowing in the light of the aircraft's controls. He was blinking rapidly – sweat was pouring into his eyes, but he couldn't take his hands off the vibrating control stick to wipe it away. 'We've got a crosswind,' he shouted over the screaming engine.

Zak girded himself. He knew what that meant. Normally, you'd want to land directly into the wind: it would help slow you down, and make it easier to keep on the right course. But a crosswind would do the opposite – blow you across the skies and make it twice as hard to keep the plane pointing in the right direction.

He looked over his shoulder. '*Hold tight!*' he shouted to his friends.

There was a terrific shattering sound of hail against the windscreen. Then they burst through the bottom layer of cloud, and Zak immediately wished they hadn't. He could see the ground, a hundred feet below, but the world looked like it was tilted at an angle. He realized the aircraft had twisted on its axis. Moriarty was struggling to straighten up. His eyes looked wild, and the sweat on his face was worse than ever.

But they were in his hands.

Seconds later, Zak caught sight of the runway. It was narrow, but dead straight – little more than a shallow impression in the ice. But Moriarty couldn't keep the nose of the aircraft in line with it. The Cessna swung left and right. It pitched and rolled and yawed. The wind buffeted it, the hail battered it . . .

They were fifty feet from the ground . . .

'Brace!' Moriarty shouted. '*BRACE!*'

Zak leaned forward and held his head in his hands. He hoped that Ricky and Malcolm were following his lead. The vibrations of the aircraft thundered through every muscle in his body. He knew that any moment they were going to hit the ice. But at what angle, and what speed, it was impossible to predict . . .

Impact!

The jolt that pummelled Zak's body was like an electric shock. It knocked the wind from his lungs for a second time, and made every muscle in his body scream. He knew the sound that battered his ears was the noise of tearing metal. He could feel the aircraft spinning, he would have been catapulted out of the cockpit if he hadn't been well strapped in. He risked sitting up. Sure enough, the plane was rotating on the ice. The port-side wing was damaged, and there were sparks in the air.

The aircraft yawed onto one side, and there was another sickening jolt as the starboard wing hit the ice. An awful cracking sound, and more sparks as the wing broke up.

And flames.

'*GET OUT OF THE PLANE!*' Moriarty roared.

They were still sliding across the ice pack, but the pilot had already kicked his door open. Zak did the same, unfastening his safety strap at the same time.

'*JUMP!*' Moriarty shouted.

Zak looked anxiously back at Malcolm. 'I've got him!' Ricky yelled. 'Go!'

Zak nodded. Looking forward again, he grabbed the portable GPS unit and ripped it from the dashboard. Then, clasping it close to his chest, he took a deep breath and hurled himself from the Cessna.

It seemed to take an age to fall from the aircraft. Time slowed down. The plane made a terrible whining noise as it slid uncontrollably away from him. Then he thudded hard against the ice, knocking the wind from his lungs yet again. He rolled over in time to see the damaged plane continue to slide across the makeshift runway, and two more figures hurl themselves out of it, into the night.

The flames on the wings of the aircraft were burning brighter. Zak got to his feet and sprinted as fast as he could over the sliding ice towards Ricky and Malcolm. From the corner of his eye, he saw Moriarty lying motionless some distance away. He reached the others ten seconds later – Ricky was staggering to his feet, but Malcolm was still flat out on the ice. Zak grabbed him with both hands and pulled him up. He pointed in the opposite direction to the plane. '*Run! She's going to explode!*'

All three of them staggered and slid across the ice, Zak clutching the GPS unit and Ricky holding Malcolm up. Suddenly, Malcolm was screaming in pain, 'My arm! *My arm!*'

'Keep moving!' Zak bellowed.

They covered ten metres . . .

Twenty . . .

And then the explosion happened. There was a huge boom. A massive waft of scorching air cut through the Alaskan night, throwing all four of them several metres forward into a heap on the ice. Zak rolled onto his back and saw the huge fireball that the Cessna had become. Snow was melting all around it.

There was a secondary explosion. Zak hugged the ground again. When it had subsided, he looked the other way.

The orange glow of the burning plane lit up the surrounding area for perhaps a hundred metres in every direction. So now Zak could see the outline of the small island emerging from the pack ice. Nothing distinct. Just a small peak, and maybe a few buildings at its foot.

He got to his feet again, wincing from several painful bruises along his abdomen. Ricky did the same, but Malcolm was squirming on the ice, clutching his right arm.

'I think it's broken,' Ricky said. Sweat was pouring down his face.

Zak nodded grimly, and looked around. 'Yesterday Island,' he said. 'We'd better move. That wasn't exactly a covert landing.'

'The inhabitants of the island will definitely know we're coming,' Ricky observed.

'Yeah,' said Zak. 'And so will anyone else who's watching.' He squinted. 'Where's Moriarty? Is he OK?'

They looked to where the pilot had hit the ice. He was twenty metres away, lying on the ground, not moving.

Zak felt sick. He ran towards the motionless heap. 'Moriarty,' he hissed. *'Moriarty . . . answer me!'*

Moriarty's face was as white as the ice, but his eyes were open. 'My knee,' he breathed. 'It's always been dodgy. I think it's bust.'

Ricky had caught Zak up. He was half carrying Malcolm, whose eyes were rolling with pain. 'We can't leave them on the pack ice,' he breathed.

Zak shook his head. He kneeled down beside Moriarty. 'We're going to lift you up,' he said. 'One of us on each side. We'll carry you. You think you can manage that?'

Moriarty's face was racked with pain, but he nodded.

IMPACT

Zak and Ricky manoeuvred themselves so that they could each grab one of Moriarty's arms. 'Lift!' Zak hissed, and together they pulled him up. Moriarty gasped with pain. His bad leg hung limply. He was heavy, and alarmingly cold.

They staggered forward. Zak managed to glance at his watch. It was seven o'clock exactly.

Five hours until midnight.

24

BETWEEN YESTERDAY AND TOMORROW

They slipped and stumbled across the pack ice, leaving the burning remnants of the plane behind them. Moriarty was a dead weight around Ricky's neck. Ricky's own legs were weak with shock, but he had to keep going. They weren't able to help Malcolm at all, but somehow he was managing to keep up, despite his injured arm . . .

After a couple of minutes, Moriarty hissed at them to stop. Ricky estimated that they were about fifty metres from shore. 'Listen,' Moriarty breathed. He was trembling badly with the pain.

They cocked their heads. Ricky heard shouting. Hardly surprising.

'Leave me here,' Moriarty said.

'No way,' Zak and Ricky told him together.

'Don't be so stupid,' Moriarty whispered. 'The

islanders will be here soon – they can sort me out, patch up my knee, get me on my feet again. But you'll never rescue Annabel with me in tow like this.' He nodded to his eleven o'clock. 'Go that way,' he panted. 'You'll come to a helicopter landing zone. Keep skirting round there and you'll find some deserted buildings where you can shelter. I'll tell the islanders that I crash-landed alone.' He nodded towards Malcolm. 'You'll have to take that one, though. He'll be too difficult for me to explain away.'

Zak nodded. Moriarty's plan made sense. They carefully laid the pilot down on the ground, but there was no time for long goodbyes – they could hear the voices of the islanders getting much closer. They turned their back on Moriarty and hurried off into the hail. But they heard him hiss – 'Hey, kids!' – and stopped to look back at him. 'I don't know what you're up to,' Moriarty said, 'but stay alive, huh?'

'We'll make a point of it,' Ricky told him.

'And save my sister,' he said. 'I don't intend to lose her for a second time.'

They hurried off again, heads bowed against the pelting hail. They heard Moriarty weakly calling to the islanders for help, but his voice soon faded.

They struggled on in silence, Ricky and Zak

supporting Malcolm whenever he looked like needing it. The ice stung Ricky's face, and his knees buckled several times. But after a couple of minutes a huge mound of rocks, fifteen metres wide and five high, emerged through the elements. There was a flat platform on top of the rocks, and on the platform was an old helicopter. It clearly hadn't been used for many days, as it had icicles dripping from the rotor blades. Its body was a dirty mustard-yellow colour, with two horizontal black stripes. Ricky was put in mind of an enormous bumblebee. The thought occurred to him that he wouldn't feel at all secure travelling in that old helicopter. He'd had enough crash-landings for one day . . .

They skirted round the landing platform, just as Moriarty had told them to do. Hugging the shoreline, they could just make out small dwellings on the hillside. There were only a very few of them, but as they staggered on, the huts became less numerous. After a couple more minutes, they came upon what looked like a deserted outbuilding, positioned just above a slope covered with icy boulders. Its slanted roof was heavy with snow, and the walls were rickety, made from sheets of corrugated iron. The door was slamming open and shut in the wind.

They scrambled up the boulders together. Outside

the building, Ricky turned to Zak and Malcolm. 'I'll check it's empty,' he said.

He approached the door and stepped quietly inside. It took a good thirty seconds to get used to the darkness. The building smelled very dank, and was empty apart from a few rusty old ice picks leaning up against the corner and, bizarrely, a couple of bales of hay at one end. It was cold, of course, but as it was protected from the wind, the chill was not so biting as outside.

He called the others, and they hurried inside. Malcolm immediately stumbled over to a bale of hay, where he sat, shivering. Ricky motioned Zak to the other end of the building. 'What now?' he asked.

Zak checked his watch. 'We've got four hours,' he said. 'Cruz's message said "between yesterday and tomorrow". If I'm reading it correctly, that means the RV point is somewhere on the ice between this island and Big Diomede.' He looked grim. 'We need to get going. It could easily take us that long to get across.'

Ricky nodded his head towards Malcolm. 'He's not up to it, mate. You can see that, right?'

Zak glanced over at their friend. Malcolm was shaking badly and his face was bleeding – they hadn't noticed that before. He was clutching his broken arm, and clearly needed medical care.

'We should never have brought him,' Ricky breathed.

'We'd never have got here *without* him,' Zak said. He sounded slightly aggressive, but then bowed his head. 'Maybe you're right,' he said. He narrowed his eyes, and walked over to sit next to Malcolm. 'Buddy,' he said kindly. 'Me and Ricky are going to take it from here.'

Ricky saw the change in Malcolm's face immediately. It turned even whiter than it already had been. 'No,' he whispered. 'I'm coming. I *have* to . . .'

'I'm sorry, buddy. You're in no state. We'll be back for you. I promise you that.'

Malcolm gave Zak a startlingly clear look. 'What if you're dead?' he said. 'What if Cruz kills you?'

'I said, we'll be back for you.' Zak strode over to the other hay bale and started pulling clumps of it apart. 'Cover yourself in this. It'll help keep you warm. And stay in here out of the wind. It's a killer. I know it hurts, buddy, but you'll have to just put up with it for a few more hours until we can get you help.'

Malcolm was in no state to answer. He collapsed, shaking, to the ground and allowed Ricky and Zak to cover him in clumps of hay. Two minutes later, they were kneeling down by his side. 'Seriously, Malcolm,' Zak said, 'don't move. Your arm injury's not life-threatening, and you *are* going to be OK. We'll be back very soon.'

Malcolm nodded weakly.

Ricky and Zak stood up.

'Ready?' Zak asked.

'Ready,' Ricky told him.

'Then let's go and finish this.'

Stepping outside the dilapidated building, they could still see, in the distance, the burning glow of what remained of Moriarty's Cessna. They could no longer hear the voices of the local Inuit. 'If they've found Moriarty, there's no reason for them still to be outside,' Zak said. Looking around, Ricky agreed. He allowed himself a moment of satisfaction. It meant Moriarty was safe. But the wind was howling. The blizzard was swirling. The cold was cutting through them like a knife. Why would anyone be out in this, if they didn't have to be?

'We need to head west, right?' Ricky said.

Zak nodded.

'How do we know when we've got to the right place?'

'Cruz will be waiting for us. Trust me.'

'And what then?' Ricky asked. 'We know we're walking into a trap. How do we know he isn't just going to pull a gun on us, shoot us there and then?'

Zak looked down at his feet, then up again.

'You've said it yourself. He could have had me killed three days ago, when one of his people murdered Michael and Felix. But he didn't. He's got something else in mind. So when we get there, I'm going to need you to do what you do best.'

'What's that?'

'Be sneaky.'

'Thank you very much.'

Zak looked out into the darkness. 'Cruz wants me for a reason. I don't know what it is yet, but when we meet, I expect him to take me somewhere. You need to stay hidden, for two reasons. One: he might have a plan for me, but he could well see you as dispensable. Two: our only chance of outwitting Cruz is for you to follow us, find out where he's taking me, and then help me escape.'

Ricky looked around too. 'Mate, I don't want to put a dampener on things, but we're going to be in the middle of the sea ice. Open ground. There won't *be* anywhere for me to hide.'

Zak shook his head. 'You'll have the darkness. And the snow, if it's still falling. That's as good a cover as any. But you'll need to remember that Big Diomede is a Russian military base and we're crossing an international border. It'll be guarded. When you follow me, you'll need to find a way to sneak onto the island.'

'Right,' Ricky said. He chewed his lower lip nervously and wondered, for a moment, how he had gone from picking pockets in the back streets of London only a month or so ago, to this. 'I guess we'd better move then, while it's still dark.' He gave Zak a forced smile. 'Ready?' he asked.

Zak smiled gratefully back. 'As I'll ever be,' he muttered.

He pulled the cab driver's torch from his pack and switched it on. Then he examined the screen of the portable GPS unit to get their bearings and showed it to Ricky. The blue dot was blinking by the tiny coastline of Little Diomede. 'Make sure you walk behind me,' he said. 'You'll be less visible behind the torchlight.' They hunched their shoulders and forced themselves on through the blizzard. They passed the snow-covered helicopter sitting on its landing pad on their right, and the burning remains of the plane on their left. As they struggled on, their faces raw and their limbs numb, the dwellings dotted on the hillside of Little Diomede slipped past, like ghostly beings in the snow. There was no sight or sound of the islanders. They were clearly avoiding the wreckage of the plane till morning.

The Bering Straits opened out in front of them, bleak and uninviting. They could see no more than ten metres at a time – the torch beam was a swirl of snow that barely seemed to penetrate the thick, icy blackness.

Time seemed to stand still. *Everything* seemed to stand still. It was as though they were walking, but not moving. Their surroundings didn't change. They just grew colder and, if Ricky was honest with himself, more frightening.

It was as if they were walking relentlessly into their own tombs.

Cruz Martinez stared at a screen, with his trusted lieutenant Calaca at his side. The screen showed the outlines of Little Diomede and Big Diomede. And between them, not one but two glowing dots.

Calaca spoke to his boss in Spanish. 'He crash-landed on the ice forty-five minutes ago. He has a single companion. We have an airborne drone with a thermal imaging camera following them. They won't be able to see or hear it in this weather. They're walking in single file. At the rate they're travelling, they'll arrive at the meeting point at five minutes to midnight.' Calaca seemed rather disappointed.

'Very good, Agent 21,' Cruz whispered softly. You could almost hear the relief in his voice. 'Punctual as ever. Do the Russians know?'

'They have a welcoming committee set up for when we escort him off the ice onto the island.'

Calaca cleared his throat. 'What if he tries to fight?'

'He will not try to fight, because he understands that if anything happens to us, there is no chance of his friends surviving.'

'There's no chance of them surviving anyway.'

'But *he* doesn't know that,' Cruz snapped. 'The weakness of trustworthy people is that they trust others in return.' He turned to his lieutenant. 'Are the dogs ready?'

'Of course,' Calaca told him. 'We can leave whenever you want.'

'I want to leave immediately,' Cruz said. 'It wouldn't do to keep our guests waiting, now would it?'

The further they walked, the more anxious Ricky became. He couldn't get it out of his head that they were walking on sea ice. How deep was it? Would it continue to take their weight? All around, he heard ominous creaking and groaning. It was as if the icy ground beneath them wanted to move, but couldn't. Every part of him was numb, and his limbs were heavy. It was an effort just to make a single step forward.

Suddenly, Zak killed the torchlight. They were plunged into utter darkness.

They stood very still.

'What is it?' Ricky breathed. His voice quavered as he spoke.

'Listen.'

Ricky closed his eyes and listened hard. At first he could hear nothing but the angry screech of the wind howling high above him, and the terrifying, echoing creak of the ice.

But then, suddenly, something else. A kind of high-pitched yelp. Impossible to be sure which direction it came from, but Ricky thought it was straight ahead. Was it a dog barking?

'Don't tell me it's another wolf,' he said weakly.

Zak shook his head. 'Not here,' he said. 'We're in the middle of the ocean, remember.'

'Oh yeah,' Ricky said dryly. 'How could I forget . . .'

Another yelp, closer this time. Ricky shivered, and peered into the darkness. 'So what is it?'

Zak didn't answer. They could both suddenly see, in the distance, a light burning through the blackness.

It was approaching them.

'Get back,' Zak said tensely, thrusting the GPS unit into Ricky's hands. 'Keep low. Hug the ground if you have to. Whatever happens, don't interfere.'

Ricky staggered back. Then he turned and ran.

His feet slipped badly, but he managed to cover a good twenty metres before hitting the ground. He pressed his body hard down onto the ice, facing Zak. He winced as the wind blew frosty ice particles into his face. But he kept his eyes on Zak, a solitary figure standing in the bleak terrain. Shoulders hunched against the elements. Waiting.

The barking grew louder. After a minute, Ricky saw that it was a sledge, pulled by a pack of eight huskies. Mounted on the sledge was a large spotlight that brightly lit up the ice before it. But he could see the silhouettes of two people sitting either side of it. The sight of them chilled him more than any ice or wind. He felt a moment of panic. The light was going to illuminate *him*. When the huskies and the sledge were twenty metres beyond Zak, however, they suddenly curled round to draw up alongside him. With the spotlight pointing at ninety degrees, Ricky remained hidden. The blades of the sledge hissed on the ice, then the sound faded away as it eased to a halt. The huskies' breath steamed in the cold air.

Silence.

One of the figures stepped off the sledge. The first thing Ricky noticed was that he had a weapon strapped around his body – from Felix's firearms lessons, he recognized it as an MP5 sub-machine gun. The second thing he noticed was his face. The man only had one eye. The empty eye socket was covered with a patch of smooth skin.

'A long way from Incarceration Unit Three-B, Calaca,' Zak called. The wind carried his voice very clearly to where Ricky was lying. 'You'll have to tell me how you did it, one of these days.'

'It's amazing how well greed and explosives go together,' Calaca sneered. 'But you're probably too weak to experiment with such ideas.'

The second figure stepped off the sledge. Ricky peered at him. He was well protected in snow gear, but Ricky could make out a young man not much older than him, with very dark eyes and a hard, haunted expression.

'Eleven fifty-eight p.m.,' the figure called. His voice had a slight accent. 'There were some people who thought you wouldn't make it. But I never doubted you, Harry. Not for one minute.'

'I find your faith in me absolutely heart-warming, Cruz,' Zak said.

Cruz walked slowly towards them, stopping only when he was a metre in front of Zak, and slightly to the side so Ricky still had a clear view of him. 'Happy *Día de Reyes*,' he said. 'I hope you've brought me a gift.'

'Sure have, Cruz.'

Ricky suddenly hissed under his breath. *What was Zak doing?*

Zak's movement had been as slick and skilful as a cat's. He had raised his right hand. There was something in it: the handgun Tyler had given him. The barrel had come to rest against Cruz's forehead.

This wasn't part of their plan! What was he doing?

'It's not quite midnight yet,' Zak said clearly. 'And right now, right here, we're still "between yesterday and tomorrow". Unless you do exactly as I tell you, *you* won't be around to see the end of your precious festival . . .'

25

PLAN B

Zak was out of control. He hadn't planned this. It was as if he was being governed by his anger and not by his mind. His hand was shaking and his whole body was burning up. He hoped Ricky had the sense not to interfere.

For a few seconds, Cruz's cold face was expressionless. He stared deep into Zak's eyes.

Then, slowly and nastily, his lip curled into something very close to a smile. 'Is that the best you can do, Agent 21? Threaten to kill me?'

'Why shouldn't I?' Zak breathed. 'You've no intention of letting Raf and Gabs go.' He felt nothing but hatred, and his finger twitched on the trigger.

Cruz's smile became more pronounced. 'But I *know* you, Harry. A tiny portion of your brain is thinking, if you keep me alive, I might lead you to them. There's no way you're going to kill me, not when there's a chance I might be of use to you in one of your desperate displays of heroics.'

Nobody moved.

'Go ahead, Harry,' Cruz breathed. 'Pull the trigger. Lay me out cold on the ice, if that's what you want. But I'm the only one who can take you to them. Remember that.'

Zak felt his eyes narrowing. There was a bitter taste in his mouth as Cruz's words echoed in his head. And they joined other thoughts, which were just as potent. He was looking into the face of a murderer. But what would he, Zak, be if he pulled that trigger? No better than Cruz himself. He heard Moriarty's voice in his head. *Every night, when you put your head on the pillow, you hear them. The screams of the ones you killed. And you can never escape them, even when you run to the ends of the earth . . .*

And then he heard another voice. It was Michael's, crisp and angry from beyond the grave. *What are you playing at, Agent 21? You need him alive, if you're going to find out where Raphael and Gabriella are.*

Shamed by those invisible voices, Zak lowered his gun and bowed his head, a crushing sense of failure weighing down on him.

'Smart choice, Harry,' Cruz said. He looked over his shoulder. 'Now then, why don't you and your little friend join me on the sledge?' He clearly saw the flicker that crossed Zak's brow. 'Oh, *please*,' he said. 'Did you really think that I didn't know you had company?' He looked up into the dark sky. 'My Russian friends have a small drone above us with a thermal imaging camera. We've been tracking your progress since just after your spectacular landing. I must say, I expected your flying skills to be a little more on the money than that.' Cruz peered into the darkness around them. 'Come out, come out, wherever you are!' he called in a sing-song voice.

'Your equipment's faulty,' Zak said. 'There's nobody else here. Only me.'

'If you keep lying to me, this will become very difficult,' Cruz said. He turned towards Calaca, who was still standing by the sledge, clutching his MP5. 'Calaca,' he called. 'Fire a few bursts all around us. Maybe that will flush our hidden companion out.'

An unpleasant smile crossed Calaca's face. He stepped forward, raised his MP5 and pointed it into the darkness to Zak's three o'clock – a full ninety degrees from where he expected Ricky to be lying. Calaca squeezed the trigger. Two seconds of deafening automatic fire burst from the sub-machine gun. The huskies grew agitated. One of them barked. Calaca turned forty-five degrees clockwise and fired another burst. This time, Zak heard rounds ricocheting off the ice. A couple of them sparked. The huskies barked some more.

Calaca turned again. He was facing almost exactly in Ricky's direction.

He raised his weapon.

'Stop,' Zak said tersely.

Cruz raised one hand, indicating to Calaca that he should hold his fire. 'Well?' he breathed.

Zak turned round. 'Show yourself,' he called. 'We don't have a choice.'

The dark figure that was Ricky slowly rose from the ice.

'Join us!' Cruz shouted. He sounded delighted, as if an old friend had turned up at a party. 'Who is this, Harry? Another agent? You will introduce us, won't you?'

Zak's mind was turning cartwheels. Their strategy was in bits, and they had no plan B. A particularly brutal gust of wind sapped all the remaining warmth and hope from him as Ricky paced over to them.

'Welcome,' Cruz said as Ricky drew near, holding the GPS unit. 'My Russian friends will be very pleased to see you. Two for the price of one.'

'Why do they want us?' Zak asked. His voice was cold and monotone.

'Isn't it obvious? A British programme to train up teenage spies. They want to get their hands on you.

To learn how it was done. To ascertain what skills you have learned. It's no secret, of course, that the Russians have spies in the UK, and the British have spies on Russian territory. It's no secret that members of the security services die in the line of duty. Both governments accept this – but only when it comes to adults. Even the Russians wouldn't dare to abduct a kid from British soil. Imagine the diplomatic mess that could cause. No, to get their hands on you, they needed to be very careful. And when I realized this, I knew I could make sure that *you* came to *them*, Harry. It was something I could so easily help them with.'

'In return for what?' Zak demanded.

Cruz shook his head. 'For a clever guy, you can be very stupid sometimes. Isn't it obvious that for someone in my profession, the ability to move merchandise through Russian waters without anyone asking any questions is a real benefit?'

'By merchandise, you mean drugs?' Zak said.

Cruz shrugged. 'One word is as good as another, Harry.'

'Is there anything you won't do for money, Cruz?'

'What else is there? I think it would be best if you handed me your weapon.'

As they were speaking, Calaca had approached, still brandishing his MP5. The skin over his missing eye was red with cold. His weapon was pointing firmly at Zak and Ricky. Zak had no choice. He passed his weapon to Cruz.

'Get onto the sledge,' Cruz said. 'The Russians are waiting.'

Calaca jerked his MP5 to indicate they should do as Cruz had ordered. Zak caught a glance from Ricky. He looked scared. Zak didn't blame him. 'C'mon,' he said. 'We don't have a choice.'

The sledge was ten metres away. They had covered half that distance when Zak murmured, 'As long as Cruz is alive, we've got a chance of rescuing Raf and Gabs. Try and sit behind them in the sledge. Maybe we can overpower—'

Zak never finished his sentence. It was cut short by gunshot – a loud retort, echoing across the frozen wasteland. Instinctively, Zak hit the ground, momentarily wondering if he'd been shot. He couldn't feel anything.

Ricky hit the ground too – maybe it was him who had taken a bullet? But his eyes were open and he was breathing heavily.

Cruz was still on his feet. He was looking around, clearly in a state of great confusion.

Calaca, however, was on his back. Zak could see a pool of blood spreading out around his head. His lower jaw had been shot away. Across the ice, Zak

could see the remains of his teeth, uniquely gruesome against his blood-spattered, one-eyed face . . .

And beyond him, half illuminated by the spotlight on the sledge, was a figure. Cruz raised the gun
Zak had handed to him in the direction of the
newcomer.

Zak's movements were like lightning. He sprinted
across the ice towards Cruz. Two metres away, he
dived and tackled him to the ground. The gun went
off as they tumbled, but the rounds blasted harmlessly into the air. Cruz himself was struggling
violently, his arms flailing, his eyes wild with a
sudden, brutal anger.

He still had the gun in his hand. The barrel was
pressing against Zak's cheek.

All of a sudden, Ricky was there. With one good
solid swipe, he kicked Cruz's wrist. The weapon slid,
spinning fast, across the ice.

Zak had pinned Cruz down. No one was moving.
There was a moment of silence . . .

Zak looked up to see the figure moving slowly
towards them out of the darkness. Who was it? Who
had just killed Calaca? *Who could it be?*

Zak's lungs filled with ice as he recognized the
gait. Slow. Awkward. A broken arm hanging limply
by his side.

'*Malcolm?*' he whispered.

Malcolm was ten metres away. Zak's eyes focused in on the weapon in his hand. It was red in colour – as red as the blood that was pooling around Calaca's body. Zak instantly recognized it as the gun Tyler had accused him of stealing. He suddenly understood that it had been Malcolm – quiet, unobtrusive Malcolm – who had really stolen it.

And that meant he must have had a plan after all. A plan to kill Cruz, as soon as they caught up with him.

'Malcolm,' Zak breathed in a low, dangerous voice. 'Mate, put the gun down.'

'He killed my cousin,' said Malcolm. 'I watched him do it.'

'We need him alive,' Zak said. 'Trust me, Malcolm, you *have* to put the gun down.'

But Malcolm didn't. He kept the gun pointing directly at Cruz, and continued to walk forward. His thin face was racked with cold and pain, yet the hate in his eyes burned through it. 'He killed her,' Malcolm hissed.

Zak stood up. Cruz rolled over and scrambled quickly to his feet. He staggered several metres, but didn't turn his back on Malcolm, who was still aiming at him.

Silence.

Nobody moved.

From the corner of his eye, Zak saw Cruz sneer. 'He'll never do it,' he whispered. 'Look at him. He's pathetic. Look how weak he—'

The shot from Malcolm's gun cut him short.

Zak started.

Cruz Martinez clutched his chest.

He stared down at the blood seeping from behind his hands, then back up again at Malcolm, whose own hand was shaking violently.

Then he collapsed.

The huskies started barking and howling. It was a sound of fear and panic. Zak ran to Cruz's side, his heart pumping violently. He forced Cruz onto his back, and was about to lean over to give him rescue breaths when a fountain of blood overflowed from the young man's throat. Zak grabbed his face, and turned it so that Cruz was looking at him. 'Where are they?' he demanded. '*Where are Raf and Gabs? WHERE ARE THEY?*'

Cruz's eyes rolled. More blood spewed from his mouth. The huskies were still howling. He wished they would just shut up . . .

'*Don't die!*' Zak shouted harshly. '*For God's sake, don't die!*'

But that was obviously impossible. There was blood everywhere now. It was seeping copiously from Cruz's chest, and Zak had it all over his hands and clothes. Cruz Martinez made a horrific, terminal gurgling sound as his last-ever breath escaped his lungs.

And then, from behind him, Zak heard Ricky shouting.

'*NO! ZAK! LOOK OUT!*'

Still kneeling at Cruz's side, Zak spun round. His eyes fell immediately on Calaca. He had been lying in a pool of blood perhaps seven or eight metres away. And he was still there. The blood was still there. But there was movement. Calaca was not dead yet. He had lifted his head slightly. With his jaw blasted away and his one-eyed face blood-spattered, he looked like a corpse risen from the dead.

He was weakly lifting his right hand – the hand that carried the MP5 . . .

Aiming it at Malcolm . . .

Ricky was sprinting towards him . . .

Zak hurled himself across the ice towards the dying man . . .

But too late.

The MP5 thundered noisily. A flurry of bullets rained hard into Malcolm's abdomen. His whole body shook with the impact. He seemed to fly back-wards, blood spurting from his thin body as he sailed through the air. He hit the ground with a horrific thump, just as Calaca's gun arm went as limp as the rest of his body.

Everything was a blur. Zak kicked the MP5 out of Calaca's dead hand as he sprinted towards Malcolm, shouting his friend's name, praying that he hadn't just seen what he knew he had.

Of all of them, Malcolm had been the least suited to this mission. And in Zak's eyes, that meant he least deserved to die.

But he had died. A single glance at his corpse told Zak that. The bullets had ripped a seam up his abdomen. Blood was flowing, and his eyes, still open, had rolled up into his head.

Hot fury surged through Zak's body. He felt like screaming out to the unfeeling sky. It all seemed so unreal. Like a horrible dream. He felt himself going through the motions of checking Malcolm's pulse. There was nothing.

He crouched in the snow, head in his hands. It was as if the world had stopped. He was burning up. He realized he was pounding his fist on the ice, and when he finally looked up again, he saw the frozen scenery through a veil of tears. He jumped to his feet, and ran back to where Cruz was lying. He bent down and grabbed the front of his clothes, pulling his heavy, limp body off the ice. Cruz's head lolled grotesquely. '*It didn't have to be like this!*' Zak shouted.

'You *didn't have to be like this! We could have been* friends*!'*

But Cruz's dead body didn't answer. Zak let it fall heavily to the ground, before running back to Malcolm, throwing only a cursory, hate-filled glance at Calaca as he went.

Maybe it wasn't true. Maybe Malcolm wasn't dead. Maybe it felt like a dream because it *was* a dream. He knelt down by his friend again. Felt his pulse once more.

Nothing.

He drew a deep breath, then put one hand on Malcolm's friend's thin, bony shoulder. 'I'm sorry, buddy,' he whispered. 'I'm so, *so* sorry. You shouldn't have been here in the first place. This wasn't for you.'

He looked over at Cruz's body. Then he turned to Ricky, who was wild-eyed, clearly shocked, but also obviously just as full of fury and helplessness as Zak himself.

Zak stood up and strode purposefully towards the huskies, whose howling and barking was now off the scale.

'Nobody else dies,' he shouted fiercely at his one remaining companion. 'Get in the sledge. We're going to the military base. *And nobody else dies!'*

26

THE RIGHT SIDE
OF THE TRACK

Ricky was numb with shock. He could scarcely take in what he'd just seen. It felt wrong, leaving Malcolm there on the ice. Surely they should do something for him. *He's dead*, the voice in Ricky's head snapped. *You can't do anything about it.*

– *But shouldn't we take his body? Bury him?*

– *Go ahead. Drag your heels – if you want to end up the same way as him . . .*

It was that thought which stunned him into action. Zak was bending over Calaca's body and unfastening his MP5. 'Get the other weapons!' he shouted at Ricky. Ricky quickly gathered up Tyler's two handguns – the old one he'd given them and the red one Malcolm had stolen. By this time, Zak was already sprinting to the sledge, clutching the sub-machine gun.

Ricky gave Malcolm's body one last look. He tried to think of something to say, but couldn't. And the voice in his head was right. Time was running out. He raced after Zak. By the time he had hurled himself into the sledge, Zak already had the reins in his hands. He shook them sharply. The huskies were still very agitated, but this seemed to calm them down a little.

'We'll be back for him,' Zak said through gritted teeth.

'That's what we told him back on the island.'

'*We'll be back for him,*' Zak repeated aggressively.

Ricky didn't push it. 'What do we do?' he asked breathlessly.

Zak suddenly hushed him. 'Listen,' he whispered.

Ricky fell quiet. 'What?' he said after a few seconds. And then . . . 'Oh . . .'

There was a tinny, buzzing sound. It came from above them. Ricky looked up. He was half blinded by the swirling snow, but could just make out a pale red dot glowing in the sky.

What was it Cruz had said? *My Russian friends have a small drone above us with a thermal imaging camera.*

Almost on instinct, Ricky raised the red gun. Zak, next to him, did the same with his MP5.

'On three,' Zak said. 'One . . . two . . . three . . .'

They fired in unison – a burst from the MP5, a single round from the handgun. Their aim was good. A split second later, a hunk of metal dropped from the sky and shattered on the ice.

Zak examined the MP5. 'Out of ammo,' he hissed, and he tossed the gun onto the ice, where it clattered noisily. He turned to Ricky, his face a picture of fierce concentration. 'What did they say?' he muttered.

'Who? When?'

'On the last video. Raf and Gabs. *What did they say?*'

Ricky clicked his fingers, desperately trying to recall the footage they'd watched in Anchorage airport. '*Remember the first thing I ever taught you – that your first duty is to stay alive,*' he recited.

But Zak shook his head. 'That *wasn't* the first thing he ever taught me.' He was frowning hard, as though he was desperately trying to remember something. 'It was my first night on St Peter's Crag,' he muttered, more to himself than to Ricky. 'I was in a really bad mood. Raf took me out onto the island. He showed me how to . . .' Zak looked up again. 'How to navigate by the stars.'

Ricky followed his gaze. He could barely see ten metres ahead of him, let alone see the stars.

'Sorry, mate,' he whispered. 'I don't think anyone's seen the stars in these parts for months—'

'Shhhh . . .' Zak interrupted him. His face was screwed up even harder. 'Polaris,' he whispered.

'What?'

'He taught me how to find Polaris – the North Star.' He clicked his fingers suddenly. 'I think Raf was trying to tell us that we need to get to the north of the island.'

'Are you sure?'

Zak thought for a moment. Then he said, quite confidently: 'I'm sure. Where's the GPS?'

Ricky held it up. The screen showed them as a little blue dot, halfway between the land masses of Little and Big Diomede. They were almost directly due east of Big Diomede, which meant they had to circle it in an anticlockwise direction.

Suddenly, from a westerly direction, they heard shouting, and the barking of dogs. It was very distant, as if it was being carried towards them on the wind. 'We need to move,' Ricky whispered. 'You know how to' – he pointed at the huskies and their reins – '*do* this?'

'There's a first time for everything,' Zak said. He shook the huskies' leash hard. Ricky felt himself slam back in the seat of the sledge as they immediately surged forward. The air was suddenly filled with the hissing sound of the sled's blades over the ice. The wind bit harder into Ricky's face as they hurtled into the darkness. He looked over his shoulder only once, and just saw the three dead bodies receding into the distance.

They travelled in breathless silence. Even the huskies were quiet, now that they were running again. Ricky clutched the GPS unit in his frozen hands. Occasionally he looked wildly around. His skin was prickling – he had the uneasy sensation that they were being watched, or chased – but he saw nothing other than the frozen darkness. After ten nervous minutes, he nudged Zak and pointed in a north-westerly direction – the GPS was telling him that they needed to change course if they wanted to reach the north of the island.

Twenty minutes passed. Ricky felt his body temperature lowering. He sensed Zak shivering too. He checked the GPS. There was no way of telling from their dark, monotonous surroundings where they were, but the screen told Ricky they were now almost directly due north of Big Diomede. From this position, he could see what looked like a track marked on the map of the island. It headed south from the northern edge, and seemed to be the only way onto the island from this northern coast.

'Stop!' he shouted at Zak. Zak pulled the reins

sharply and the huskies, their breath steaming, quickly obeyed the order to halt.

'What is it?' Zak said.

Ricky showed him the map on the GPS screen. 'I can't see any other way of getting onto the island from this direction,' he said.

Zak narrowed his eyes, then nodded his head. 'We'll get within a hundred metres,' he said, 'then we'll leave the huskies. They stayed put when Cruz got off them – I think they're trained to wait. If we can get Raf and Gabs back to them, maybe . . .' His voice trailed off. Ricky didn't feel the need to observe that it was a long shot. But he didn't have any better plan.

Zak flicked the reins again. As the huskies moved off, he pulled the left-hand rein and they swerved in that direction. Two minutes later, at a word from Ricky, he yanked them to a halt again. Both boys jumped off the sledge. The huskies' breath steamed heavily in the cold air, and they pawed nervously at the ice. But they didn't move. At least, not yet.

'How long do you reckon they'll stay?' Ricky asked.

'I don't know. Probably not that long when it's so cold. We haven't got much time. I don't think we can risk the torch. Cup your hand over the GPS screen so it doesn't glow . . .'

They struck out in a southerly direction, following the blinking blue dot on the GPS unit, their faces screwed up against the bitter elements. Ricky's legs were weak with exhaustion, his mind spinning with the horror of what had happened in the last hour. But he kept surging forward, jaw clenched, teeth gritted, until finally he saw the island emerging ahead of them from the darkness.

There were lights along the coastline. Five. Maybe six. Hard to tell, since they were moving around. 'Men with torches?' Ricky suggested as they took a moment to watch them.

Zak nodded. 'The coastline's guarded,' he said tensely. And then, almost to himself: 'Why did Raf tell us to come this way?'

Ricky almost pointed out that Raf had told them nothing of the sort. He'd merely given them a rather obscure message. But Zak had already started marching forward, and Ricky wasn't sure how much longer he could stand being out here on the ice. He followed.

They were no more than thirty metres from the shoreline when Zak stopped again. They crouched down and recce'd the scene in front of them.

The path they'd seen on the map was more of a valley between two small, rocky hills. 'I think the men with torches are patrolling that valley,' Ricky said. 'What do you think?'

Zak had a slightly faraway look in his eyes. *'That means you have to stay on the right side of the track . . .'* he muttered.

'Eh?'

'It's what Raf said, remember? Stay on the right side of the track. We thought he was just delirious, but I think he was trying to tell us something else. I think he was telling us something about the terrain we're about to hit.'

'But how would he know?'

'He speaks Russian. He probably overheard someone talking about it. We need to approach in single file,' he said. 'We're less obvious that way, and if anyone starts firing on us, we're not so spread out as a target. And we need to be very quiet. It's hard to predict how sound will travel in this wind.'

Ricky swallowed hard. The idea of being fired on by five Russian soldiers was not one he relished. He didn't like to admit it to himself, but he was pleased when Zak took the lead . . .

They kept five metres apart, and within thirty seconds they'd hit the island. The nearest of the torches was about thirty metres away. Its operator seemed to be concentrating his beam up and down the valley, but it wasn't strong enough to light them up just yet. The terrain was rocky and the rocks were sharp, ice-covered and slippery. Ricky and Zak crawled over them very carefully, Ricky wincing as a shard of rock almost pierced his skin. They could hear people shouting to each other in the distance, but it sounded like Russian and Ricky couldn't understand them.

They moved forward five slow metres, struggling painfully over the treacherous rocks.

Ten.

'We can't go on,' Ricky breathed. 'We'll crawl right into those guards.'

But Zak didn't seem to be listening. He didn't even seem to be watching the guards. He was looking off to the right-hand side of the track, his eyes searching . . . 'Look!' he hissed suddenly.

He pointed to their right. Ricky blinked. At first he couldn't see anything. Then he realized what Zak was pointing at. Leading away from the ravine, at a thirty-degree bearing, was a tiny track, so narrow you'd have missed it if you weren't looking for it. There was no sign of men with torches along that rough path.

Stay on the right side of the track.

Could that have been what Raf had meant?

– *You don't have much choice*, said the voice in Ricky's head. *If you keep going in the other direction, they'll catch you, no question.*

It looked like Zak had already come to the same

conclusion. He had started to scramble away from the main ravine, up along the new path. Ricky crawled after him – to stand up straight would make them too visible to the men with torches. They moved slowly. Ricky's limbs were almost totally numb now with the cold and he had to force them into action.

Five minutes passed. The shouting faded away. As Ricky looked back over his shoulder, he could no longer see the glow of the torches. Everything was black. They could do nothing but continue to follow this tiny, rough path, and hope that it led somewhere that they wanted to go.

They were heading more steeply uphill. When Ricky finally caught sight of the brow, it was about twenty-five metres in the distance. He felt as though the sweat was freezing on his forehead.

– *Is it just me*, said the voice in his head, *or is it getting brighter?*

Ricky blinked heavily. He looked around. There was no doubt about it. There was a faint glow. The light seemed to be coming from beyond the crest of the hill, which was suddenly more distinct – a craggy black line twenty metres beyond them.

'Zak,' Ricky hissed.

'I know,' said his companion. 'Keep going.'

They upped their pace – still crawling, but with a

new purpose. They covered the distance to the brow of the hill in thirty seconds. The light was very bright now. For a moment they lay flat on the ground, catching their breath. Then, together, they pushed themselves up a fraction, so that they could see the terrain beyond.

Ricky's eyes widened at what he saw.

27

1H

It was a military base, situated in what looked like an immense crater, surrounded by high, rocky cliffs. In the centre was a helicopter landing zone. Zak counted three choppers dotted around it. Two of them looked like personnel carriers of some kind. The third was plainly an attack helicopter. It had a sleek body, and guns on either side. The kind of kit that you *really* don't want on your tail. Despite the late hour, the whole base was alive with activity: trucks skirted the landing zone, and there were about thirty armed, uniformed soldiers milling around the area.

Surrounding the LZ were a number of large, square buildings: eight on the far, southern side of the base, eight on the northern side, closest to Zak and Ricky. Each of the buildings had a number and letter painted on the roof. Those on the nearest side were marked 1A, 1B, 1C . . . all the way to 1H. On the far side, they were marked from 2A to 2H. As Zak and Ricky watched, the large, wide doors of the building marked 2C slid open. Bright light burst from inside and a small truck emerged, pulling another attack helicopter out onto the landing zone.

'Aircraft hangars,' Zak breathed. And then his eyes widened for a moment. 'What was it Gabs said?' he whispered urgently.

A look of dawning realization had crossed Ricky's face too. '*Be careful of hangers-on.* Something like that.'

'No,' Zak said. 'What were the *exact* words?' He closed his eyes, and tried to replay that horrible video in his head. He saw Gabs's bruised face and her shivering body. And he heard her weak, trembling voice. *Be careful . . . of hangers-on, eh, sweetie.* His eyes widened even more. 'Come with me,' he hissed. He clambered a few metres back down the hill, Ricky following. Casting around, he saw a flat patch of rock, covered with an icy, frosty layer. He pulled off his glove and, with one fingernail, scratched some words into the ice:

Hangers-on, eh?

'You see what she's saying?' Zak said, barely able to keep a note of excitement from his voice.

Ricky nodded and made a small hissing sound under his breath. With his own finger, he drew two vertical lines in the ice:

Hangers | on, e | h?

'They're in Hangar One-H,' Ricky whispered. 'Their messages have been leading us here all along.'

'You bet,' Zak answered. He crawled back to the crest of the hill. Hangar 1H was at the end of the line of hangars on the near side of the base. Zak and Ricky moved further along the ridge, about forty metres, until it was directly opposite them. Distance: fifty metres as the crow flies, but the hillside looked rocky and hazardous. 'The hangar will be guarded,' Zak told Ricky, who had crawled up beside him again. 'We're going to need a diversion.'

'Again?' Ricky asked, a bit sourly.

Zak furrowed his brow, thinking his way carefully through the next few minutes. They could only see the back end of the hangar, where there was clearly no entrance. In order to make a plan they needed to know how many guards there were at the unseen entrance. Impossible from this vantage point. But then . . .

'We've got eyes on the inside,' he breathed.

'What?' Ricky asked.

'Follow me,' Zak said. 'Keep very low. If I raise my hand, hit the ground.'

'Care to tell me what we're doing?'

Zak gave him a sharp look. 'Rescue mission,' he said shortly. 'What else?'

Without another word, Zak rolled over the crest of the hill to reduce the chance of revealing himself along the ridge. When he was a couple of metres over the brow, he saw Ricky doing the same. He crouched low and started crawling down the hillside.

It was treacherous underfoot. Several times his boots slipped on the rocky, icy slope, and his body thwacked hard against the hillside. He tried to keep one eye on the military base down below, but the lower they went, the more the hangars on the near side of the LZ blocked their view. As they got closer, however, they could hear increased sounds from the base: the roaring of engines, and people calling to each other in Russian. They were halfway down when a sudden burst of shouting hit Zak's ears. He immediately raised his right hand. He and Ricky dropped to the ground. Not a second too soon. From somewhere, a floodlight shone across the hillside, moving quickly from west to east. It missed them only by a matter of metres.

Zak found himself breathing and sweating heavily, despite the cold. They stayed flat on the ground, not moving, for a full two minutes before setting off again.

It took fifteen minutes to reach the bottom of the hill. Zak's every sense was on high alert. They were now positioned just twenty metres from Hangar 1H. To their left was Hangar 1G. There was the noise of some kind of engine from inside that one, but so far as they could tell from here, 1H was quiet.

They crept forward. Zak's skin was prickling. A Russian soldier could appear behind these hangars at any moment. And if that happened, it would be game over . . .

It was with a deep sigh of relief that they reached the back of Hangar 1H. Zak felt it carefully. The building was cheaply made – this back wall was a thin sheet of corrugated iron. Good. That meant it would be resonant enough. He stepped back slightly and then, very gently, started tapping on the metal wall.

'What are you doing?' Ricky hissed.

'Shhh . . .' Zak replied, and continued tapping. His taps were a series of short and long beats – the Morse code his Guardian Angels had taught him so long ago.

It took him twenty seconds to complete his message, at the end of which Ricky whispered an immediate translation. '*How many guards are there?*' He looked at Zak. 'You think they'll be in a position to answer? They looked in a pretty bad way on those videos.'

Zak didn't answer. All they could do now was wait.

A minute passed.

Two.

The sick feeling in his stomach grew more intense. What if they weren't there? What if word had reached the Russians that Cruz was dead? What would that mean for Raf and Gabs?

He tapped his message on the hangar again.

'Mate,' Ricky whispered, 'I don't think we can stay here too much—'

He paused. From the other side of the metal wall was a tapping sound. It was slightly hesitant, as if the person making it was struggling.

Dot. Dot. Dash. Dash. Dash.

'*Two,*' Zak translated immediately.

And then the tapping came again. Still struggling. Some taps weaker than others. But fluent enough. Zak and Ricky's eyes narrowed as they translated.

'*Coming . . . your . . . way . . .*'

They exchanged a sudden alarmed look.

More tapping.

'*One . . . on . . . either . . . side . . .*'

Zak pointed to the left-hand corner of the hangar, but he didn't need to – Ricky was already running in that direction. Zak himself sprinted to the right-hand corner and waited, his heart pumping, his back pressed up against the metal rear wall. He felt himself flexing his fingers . . .

There were footsteps approaching along the side of the hangar . . .

He raised his left arm, and with a quick glance could see Ricky on the other corner, raising his right.

The two Russian guards appeared at the same time. Zak instantly recognized the weapons his guy was carrying – an AK-47. But the soldier had made a bad error. The weapon was pointing forward from his body in the firing position, which meant it appeared from the side of the hangar, at right angles to Zak, before the soldier was even visible. Zak didn't hesitate for a second. He slammed down his raised hand and grabbed the far end of the barrel and, before the soldier had a chance to squeeze the trigger, he yanked the butt hard into his chest.

The soldier grunted in pain and stumbled

forward like a drunk. Zak wasn't finished yet. His guy had let go of his weapon in an attempt to clutch his chest. It was still strapped round his body, but Zak had a good amount of control over it. He angled the weapon so the butt was pointing up towards the soldier's head, then slammed it hard into the area just between the eyes.

The soldier's eyes glazed over. He slumped heavily to the ground. Zak grabbed him by his ankles and dragged him fully round to the back of the hangar. Then he checked the guy's pulse. It was there, strong enough. He'd live. But he'd have a hell of a headache when he woke up.

Zak looked over towards Ricky. He saw almost a mirror image – Ricky's guard was out cold too, lying on his back behind the hangar. They both unclipped their guard's AK-47 and, breathless, met back in the centre of the hangar.

'They could wake up any time,' Ricky said, fumbling with the weapon, trying to put the safety catch on.

Zak nodded his agreement. 'We're going to have to move fast.' He looked uncertainly at the weapons. 'Nobody dies,' he reiterated.

'Nobody dies.'

'And Ricky?'

'Yes?'

'You have used one of these before, haven't you? We don't need any accidents . . .'

Ricky nodded. 'Day on a range with Felix,' he said. 'The bullets come out this end, right?'

Zak gave him a severe look. 'Don't fire unless you have to. We'll go this way.'

They ran back to where Zak's guard was lying. Then, side by side, they turned the corner and advanced silently to the front of the hangar.

They were on the very edge of the military base here. There were no personnel up ahead. Just the far end of the landing zone. Hangar 1H was about thirty metres in length. They covered that distance in ten seconds. When they reached the front corner, they pressed their backs against the wall. There was light spill coming from the front of the hangar – a clear indication that the guards, in their hurry, had left the door open.

Zak turned to Ricky. 'Ready?' he whispered.

'As I'll ever be.'

They swung round the corner, brandishing their weapons. Zak felt his stomach lurch. The landing zone was teeming with people – he estimated twenty-five soldiers at least. But the nearest of them were twenty metres away, and facing in the opposite direction. Distance to the entrance of the hangar: five metres. If they were quick – *very* quick – they

329

might just manage to get into the hangar without anyone seeing . . .

They sprinted, catlike, then swung round into Hangar 1H.

Zak's eyes burned momentarily from the brightness of the light. He squinted hard, and it took a good three or four seconds before the dazzle left him.

When it did, his mouth went dry.

Raf and Gabs were there, but they looked barely alive. They were slumped against the back wall, their hands tied together. Their faces were as bruised and bloodied as they had been in the videos Cruz had sent. More so. Their heads lolled listlessly and, although their eyes were open, they were staring into the middle distance, as though not even aware where they were.

Zak sprinted towards them. He was aware of Ricky behind him, moving back into the hangar, but facing the entrance, his weapon covering it. He let his own weapon fall to the side as he slid to his knees right by his Guardian Angels.

Gabs blinked. She turned to look at him, and spoke in a hoarse voice, a shadow of what it once was.

'What kept you, sweetie?' she said.

Zak raised an eyebrow. 'Ran into a couple of obstacles,' he muttered.

'Cruz?'

Zak frowned. 'Won't be bothering us any more. Nor will Calaca.'

'Does Michael know you're here?'

Zak looked her in the eye. 'Michael's dead. And Felix. And . . . and Malcolm. We're on our own. No backup. No support.'

For the briefest moment, a look of unspeakable anguish crossed Gabs's face. It was almost too much to bear. Zak glanced over at Raf, whose face was a mixture of anger and confusion. Then he looked down at the cable ties that bound their wrists and ankles. They were digging deeply into their skin – their wrists were bleeding. He pulled out the hunting knife he'd stolen from the cab driver's car, and with four quick slashes cut through the plastic ties.

'There are dogs and a sledge,' Zak said abruptly. 'It's about a twenty-minute tab. Think you can make it?'

'Only one way to find out,' Gabs whispered with an unconvincing smile. 'But we'd better move fast. If they find out we're gone . . .'

Ricky nodded in agreement. Right then, however, Raf spoke.

ENDGAME

'Behind you,' he breathed. His eyes flashed.

It was as Zak was spinning round, weapon engaged, that he heard the first burst of fire.

28

ATTACK

Ricky felt like the air had been punched from his lungs.

Three Russian soldiers had suddenly appeared at the entrance to the hangar. They were armed, and were advance. One of them barked an order. Ricky didn't recognize the word he spoke, but he could definitely tell what it meant: '*Fire!*'

Time slowed down. As the Russian soldiers continued to advance, Zak's mantra rebounded in his head: '*Nobody dies.*'

He angled his AK-47 down a few degrees and let rip a burst of fire. The sharp recoil caught him by surprise, but the rounds exploded onto the ground less than a metre from the soldiers' feet. As sweat trickled stingingly into Ricky's eyes, he saw the soldiers diving out of the way. The exit was clear. He didn't know how long for.

'Move!' he roared, looking over his shoulder as he did so. He saw Zak standing up. His AK-47 was pressed expertly into his shoulder. The thought shot through Ricky's mind that, for the first time since he'd known Zak, he looked like a fully-fledged adult. Not a kid any more.

Behind him were Raf and Gabs. To start with, they were still crouching on the ground. But slowly they rose, phoenix-like. They were beaten up, and in very bad shape, but there was something encouraging about the way they stood, flanking Zak. Raf had broad, muscular shoulders and a face like thunder. Gabs was slimmer and sleeker, but appeared, if anything, more dangerous. She was holding a pistol. Ricky recognized it as the red one. From his own snow jacket he withdrew the second handgun – the bulky old one Tyler had given them. Zak, Raf and Gabs moved forward in grim formation. Ricky handed the gun to Raf, who took it, cocked it, and held it – double-handed like Felix had taught him – in front of him.

They stood in a line – Raf, Ricky, Zak, Gabs – facing the open exit of the hangar. They could hear shouting outside.

'Nobody dies,' Zak said, his voice like steel.

'Whatever you say, sweetie,' Gabs croaked. 'Rifles to semi-automatic. Fire.'

Ricky flicked the switch on his AK-47 and fired a single shot. At the same time there were three shots from his three companions. The rounds fell harmlessly at the mouth of the hangar, but the sound they made echoed loudly. Only an idiot would put themselves in that line of fire.

'Forward,' Raf said.

They advanced in a line, weapons engaged. Ricky's eyes flickered left and right – he couldn't help noticing that Raf and Gabs were both limping. Walking was clearly very painful for them.

Ten metres from the exit, they heard another surge of voices outside.

'Fire!' Gabs ordered.

A second set of bullets kept the exit clear.

'We need to turn right and get up the hill,' Zak said, his voice as taut as a wire.

'I'll cover you,' Raf said.

Ricky turned to him. 'Mate,' he panted. 'Are you sure you—'

He fell silent at a single glance from Raf. He might have been all messed up, but Ricky had never seen such a look of fierce intensity. 'Yeah,' Ricky muttered after a second. 'You cover us.'

Raf moved forward into the doorway, where he automatically fell to one knee, the old firearm firmly in his double-handed grip. He took a moment to aim, then fired a single shot.

'*Go!*' Zak hissed.

Gabs surged forward, Ricky following, Zak bringing up the rear. As Raf fired a second covering shot, they swung quickly out of the hangar, turning hard right. From the corner of his eye, Ricky saw numerous figures on the landing zone. Too many to count. He lost sight of them as he followed Gabs round the corner of the hangar, but then he heard Zak, behind him, firing a burst from his AK-47 before he and Raf joined them.

Gabs, still in the lead, was limping heavily.

– *She'll never make it up the hill*, the voice in his head fretted. *And what if the dogs have gone? What, then?*

Ricky ignored the voice. Looking over his shoulder he saw Raf and Zak. They were walking backwards, their guns pointing towards the front of the hangar. When a Russian soldier appeared fifteen metres from their position, Raf fired another single shot. Ricky caught a muzzle flash, and knew the round must have passed inches from the soldier – he shouted in alarm, then dived back behind the protection of the front of the hangar.

Ten seconds later, they were behind the hangar in a huddled group. Raf and Gabs were sweating profusely, their faces racked with pain. They looked toward the hill and its rocky, icy slope. It was surely obvious to everyone, Ricky thought, that the two adults would find it almost impossible to climb, in their state.

'That way?' Gabs asked quietly.

'I'm afraid so,' said Zak.

Gabs nodded. 'Listen to me, you two,' she said. 'Whatever happens on that slope, you keep going. You've done enough already. You've got us out of that hangar – now it's up to us to make it to your dogs. Your body's going to hurt, but forget about that. This battle will be won in your head. If we all keep our mental toughness, we stand a chance. Understood?'

Neither Ricky nor Zak answered.

'I said, under—'

'We haven't got time,' Raf said grimly. 'They'll be swarming round us any minute. Move.'

They didn't need any more encouragement. As a group, they sprinted towards the hillside, covering the twenty metres of open ground in as many seconds. Ricky expected to hear gunshot any moment. But it didn't come. Not yet, anyway . . .

'Go,' Gabs hissed at the bottom of the hill. 'Both of you go first. Don't look back – we'll cover you if we need to.'

There was no arguing with her. Ricky and Zak set off up the slope. Their feet slipped badly on the perilously icy rocks, and within thirty seconds Ricky's lungs were burning with the effort of the climb. His AK-47 clattered hard against the rocks, and it was an effort just to carry it. But he didn't dare discard the weapon. He might be needing it.

Ignoring Gabs's instruction, Ricky looked over his shoulder. They'd ascended maybe fifteen metres. Only another twenty to go. Zak was alongside him, while Raf and Gabs were five or six metres behind. They were obviously struggling. Every movement seemed to be a colossal effort, and their faces were etched with pain and exhaustion. He allowed his eyes to move further down the slope. A confused look crossed his face.

'Why aren't they chasing us?' he gasped breathlessly at Zak. 'What's going on?'

Zak stopped and looked back. He frowned. 'I don't know,' he said. 'I don't like it.'

'Keep going!' Raf shouted from behind them. 'They're planning something. We need to get under cover. *Go!*'

Ricky suppressed a shiver of panic. He faced back up the hill and redoubled his efforts. But it was like a nightmare – the faster he moved his limbs, the slower he seemed to go. He fixed his gaze on the brow of the hill, willing it to come closer, expecting any moment to hear the sickening retort of gunfire that meant they were being fired upon.

Ten metres from the ridge, however, he heard a very different sound.

It was a harsh, mechanical grating. It came from further into the base. Something about it sent a cold shock through Ricky's body. It clearly did the same to the others – they'd all stopped and were looking back towards the base, trying to identify the source of the noise.

Raf and Gabs turned in unison towards them. 'Did you get a view of the base when you arrived?' Raf asked, his voice breaking as he spoke.

Ricky and Zak nodded.

'Did you see helicopters?'

Another nod.

'What sort?'

Ricky and Zak exchanged a look. It was Zak who answered. 'Two utility choppers. One attack helicopter.'

A shadow crossed Raf's beaten-up face. 'That's what that noise is,' he hissed. 'That's why the soldiers aren't following. They'd just be in the way. *Get moving!*'

They started climbing even more furiously. Ricky's hands were bleeding from contact with the rocks. His heart was pumping two beats to a second.

'Attack helicopter . . .' he breathed as they went. 'That's . . . that's bad, right?'

'One missile from an attack chopper will destroy half this hillside . . .' Zak responded without slowing down. 'That's if they even bother with it – the chopper's guns will see us off easily . . .' He stopped for a split second and threw down his weapon. 'These are no good to us any more. We'll move faster without them.'

Ricky followed his lead. Just as he discarded his weapon, he saw a shape rising slowly above the nearest hangars.

The attack helicopter was brightly lit, sleek and sinister. It continued to rise higher into the air, its nose pointing downwards slightly, its searchlights fixed on the hillside.

'*We can't outrun that thing!*' Ricky shouted.

'*We've got to try!*' Zak countered.

Their scrambling became more frenzied as they desperately tried to make it to the top of the slope. The sound of the attack helicopter was getting louder. *Much* louder. It was hovering directly above Hangar 1H now, and the beam of its spotlights slammed straight into them, illuminating them as if it was the middle of the day.

Ten metres to the top of the hill. Ricky's bloodied hands kept grabbing for the rocks. He didn't dare look back. Didn't dare waste his precious breath by shouting out. If they could just get over the hill, maybe – *maybe* – they stood a chance.

Gunfire!

The noise was like an axe at the back of Ricky's head. It went right through him. Heavy-calibre rounds exploded on the rocks all around them. Ricky slammed his body flat onto the hillside, fully expecting to feel one of those rounds rip through him at any second.

The gunfire subsided. He heard Gabs's voice. 'Keep moving! *Keep moving!*'

Ricky could barely obey. He felt paralysed with fear. If he moved, surely they'd see him. Surely they'd *kill* him . . .

'*They're not shooting by sight!*' Gabs yelled. '*They'll have thermal imaging. The more you move, the harder it is to hit you . . .*'

Ricky surged forward, wincing with pain as the jagged rocks needled his bleeding hands.

Five metres to the crest of the hill.

And, suddenly, another sound. The grinding rumble of a second engine. It was coming at them from beyond the hill.

'They're surrounding us!' Ricky yelled. '*They're surrounding us!*'

He looked over his shoulder. The attack helicopter was still hanging threateningly in the air above them.

Raf, Gabs and Zak were all staring towards the top of the hill, their faces fixed with terror.

Time slowed down. Ricky turned to face forward again. He saw the spinning rotor blades of a second chopper rising above the ridge.

His heart in his throat, he watched it come slowly into view.

He blinked.

Ricky recognized that chopper. Its body was mustard yellow, with black horizontal stripes. Like a bumblebee.

He squinted and stared through the windscreen of the aircraft. The pilot had receding hair, and a scar that stretched from his forehead up to his scalp. He was chewing on an unlit cigar, and his eyes, even from a distance, were a sharp, piercing blue.

'Moriarty!' Ricky bellowed at the top of his voice. '*It's Moriarty!*'

29

EVERYBODY DIES

Zak couldn't believe his eyes. The last time they'd seen Moriarty, he couldn't walk. How come he was flying that old chopper? How had he found them?

Those questions would have to wait. The chopper was settling on the top of the ridge. They had to get into it. Fast.

He turned to Raf and Gabs. Somehow they'd managed to keep up, and were just a couple of metres behind him. But they were a mess. He scampered down to them, buffeted strongly by the downdraught of the yellow chopper, and grabbed Gabs's arm. She cried in pain, but allowed him to drag her up the hill towards the chopper. Zak's eyes flickered in the direction of the attack helicopter. It was still hanging in the air, and he expected another burst of fire any second. But it didn't come.

Not yet.

The side door of Moriarty's chopper was open. Ricky was standing there, his hair blowing wildly in the downdraught, screaming urgently at them – but his voice was totally drowned out by the deafening sound of the two aircraft. Zak, Gabs and Raf stumbled towards him. Zak's eyes flickered towards Moriarty. He expected him to be looking at his sister, but he was surprised. The pilot's brow was furrowed, his face white with pain, and his gaze was firmly fixed on the attack helicopter facing off in front of them.

If he was scared, he didn't look it.

All three of them were gasping for air by the time they reached the door. Ricky ushered them inside. Zak caught a glimpse of a white bandage strapping up Moriarty's knee as they fell heavily into the body of the chopper, a bundle of bruised, beaten bodies. Zak felt a moment of weightlessness as the chopper lifted into the sky.

He pushed himself to his feet, just as the aircraft banked sharply, throwing him to one side. From the corner of his eye, he glimpsed the attack chopper. It was advancing.

'*That thing can put us down any moment it likes!*'

'*Thanks, kid!*' Moriarty yelled back. '*You think I don't know that? We're in Russian airspace. They're within their rights to shoot us down if they want to.*

Our only hope is to get back over the date line, into US territory. Then they might think twice . . .'

The chopper surged forward. Through the windows, Zak saw the familiar blast of snow and cloud. The others were getting to their feet. Gabs was staring hard at Moriarty, but it seemed as if the pilot himself was steadfastly refusing to look at her. With a flash of insight, he realized that Moriarty couldn't bear to be reunited with his sister, only to be parted from her immediately, when the attack helicopter put them down.

That thought made Zak lurch to the side window and press his face against it. At first he couldn't see their enemy – they were surrounded by thick cloud. But a few seconds later, through a gap in the mist, he caught a glimpse of its evil shape as it sped past them. Outrun it? In this old aircraft? Impossible. Fight it? Get real.

They needed a better idea. Or they were dead.

Zak closed his eyes. He found the events of the previous few days spinning through his mind. Michael and Felix, dead . . . Malcolm . . . Cruz, luring them here on behalf of the Russians . . . And the Russians themselves, wanting to get their hands on a precious teenage spy, but unwilling to risk the fallout of abducting him themselves . . .

His eyes pinged open.

'Moriarty,' he said sharply. 'Is there a radio on this thing?'

'Yep,' Moriarty growled. There were beads of sweat on his brow as he struggled to keep the chopper level. 'But unless you speak Russian—'

'Tune it in to the aircraft emergency frequency,' Zak barked. '*Now!*'

'Kid, we've got an attack chopper on our—'

'We'll never escape it. Tune it in!'

'Do it, Moriarty!' Gabs's voice was like a whip. 'He knows what he's talking about.'

The sound of her voice had an immediate effect on the pilot. He jolted sharply and blinked furiously. He leaned towards his controls and, with his free hand, switched on the old radio set and passed the handset to Zak.

'Hover,' Zak said. Moriarty hesitated. '*Hover!*'

There was a sudden lurch as the chopper slowed down. Zak could see almost nothing – they were shrouded in mist and cloud. But then, through the windowscreen, he saw the shape of the attack helicopter emerge through the mist. It hung in the air, no more than fifteen metres from the yellow chopper. On either side were two missile launchers. Zak's heart almost stopped as he saw them slide upwards, locking into place.

'*I KNOW YOU'RE MONITORING THIS*

CHANNEL,' he shouted into the radio handset. '*I KNOW YOU CAN SPEAK ENGLISH. THERE ARE THREE CHILDREN IN THIS HELICOPTER! THIS IS BEING BROADCAST OVER A PUBLIC DISTRESS CHANNEL. ANYBODY COULD BE LISTENING. IF YOU WANT THE WORLD TO KNOW THAT A RUSSIAN MILITARY AIRCRAFT HAS KNOWINGLY SHOT US DOWN AND KILLED US, GO AHEAD AND FIRE.*'

Nobody, and nothing, moved. The choppers faced each other, surrounded by mist. Zak's eyes didn't move from the missile launchers.

'*This is what I know,*' he continued, his voice tense and clipped. '*You paid Cruz Martinez to kill two security personnel in the UK. You paid him to kidnap two more, knowing that I would do whatever it took – and go wherever I needed – to find them. There's already one UK citizen dead on the ice. If you shoot down this chopper, you'll have more than a diplomatic incident on your hands.*'

Zak's eyes narrowed.

'*You'll have a* war,' he said. It felt like everyone in the chopper was holding their breath.

'*Do what you have to do,*' Zak said quietly. He released the pressel on the handset, and calmly passed it back to Moriarty.

Nothing happened. The attack helicopter remained

where it was, hovering just ahead of them. The missile launchers remained engaged.

'You like a high-stakes game, kid,' said Moriarty.

Zak didn't – couldn't – take his eyes off the chopper. 'You too, Moriarty,' he said. 'How did you know where to find us?'

'The Little Diomede islanders told me where the military base was. They're good people. I figured you might need a bit of help . . .'

'You figured right.'

There was movement in the cabin. Gabs struggled forward. She put one hand on Moriarty's shoulder. For the first time during the stand-off, the yellow chopper wobbled. Zak saw a tear run down Moriarty's grizzled face. 'Good to see you, sweetie,' he said in a broken voice.

Just then, there was movement up ahead. The tail of the attack helicopter had risen slightly. Zak caught his breath. His message had failed.

'Nice knowing you all,' he said weakly. From the corner of his eye, he saw Gabs squeeze Moriarty's shoulder a little harder.

He closed his eyes.

Nothing happened.

Opening them again, he saw the attack helicopter still hanging in the air. But its missile launchers were moving again.

They were sliding back to their original position. Disengaging.

Zak felt a sudden, wild leap of hope. Slowly, the attack helicopter retreated, disappearing into the mist, like a ghost fading away.

For a moment, nobody spoke. Zak realized that he'd somehow cut off all external noise. Now the hum of the yellow chopper's engines assaulted his ears again. And he suddenly felt so weak that he thought his knees would collapse underneath him.

'How about you get us out of here, brother of mine?' Gabs whispered. If she felt any sense of relief, it wasn't evident in her voice. In fact, the whole cabin was sombre. Ricky's head was hanging low, while Raf looked barely conscious. Moriarty's grizzled face was still tear-dashed. But he moved his control stick and the chopper banked sharply off to the right.

'Wait,' Zak said. His voice shook as much as his limbs and a heavy sense of despair weighed down on him. He looked over at the pilot. 'Can you get down below the cloud line?'

Moriarty nodded. There was a slight lurch as the chopper lost height. The dark, icy landscape came into view.

'Get us to the date line,' Zak said, 'between the two islands. We've got one more passenger to pick up.'

They flew in silence, with just the beating of the rotors for company. Less than a minute later, they approached the position where they had made contact with Cruz. Zak's eyes were magnetically drawn to the three bodies lying on the ice.

But to one body in particular.

'Can you put us down on the ice?' Zak asked quietly.

Moriarty didn't answer, but moments later the yellow chopper was settling onto the frozen wasteland. Zak moved towards the side door, but Ricky was already there.

'I want to do it,' Zak said.

Ricky gave him a supportive smile. 'Together?' he said.

Zak nodded.

They opened the door and jumped out onto the ice. Malcolm's body was lying ten metres away. They hurried over, then bent down and picked it up, Zak taking the head end, Ricky the feet. The body was horribly cold. Cold enough to suck any remaining warmth from Zak himself.

He looked across the ice, to where Cruz and Calaca were lying. Zak frowned, then realized that Raf and Gabs had exited the chopper, and had walked over to stand by them.

'It's not your fault, sweetie,' Gabs said. 'None of this is your fault.'

'I thought I could change him,' Zak said. 'Cruz, I mean. I've always thought I could change him back into the person he was.'

'Cruz made his own choices, Zak,' Raf told him.

Zak nodded at the corpse in his arms. 'What about Malcolm? We shouldn't have brought him with us. He wasn't cut out for this.'

Raf's face tightened. 'Maybe he wasn't. But he also wasn't a fool. He made his own choices too, buddy.' He looked over at Ricky. 'We all did.'

'Does it get easier?' Zak asked. 'Losing people?'

'Never,' Raf said. 'Not one bit.'

An icy wind blew against them. Zak found himself vocalizing a thought that had been his constant companion for the past few days. 'I'm not sure I'm cut out for this,' he said quietly. 'People seem to die around me. I don't want that to happen any more.'

Gabs walked up to him. She looked steely. 'You think that if you weren't around, people wouldn't die? Think again.'

'But Malcolm . . . Felix . . . Michael . . .'

'If Michael were here, he'd tell you that everybody dies, Zak. Every single person. Some sooner, some later. The question is, what do we do with the time we have? Do we let it slip by? Or do we do something worthwhile with it? Do we make our life mean something, until the time comes for *us* to . . . ?' She nodded towards the dead bodies, and Zak knew what she meant. 'That's the choice you have to make, sweetie. It's the choice we all have to make.' She looked back at the chopper. 'If you'll excuse me,' she said, 'my brother and I have quite a lot to catch up on.'

She turned and walked back to the chopper, bowing her head against the downdraught. Raf followed her.

'I guess she's right,' Ricky said.

'Yeah,' Zak replied. 'I guess.' He paused. 'You did well, Ricky,' he said. 'Really well. I can see why Felix picked you out.'

'I'd say we make a good team,' Ricky replied. He held up a clenched fist, and Zak met it with his own.

Then Zak took a deep breath. 'We'd better . . . you know . . .' He nodded at the yellow helicopter.

Agents 21 and 22 moved towards the aircraft. Their shoulders were hunched, and their footfall was heavy as they carried their fallen companion home.

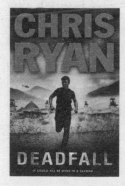

In a CODE RED situation
what would you do . . . ?

READ *THE ONE THAT GOT AWAY*, CHRIS RYAN'S FAMOUS, REAL-LIFE STORY OF COURAGE AND SURVIVAL, NOW RETOLD FOR A NEW GENERATION.

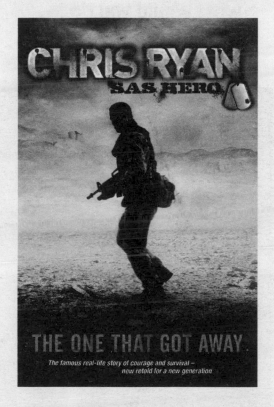

'It was a tough decision. My last friend had disappeared . . . I checked my compass and started walking north. Alone . . .'